Praise for Leslie Meier an[illegible]
her Lucy Stone Mysteries!

TURKEY TROT MURDER

"Timely . . . Meier's focus on racism gives this cozy a serious edge rare for this subgenre."
—*Publishers Weekly*

BRITISH MANOR MURDER

"Counts, countesses, and corpses highlight Lucy Stone's trip across the pond . . . A peek into British country life provides a nice break."
—*Kirkus Reviews*

CANDY CORN MURDER

"Meier continues to exploit the charm factor in her small-town setting, while keeping the murder plots as realistic as possible in such a cozy world."
—*Booklist*

FRENCH PASTRY MURDER

"A delight from start to finish."
—*Suspense Magazine*

CHRISTMAS CAROL MURDER

"Longtime Lucy Stone series readers will be happy to catch up on life in Tinker's Cover in this cozy Christmas mystery."
—*Library Journal*

EASTER BUNNY MURDER

"A fun and engaging read. It is quick and light and has enough interesting twists and turns to keep you turning the pages. If you like this type of mystery and this is your first meeting with Lucy Stone, it will probably not be your last."
—*The Barnstable Patriot*

Books by Leslie Meier

MISTLETOE MURDER
TIPPY TOE MURDER
TRICK OR TREAT MURDER
BACK TO SCHOOL MURDER
VALENTINE MURDER
CHRISTMAS COOKIE MURDER
TURKEY DAY MURDER
WEDDING DAY MURDER
BIRTHDAY PARTY MURDER
FATHER'S DAY MURDER
STAR SPANGLED MURDER
NEW YEAR'S EVE MURDER
BAKE SALE MURDER
CANDY CANE MURDER
ST. PATRICK'S DAY MURDER
MOTHER'S DAY MURDER
WICKED WITCH MURDER
GINGERBREAD COOKIE MURDER
ENGLISH TEA MURDER
CHOCOLATE COVERED MURDER
EASTER BUNNY MURDER
CHRISTMAS CAROL MURDER
FRENCH PASTRY MURDER
CANDY CORN MURDER
BRITISH MANOR MURDER
EGGNOG MURDER
TURKEY TROT MURDER
SILVER ANNIVERSARY MURDER
YULE LOG MURDER

Published by Kensington Publishing Corporation

EASTER BUNNY MURDER

LESLIE MEIER

KENSINGTON BOOKS
www.kensingtonbooks.com

KENSINGTON BOOKS are published by

Kensington Publishing Corp.
119 West 40th Street
New York, NY 10018

All Kensington titles, imprints, and distributed lines are available at special quantity discounts for bulk purchases for sales promotion, premiums, fund-raising, educational, or institutional use.

Special book excerpts or customized printings can also be created to fit specific needs. For details, write or phone the office of the Kensington Sales Manager: Kensington Publishing Corp., 119 West 40th Street, New York, NY 10018. Attn. Sales Department. Phone: 1-800-221-2647.

First Kensington Hardcover Edition: February 2013

First Kensington Mass-Market Edition: March 2014

ISBN-13: 978-0-7582-8630-7 (ebook)
ISBN-10: 0-7582-8630-9 (ebook)
Kensington Electronic Edition: February 2013

ISBN-13: 978-1-4967-2219-5
ISBN-10: 1-4967-2219-1
First Kensington Trade Paperback Printing: March 2019

10 9 8 7 6 5 4 3 2 1

Printed in the United States of America

For Calvin X

Chapter One

It was not the sort of thing you expected on a beautiful April morning. The sun was pouring through the kitchen windows and, outside, long wands of yellow forsythia blooms were waving in a gentle breeze. The newly installed granite countertop gleamed expensively beneath two dozen Easter eggs, freshly dyed in a rainbow of colors. Lucy Stone was admiring her grandson Patrick's handiwork, which featured crayon scribbles and garish color combinations, when she heard the scream.

It was a truly ear-piercing, heart-stopping sound. What was happening? Had the just-turned-three-year-old poked a finger into an electric socket? Had he run with scissors and stumbled, gashing himself? A second scream, even louder than the first, sent her flying up the stairs.

"What's the matter?" she cried, racing into Patrick's sunny little room, which was decorated with trucks. There was a parade of red, blue, and yellow trucks on the curtains, on the wallpaper border, and on his bedding.

"Nothing at all," sighed Patrick's mother, Molly, who was sprawled on the blue rug. She was attempting to restrain her wiggly son in something resembling a wrestling hold, with one arm firmly clamped across his chest. In the other hand, she had a miniature necktie.

Lucy, an experienced mother, grasped the situation immediately. "Patrick, don't you want to wear a necktie, just like Daddy does?" Actually, this was a bit of a stretch. Lucy knew her son, Toby, Patrick's father, rarely wore a necktie and then only under protest. His current occupation as a college student only required casual clothing, and he donned sturdy work clothes when he snagged occasional employment as a carpenter's helper or landscaper.

"No!" Patrick kicked a small foot, clad in brand-new brown leather oxfords, sending his shoe flying across the room.

"Patrick! That's enough! Now sit still so we can finish getting you dressed!"

Molly's tone was firm and Patrick paused in his protestations long enough to allow his grandmother to scoop him up and set him on her lap, where he continued to show his displeasure by shoving his lower lip out in a resentful pout.

"Now, now," crooned Lucy. "That's no way to behave. We're going to see the Easter Bunny! And there will be treats for good little boys."

"I don't know," murmured Molly, struggling to shove Patrick's small foot into the stiff shoe. "Maybe this isn't such a good idea."

"But he looks so handsome," said Lucy, nuzzling the little boy's silky blond hair.

Patrick was indeed the very picture of a proper little gentleman. In addition to the new shoes, he was wearing a pair of kelly green pants, a blue, green, and white argyle vest, a white shirt, and—hopefully—the matching green necktie.

"What if he has a tantrum there?" fretted Molly, brushing a lock of hair out of her eyes and leaning back on her heels. "I'd be so embarrassed."

"Tantrums happen," said Lucy with a shrug. "If he blows, we'll just pick him up and take him home. But it would be a shame to miss the Easter egg hunt just because he might have a tantrum. He'll probably be fine."

"If you ask me, I think Patrick has a point," said Molly, handing the necktie to Lucy. "I don't see why the kids have to dress up when they'd be so much more comfortable in their play clothes."

Lucy bent down and buried her nose in Patrick's neck, giving him little kisses at the same time she deftly fastened the miniature clip-on tie to his collar. "VV is a generous hostess. She spares no expense on the Easter egg hunt and the refreshments afterward, and she expects her guests to show their appreciation by dressing up a bit." She tickled Patrick, who responded by giggling. "And by using their very best manners."

"It's a lot to expect of a three-year-old," said Molly, gathering up Patrick's T-shirt and jeans, stained with dye. "And eating candy sends him into the stratosphere."

"There's more than candy in those plastic eggs," said Lucy. As a part-time reporter for the local weekly, she had covered Vivian Van Vorst's annual Easter egg hunt at her magnificent private estate, Pine Point, for many years. "Some of them have gift certificates, savings bonds, even tuition vouchers. Wouldn't you love to get a free month or two of day care?"

"Actually, yes, I would," said Molly, getting to her feet. "Come on, Patrick. This is going to be fun."

When Patrick was firmly belted into his car seat, Lucy and Molly resumed their conversation.

"You know, I don't remember going to the Easter egg hunt when I was a kid," said Molly.

"No, you wouldn't," said Lucy, pausing at the end of Prudence Path before turning onto Red Top Road. "VV started it about twelve years ago, and it's only for children eight and under. You were too old by then."

Molly gazed out the car window as they drove along, noticing the bright yellow forsythia bushes and the green shoots of spring bulbs that had popped up around the modest gray-shingled and white clapboard houses that were dotted along the road. "How did VV get all her money, anyway?"

"She did it the old-fashioned way; she married it. She's a local girl. I heard she grew up on a poultry farm but it's long gone. Anyway, at some point she left Tinker's Cove and met Horatio Van Vorst and captured his heart. Or maybe something else."

Molly chuckled.

"He was a big industrialist and was immensely rich. I think they came here to Tinker's Cove sometime in the 1950s and began buying up land, accumulating some two hundred acres and building the house. It's enormous, but they only came in the summers while he was alive. He died some years ago, leaving VV very well off. She's in her nineties now and she lives here year-round."

"I've heard she's the richest person in town," said Molly.

"She sure is," said Lucy, making the turn onto Shore Road. "These houses are nothing compared to Pine Point," she said, pointing to the McMansions that had sprouted up on the rocky bluff overlooking the Atlantic Ocean. "But she's a very generous benefactor. She's given lots of money to the library and the hospital. The town wouldn't be the same without her."

Molly's expression hardened as they drove past one huge, empty house after another. "Look at them, nobody's home at most of them. Their owners only use them in the summer. It's enough to make you a communist! Toby and

I are struggling to pay our bills and these people have houses they don't even use."

"You just had your kitchen remodeled," Lucy reminded her, thinking of all that gleaming granite and stainless steel.

"That was my dad. He said we had to upgrade or we'd never be able to sell the house—and he paid for it."

Lucy was immediately alarmed; she liked having Molly and Toby and Patrick living so close to her old farm house on Red Top Road. "Are you planning on selling?" she asked, braking well in advance for the sharp turn where Shore Road clung to the bluff and curved high above the tiny cove known as Lover's Leap. The view of the bay was spectacular but Lucy didn't notice; she kept her eyes on the road, fearful of plunging down into the roiling water below.

"No. I love that house; I don't want to sell. And, frankly, I was perfectly happy with the old kitchen. I would much rather have had the cash, what with Toby's tuition and all. But Dad said we had to have granite."

"Well, getting a new kitchen isn't exactly a hardship," said Lucy, joining the line of cars snaking down the drive to Pine Point. "I don't know if that disqualifies you from membership in the Communist Party."

Molly laughed. "You think I should count my blessings."

Lucy nodded. "Whenever I complained that my friends had nicer things than I did, my mother would say, 'Envy's a green-eyed monster that comes hissing hot from hell.' " She looked over her shoulder at Patrick, whose chin had dropped onto his chest. "Uh-oh. Guess who's asleep?"

"I thought he was awfully quiet," said Molly, as the car crept along.

In past years, Lucy remembered, parking had been allowed along one side of the long driveway and was supervised by young men hired for the day, equipped with whistles and red flags. There were no attendants on the job this year, but most people remembered the drill and pulled off to the right, lining up neatly on the gravel verge. A few others, however, parked any which way on the lawn, at which Lucy clucked her tongue in disapproval. "That lawn is VV's pride and joy," she said, pulling into the next available spot, "and those cars are going to leave tire marks."

"At least they're not blocking the drive," said Molly, who was busy unfastening the straps on Patrick's car seat. The little boy stirred, yawning adorably and stretching his little arms.

Lucy, meanwhile, got out of the car and unfolded the umbrella stroller and in a moment Patrick was settled and they joined the other families walking up the drive toward the house. There was a sense of happy anticipation. It had been a long, hard winter and everyone was enjoying the fine weather and looking forward to the afternoon's entertainment. The Easter egg hunt was always lots of fun; the kids were cute as they scrambled across the lawn, first racing to grab the obvious eggs scattered on the grass and, then, encouraged by shouts from their parents, searching for the more valuable eggs that had been hidden in the shrubbery, beneath flowers, and behind statuary.

Then, when all the eggs had been collected, VV would award prizes. She would stand on the front steps of the magnificent mansion, dressed in a lovely pastel suit topped with a flowery hat, beaming at the assembled children. There were always so many certificates and ribbons that everybody got one: most eggs, fastest collector, most polite collector, best blue outfit, best pink outfit, shiniest shoes, curliest hair, and on and on, until every child had been recognized for some special attribute.

Later, after all the prizes had been distributed, Willis, the butler, would open the massive front doors and everyone was invited to partake of refreshments in the hall. This was Lucy's favorite part, because the oval hall was always beautifully decorated with garlands of spring flowers. They were clustered on the crystal chandelier, they twined around the railing on the floating staircase, and they were looped on the overloaded buffet tables.

The food was always delicious, served up by uniformed caterers. There was something for everyone: fruit punch for the kids, tea for the teetotalers, and wine punch for those who enjoyed a drop of something stronger. Of course, there were always tons of deviled eggs, as well as mountains of tiny sandwiches and platters of cookies and cupcakes, all iced in pretty pastel colors. Most tempting of all, perhaps, were the fruit tarts, each one heaped with a generous mound of glistening berries.

But before diving into the buffet, Lucy always took a moment to admire the priceless Karl Klaus sculpture that was VV's pride and joy. The sculpture, aptly titled *Jelly Beans*, was a group of four ovoid shapes clustered together—orange, pink, and lavender were on the bottom, yellow on top. The sculpture was always displayed on the round table in the center of the hall, but on the day of the Easter egg hunt, it was featured in an elaborate ice sculpture depicting the Easter Bunny with his nest of eggs.

All this was running through Lucy's mind as they walked along the drive, toward the curve and the final approach to the mansion, where budding Japanese cherry trees flanked the drive leading to the elaborate iron gates. Those gates were always thrown open for the Easter egg hunt, but today they were inexplicably closed, and a sizeable crowd had gathered in front of them.

"I wonder what's going on," said Lucy.

"Are you sure this is the right day?" asked Molly.

"Absolutely. It's always the Saturday before Palm Sunday, a full week before Easter," said Lucy. "At noon. Precisely."

"They must have forgotten to open the gates," said Lydia Volpe, a retired kindergarten teacher who had brought her two grandchildren, twins, dressed identically in pink gingham jackets.

"I dunno," said a bearded and tattooed young man Lucy recognized from the Quik-Stop. "I don't see any eggs on the lawn."

"And the gate's not decorated," added his companion, a pasty-faced young woman who was bouncing a doughy baby on her hip.

"If you ask me, the garden looks a bit run down," whispered Rebecca Wardwell, an elderly woman who Lucy knew was a dedicated gardener. "That quince needs pruning and those daffodils are tired; most of them don't even have buds."

"I noticed that, too," said Lucy, who had always admired VV's impeccably tended grounds. "And there were no parking attendants. I'm beginning to think they decided not to have the egg hunt this year."

Her comment sparked a little buzz as people speculated whether or not the hunt was going to take place. Despite the disturbing evidence to the contrary, most people insisted it must be on, perhaps just delayed for some reason. After all, there was always an Easter egg hunt at Pine Point.

Then a sudden hush fell over the crowd as VV's butler, Willis, was seen opening one of the French doors that opened onto a stone terrace. He carefully closed the door behind him, then began a stately walk across the terrace, down the stone steps and then proceeded along the paved walk to the oyster shell drive. As always, he was dressed in a black suit with a white shirt and striped tie and his gray hair was combed straight back from his lined face.

Reaching the gates, he paused and cleared his throat. He was about to speak when a collective gasp arose from the crowd. The Easter Bunny had appeared! Everyone could see him standing in the elaborate front doorway, where two double doors were now open behind a protective metal grille. He was a big bunny, at least seven feet tall, covered in white plush with a pink felt stomach and a huge round head, complete with big blue eyes, a pink nose, toothy smile, black whiskers, and enormous pointy ears, one of which flopped down over one eye. An absolutely huge basket filled with colorful plastic eggs was looped over one arm.

"There he is!" shrieked a little girl, whose black hair had been twisted into braids tied with crisp polka-dot bows.

"It's the Easter Bunny, it's really him," said a serious little boy wearing wire-rimmed eyeglasses.

Lucy scooped up Patrick, holding him up so he could see the Easter Bunny for himself. "See!" she said, pointing. "He's going to hop, hop, hop down the bunny trail."

Patrick chortled merrily. Like everyone else, his eyes were glued to the big bunny, who raised one paw in a wave to the crowd before he grabbed the metal grille to push it open. For a moment, he seemed to stagger, and everyone held their breath: Was something the matter with the Easter Bunny?

Then there was a collective sigh of relief as the bunny seemed to recover, shoving the grille open and leaping awkwardly down the steps to the lawn, where he began a clumsy gallop toward the gates, dropping a few plastic eggs on the way.

Patrick was getting heavy and Lucy was passing him to

Molly when the bunny reached Willis, swayed on his feet, and suddenly collapsed, dropping the basket. The colorful eggs rolled every which way as the bunny convulsed and then was still.

The crowd stood in shocked silence, until the little girl with braids began to cry. "The Easter Bunny is dead," she sobbed.

Chapter Two

"No, no," said her mother, giving the little girl a hug. "That's not the real Easter Bunny, it's just someone dressed in an Easter Bunny suit."

"Are you sure?"

"Absolutely," said the mother, covering the child's eyes as Willis bent over the fallen figure and eased off the big round bunny head, revealing the face of the man inside.

It wasn't a pretty sight; his blue lips were twisted in a ghastly grimace. Lucy inhaled sharply, recognizing him.

"Do you know him?" asked Molly, who was holding Patrick close.

"Van Vorst Duff, VV's grandson." She paused, suddenly remembering that she was a reporter and this was news. "Everyone calls him Van," she added, pulling her camera out of her shoulder bag and snapping some photos of Willis leaning over Van's fallen figure.

Getting no response from the fallen man, Willis ran to the gate and punched some numbers into the intercom located there. "Mr. Duff has had an attack of some kind. Call nine-one-one," he said. Receiving an affirmative squawk in reply, he turned to the assembled and silent crowd. "This is most unfortunate," he said. "But we need to clear the area for the rescue squad."

Nobody budged. Peering through the bars of the gate, Lucy saw a nurse dressed in green scrubs appear at the doorway and begin running awkwardly down the walk. When she reached Van, she immediately began performing CPR. Feeling a bit like a ghoul, Lucy snapped a few more photos, of the petite, dark-haired woman laboring over the fallen Van. A moment later, the distant wail of an ambulance siren was heard.

"Please, please move away," begged Willis in a shaky voice. His face had lost its usual ruddy glow and he seemed in need of assistance himself, appearing a bit unsteady on his feet.

The siren grew louder, but people were reluctant to move, stepping aside only when the ambulance came into view and the gates began to swing open. "Go on home," urged Willis. "There's nothing to see here."

He was wrong, of course. This was the most exciting thing that had happened in Tinker's Cove for quite some time and everyone was determined to see how it played out. So they all squeezed together to let the ambulance by and then closed ranks, waiting to see what happened next.

An EMT in a dark blue uniform was already opening the rear doors of the ambulance and pulling out a heavy plastic case. The driver was kneeling on the ground, examining Van and questioning Willis and the nurse. More sirens could be heard, as well as the rumble of the ambulance's diesel engine, but everyone in the gathered crowd seemed to be holding their breaths.

Suddenly the EMTs were on the move, pulling a wheeled stretcher out of the ambulance. In a moment, they had slapped an oxygen mask on Van's face and lifted him onto the gurney, covered him with a blanket and fastened a couple of straps, and pushed him the short distance to the ambulance. Doors slammed and the ambulance began to roll at the same time a police cruiser appeared at the end of the drive. Lucy watched as the two vehicles passed, one leaving and one approaching. When she turned back, she saw the gates had closed once again and Willis was standing behind them.

The crowd parted once again as the cruiser drew up to the gates and stopped, its blue lights flashing, and Officer Barney Culpepper climbed out. "All right, folks," he said, placing his hands on his hips. "The excitement's over. It's time to go home."

A few people began to drift away but others hesitated, fearful of missing something.

"This is private property," said Barney in a firm voice. "I don't want to have to start arresting you folks for trespassing."

"But what about the Easter egg hunt?" asked the guy with the tattoos.

"There's no Easter egg hunt," said Willis, shaking his head before turning and walking slowly toward the house.

"You heard him," said Barney. "Now get moving before I call for reinforcements."

People finally began to leave, taking their dressed-up children by their hands and returning to their cars. Lucy, who had been friends with Barney ever since the days when they'd both served on the Cub Scout Pack Committee, pulled her notebook out of her bag. "Why don't you take Patrick back to the car and wait for me there?" she suggested to Molly, giving her the keys. "I want to get a comment from Barney."

"Okay," agreed Molly, plunking Patrick back in the umbrella stroller.

Lucy gave Patrick a big smile and a little wave as his mother began pushing him down the drive, then went up to chat with the tall, well-padded officer. "So, Barney, what can you tell me?"

"Not much," he said. "We got two calls. One that an

unresponsive male needed assistance. Shortly after that, the second call came asking for crowd control."

"There's usually an officer or two here for the Easter egg hunt," said Lucy. "But there were no officers here today."

Barney shrugged. "That would be a private detail, not part of the department's regular duties. Folks have to make a special request and pay for the officers' time."

"They didn't do that?"

Barney shook his head, looking like a big old bulldog. "Not that I know of. They usually post requests for special details on the bulletin board, but I didn't see anything. I watch out for it; it's easy duty and they always had a plate of food for us afterward."

"What about Van?" asked Lucy. "Do you think he'll be all right?"

Barney sighed. "They didn't put the blanket over his face."

"Meaning he was alive when they took him away?"

"Don't quote me," he cautioned, raising a bristly gray eyebrow. "This is off the record. You can get the official information from the department."

"Of course." Lucy smiled. "So, how are Marge and Eddie?" she asked, naming his wife and son.

"Fine, just fine," said Barney, fastening his gaze on a man who was about to pluck an early daffodil bloom. "Hey!" he yelled, marching toward the offender. "Stop that!"

Lucy began walking back toward the car, hurrying to join a young mother with three little ones in tow. "I'm Lucy Stone, from the *Pennysaver*," she said. "Can I take your photo? You and the kids?"

"Sure," said the woman. "This was a real bummer. It'll be fun to see our pictures in the paper, though, right, kids?"

Lucy arranged the little group—the mom in back, holding the youngest, Saffron, eighteen months, with the boys, Scott, five, and Todd, three, in front. The mother supplied the names, as well as her own, Angie Toth. She hesitated about giving her own age but finally divulged the information. She was thirty-one.

"So what's your reaction?" asked Lucy.

"I'm disappointed. I got the kids all dressed up in their Sunday best, expecting a terrific afternoon. Last year, Scott got a Children's Shoppe gift certificate for a hundred dollars and Todd got a fifty dollar savings bond. They didn't care, of course, it was just paper to them. They just loved the jelly beans and toys."

"I got a Bakugan," volunteered Scott.

"Me, too," said Todd.

"You did not," said Scott, with a smirk. "You got a pink pony."

"I did not!"

"Did too!"

"That's enough, boys," said Angie.

"I'll let you go," said Lucy, chuckling. "Thanks."

She stood for a moment, watching Angie getting the kids settled in the family van, then looked around for more people to interview. Most everyone had gone, however, so she hurried along to join Molly and Patrick.

When she reached the car, Molly had already strapped Patrick into his car seat and was sitting in the front passenger seat. She'd turned on the radio and was singing along to the Beatles' "Yellow Submarine." Patrick was waving his arms and kicking his legs in appreciation.

"This was lucky—it's Beatles hour on the oldies station," she told Lucy. "Patrick loves the Beatles."

"He has good taste," said Lucy, settling herself behind

the wheel and turning the car around very slowly, mindful of the people who were still walking in the drive.

"What did Barney have to say?" asked Molly. The Beatles were now singing "I Want to Hold Your Hand" and Patrick was oo-ooing along with them.

"Not much. He seemed to think Van was alive when they put him in the ambulance, but he wasn't sure."

Molly was silent for a moment. "It's scary to think a person could just collapse like that. I hope he's all right."

Lucy was silent, thinking of a popular high school teacher who had died recently from a heart attack at the ripe old age of fifty-two. "Van's not very old," she said. "I think he's only in his forties."

"He'll probably pull through, then, don't you think?"

"I hope so," said Lucy, remembering Van's agonized expression and unhealthy blue color. The brake lights on the car in front of them suddenly lit up and she braked, too, realizing they'd reached the curve at Lover's Leap.

"I bet he's a really nice man," said Molly. "After all, there aren't too many guys who'd dress up like a giant bunny."

Lucy found herself chuckling. "Not Bill," she said, naming her husband, a restoration carpenter. "That's for sure. And probably not Toby."

"No, not Toby."

"Van's always been a party animal," said Lucy. "I remember when we first moved to Tinker's Cove, he was quite the playboy. He had a fancy English car, a Morgan or something, and there was always a gorgeous girl sitting in it."

"Did he ever marry?"

"I don't know if any of those fabulous blondes ever snagged him." Lucy was humming along to "Norwegian Wood." "I do know he's been to rehab a few times. He's always starting projects and then dropping them. He was going to row across the Atlantic. He had a fancy boat built especially for the venture, but he ended up crashing it on the rocks at Quisset Point. Then he had some idea about adding recycled glass to asphalt to make it more durable, but that never worked out. He had another idea about vacuuming up oil spills. He tried to get them to use it after the BP disaster in the Gulf of Mexico but nobody was interested."

"I suppose he can afford to dabble," said Molly.

"I think he must have a trust fund or something," said Lucy. "Rumor has it that his mother, Little Viv, got herself disinherited when she divorced her husband and ran off with a defrocked priest. VV did not approve."

"Does that mean Van gets everything when VV dies?" Molly smiled. "Maybe I married the wrong guy."

"I'm pretty sure you married the right guy," said Lucy. "Just look at Patrick."

Patrick was quietly studying a little toy truck, looking every bit the angel he wasn't. "He drives me crazy most of the time," admitted Molly, "but I can't imagine disinheriting him. Not that we've got all that much to leave him."

"I guess VV had her reasons," said Lucy. "For all I know Little Viv is back in the will. I heard she divorced the priest, too."

"Sounds like quite a family," said Molly, a hint of disapproval in her voice.

"Little Viv has a daughter, too. Vicky."

"And what's Vicky like?" asked Molly. "Is she a playgirl like Van?"

"Not at all, she's terribly proper," said Lucy, listening to John Lennon singing about money on the radio. "Her wedding was a big deal. They had a tent at Pine Point and the town was flooded with famous people. It was the first big story I covered for the paper. It was the talk of the town. Nobody here had seen anything like it."

"And the marriage lasted?"

"Oh, yes. Every once in a while I see them. Her husband is Henry Chatsworth Allen . . ."

"My, my. That's a rich-sounding name."

"It sure is. Well, Mr. and Mrs. Henry Chatsworth Allen are often pictured in the society pages, generally looking as though they'd rather be somewhere else." She sighed, turning into Prudence Path. "You know, it's a cliché to say that money can't buy happiness, but it seems to be true for VV and her family."

Lucy braked in front of Molly and Toby's house, noticing with disappointment that Toby's old truck was missing, which meant he wasn't home. She brightened when Molly invited her to come inside and take some of the dyed Easter eggs. "We can't possibly eat them all," she said, lifting her child out of the car seat.

Inside the kitchen, she settled Patrick in his high chair and gave him a few animal crackers and a juice box. Lucy was choosing some of the colored eggs and packing them in a cardboard egg carton.

"I'll take blue," she said, showing the egg to Patrick.

"Bloo," he repeated.

"And this red one."

"Red," exclaimed Patrick, kicking his legs.

"How about green?"

"Grrr," growled Patrick. "Grrr. Grrr."

"He loves growling," said Molly, who was filling the kettle. "You know, it seems to me that Van must have decided at the last minute to have the Easter egg hunt. It didn't seem as if it was planned. The gate was closed and there were no eggs in sight, except the ones in his basket."

"I know. It was odd. And Barney said they hadn't requested a special detail, like they usually do."

"And there was no sign of VV. It's her shindig, isn't it? You said she gives out prizes and stuff."

"You're right. I wonder if her health is failing." Lucy was closing the lid on her half-filled egg carton.

"Can you stay for some tea?" asked Molly.

"No, thanks. I better get going. I have to call Ted." Ted Stillings was Lucy's employer, the editor, publisher, and chief reporter for the town's weekly newspaper, the *Pennysaver*. "I have a feeling this is going to be a big story."

"Keep me posted," said Molly.

Lucy bent down and kissed Patrick on the top of his head. "Be a good boy," she said.

"Grrr," he replied.

Lucy was smiling when she got back in the car for the short drive out Prudence Path and down Red Top Road to home. The old farmhouse was as welcoming as ever, with its sharply peaked roof and spacious porch, but when she stopped at the mailbox, she noticed the blue sky was filling with clouds. Typical in Maine, where people said if you didn't like the weather, you should wait a minute.

When she lowered the window to reach into the mailbox, she noticed the temperature was falling and felt cold drops of rain on her hand. It looked as if spring was over, at least temporarily. She parked the car in her usual spot and hurried along the brick path lined with shivering crocuses, clutching her light jacket tightly at the collar and dodging the pelting sleet that was quickly turning into a downpour.

Inside the warm kitchen, Libby, her lab, rose slowly from her bed and stretched, wagging her tail in greeting. Lucy set the carton of Easter eggs along with the bills and a plastic-wrapped issue of *Glamour* magazine on the kitchen table, thinking that her daughters, Sara and Zoe, would probably get in a fight over it. Then she took her jacket off and hung it on the hook, giving her damp hair a shake.

Nobody seemed to be home. It was the perfect time to wrap up this story, so she called for an update on Van's condition.

Willis answered, announcing "Pine Point" in his usual clipped tone.

"This is Lucy Stone, from the *Pennysaver*," she said. "I was just wondering if there's any news about Mr. Duff's condition."

There was a long silence while she waited for a reply. Finally, Willis spoke, but seemed to have a difficult time getting the words out. "I'm very sorry to say we've just learned that Van Vorst Duff passed away en route to the hospital."

Chapter Three

Lucy was thoughtful as she drove to work on Monday morning. She knew Van's death would be a big story and she wasn't all that eager to cover it. She wasn't getting any younger, she noted wryly, and neither was Bill. The sudden death of a man who seemed to be in his prime was a grim reminder of their own mortality. How would she cope if Bill suddenly had a heart attack? And what about poor Bill, if she died suddenly? Did he even know where she kept the important papers—the birth certificates, the insurance policies, and the deed to the house? Would he know what bills to pay first, and which could wait? Could he tell the difference between her good jewelry and the costume stuff? What if he sent her mother's pearls to a thrift shop? And what about the silver? Could he tell it from the stainless? My goodness, she realized with a shock, they didn't even have wills.

She had a horrible feeling in the pit of her stomach by the time she reached the *Pennysaver* office, which was in a Main Street storefront, and swung into the parking area behind it, and was resolving to have a serious talk with Bill as soon as possible. This very evening, if she could pull him away from the Bruins game on TV.

"Why are you looking so glum?" asked Phyllis, when she entered the office. "The sun's shining, the birds are singing, it's a beautiful spring day."

"It's probably global warming," muttered Lucy, hanging up her jacket on the coat tree. "We're doomed. The ice caps are melting, the ocean's rising, and soon we'll be swimming for our lives."

Phyllis perched her harlequin reading glasses on her nose. "You know what they say. *No one gets out alive.*"

"You're right. But I'd rather leave later than sooner. Not like poor Van—he was only in his forties."

"Ouch," said Phyllis. "Wilf is fifty-two. Of course, he's in excellent shape; he walks all day long." Phyllis's husband, Wilf, was a mail carrier. She furrowed her brow and examined her manicure; her nails were painted a bright shade of green. "He does eat fast food for lunch, though. I wish he wouldn't. Just one soft drink a day is supposed to be bad for you, even if it's diet. And the fries, well, everyone knows they go straight to your arteries and clog them up."

"Tell me about it. Bill won't touch brown rice—I lost that battle years ago. He's a meat and potatoes man and he has to have meat loaf at least once a week." Lucy sat down at her desk and booted up her computer. "He'll eat salad—if it's slathered with blue cheese dressing. And fruit . . ."

"If it's in a pie served with a scoop of ice cream," finished Phyllis.

"How are we going to keep them alive?" asked Lucy.

"It's not going to be easy," said Phyllis, with a sharp nod. "I heard on some financial planning show that the average age women become widows is fifty-eight."

Lucy's jaw dropped. "No."

"Yes. It's a statistical fact." Phyllis shuffled some papers. "Look at VV. I bet she's been a widow longer than she was married."

Lucy's computer was finally ready and she Googled Vivian Van Vorst, learning that Phyllis was right. "She was married for twenty-five years. Old Horatio died in 1969. She's been a widow for more than forty years." Her eyes met Phyllis's. "Is that what we have to look forward to?"

"I hope not. Wilf and I have only been married a couple of years," said Phyllis. "Did I mention that Elfrida is the new cook up at Pine Point? She says it's pretty dismal there these days."

"Elfrida!" Lucy's eyebrows shot up. Elfrida, Phyllis's niece, was known for her numerous marriages and even more numerous offspring. "I didn't know she was a cook."

"She's not, but things have gone downhill at the mansion. There are no more fancy dinners, she says. Just invalid food for VV and soup and sandwiches for the staff."

"Invalid food? What's that?"

"You know, mostly those vitamin shakes that come in a can. Sometimes she gets a little soup or yogurt."

"Poor old thing."

"Elfrida says she's confined to her room. There are a couple of nurses who live in the house and they take turns caring for her. She doesn't have any visitors anymore, just her granddaughter Vicky and Vicky's husband, Henry. Elfrida says the staff all hate them, and that lawyer, too." She paused, thoughtfully sucking on a finger. "Weatherby, George Weatherby. That's his name. When he shows up, Elfrida says, they all make themselves scarce. They say that if he finds you, he'll probably fire you; they're cutting back on staff."

That explained a lot, thought Lucy. "So there were no plans for the Easter egg hunt after all?"

"No. Elfrida says Van arrived Saturday morning and was really upset when he learned there wasn't going to be a hunt. He went up to the attic and dug out the bunny costume and then he went into town and bought up all the plastic eggs and candy he could find. When he got back to the house, he had a big argument with Willis. Willis didn't want to let the people into the estate. But when they began gathering at the gates, Willis finally agreed to let him give the eggs to the kids."

"That's when he died," said Lucy.

"VV's the one I feel sorry for," said Phyllis. "Elfrida said Van asked the nurses to get her to the window so she could watch, and she saw the whole thing. She was horribly upset, they had to sedate her, and it's no wonder. Imagine outliving your grandchild. It's not normal."

"You said it," agreed Ted Stillings, whose arrival had set the little bell on the door jingling. "That's the trouble with living to a ripe old age. You end up without any friends and hardly any family."

"You're bright and cheerful today," said Lucy, watching her boss hang up his jacket and seat himself at the old-fashioned roll-top desk he'd inherited from his grandfather, a legendary New England newsman.

"I'm just trying to look on the bright side," said Ted, in a defensive tone. "Die young, stay pretty. Now Van won't have to get old and frail like his grandmother. He died in his prime. It's not such a bad way to go."

"Speak for yourself," said Lucy. "I'm planning on living to a ripe old age. I want to see little Patrick grow up into a fine young man, and I want a lot more grandchildren, too. I won't mind getting wrinkles and white hair, not if I can stay interested and involved."

"But that's the rub. Poor VV isn't interested or involved anymore," said Ted.

"She looked great at the egg hunt just last year," protested Lucy. "She was dressed to the nines—I think she was wearing a Chanel suit—and she had a gorgeous flowery hat. White gloves, even. She looked like the queen. She was healthy and clearheaded and she really enjoyed herself when she handed out those silly awards. Reddest hair, most freckles, you know the drill."

"That was then, this is now. A year can make a big difference. She's failing," said Ted. "She's ninety years old, after all."

"You know, that's why I don't like to read biographies," said Phyllis. "They start out just fine, the little genius is born and grows up, overcoming obstacles and achieving great things, and then there's the inevitable decline and death. It's the same story, over and over."

Lucy realized she had to agree. She'd just finished a new, highly acclaimed account of Jacqueline Kennedy Onassis's life and had found the last chapter terribly sad and depressing. Wealth and fame, even beauty, didn't really matter. In the end, it all came down to the same thing. "I wonder when she began to fail," said Lucy.

"Sometime over the summer, I think," said Ted. "Pam told me VV didn't make her usual August contribution to the Hat and Mitten Fund. She always donated a thousand dollars for school supplies." Ted's wife, Pam, was one of Lucy's best friends and chaired the Hat and Mitten Fund, which provided school supplies and warm clothing for the town's underprivileged kids.

"When the check didn't arrive, Pam called Pine Point and they referred her to VV's lawyer, George Weatherby. He told her he'd get a check in the mail immediately, and he did, but it was only for twenty-five dollars!"

"You're kidding!" exclaimed Lucy.

"Nope. You can ask Pam."

"I will," said Lucy, reaching for the phone. It wasn't often that she got permission to talk with her friends when she was at work.

Pam didn't have time for a long chat, however. She was

getting ready for the yoga class she taught at the senior center. "I really had to scramble to make up for VV's missing donation," she told Lucy. "The Seamen's Bank gave me two hundred and I got a hundred each from the Methodists and Baptists. The Lions and Rotary pitched in, too, but I ended up filling up the backpacks with donated snacks from the IGA instead of school supplies."

"The kids probably liked the snacks better," said Lucy with a chuckle.

"You're probably right. But I really missed having tea with VV. She used to invite me up to the house to give me the check and I always had a lovely time. We'd sit out in the garden and she was so funny and engaged; she'd ask me about the kids we were helping. She knew quite a few of them by name, you know, and followed their progress." Lucy heard her sigh. "I called the house and asked if I could visit VV, but Willis said no, she wasn't up to it. It's really sad. I guess one good thing is she probably doesn't know what happened to Van."

"That's not what I heard," said Lucy. "It seems she was watching from the window and saw the whole thing."

"Oh, that's too bad," moaned Pam. "Well, I gotta go. My elderly yoginis will be wondering where I am."

Lucy was thoughtful as she replaced the receiver on her phone. It seemed as if this lawyer, George Weatherby, was getting awfully involved in VV's affairs, and she was beginning to wonder whose interests he was truly representing. It was hard to believe that VV's finances were in such dire shape that she couldn't afford to maintain staff and to make her usual charitable contributions. The stock market had taken a terrible tumble recently, but it was recovering. It wasn't that long ago that VV had been included in *Maine Business Journal*'s list of the state's richest residents. She wasn't at the top of the list, but she was there. What had happened? Where had all her money gone?

Phyllis interrupted Lucy's thoughts, handing her a stack of press releases. "Ted says space is tight this week and he wants to know how many inches we need for listings," she said.

"I'll get right on it," Lucy said. She was leafing through the press releases, organizing them by date, when her phone rang. It was Roger Wilcox, chairman of the town's board of selectmen, but he had other business on his mind.

"I'm just checking to make sure you got the press release about the hospital auxiliary's Las Vegas night," he said.

"Good timing," said Lucy. "I was just getting started on the events listings." She flipped through a few sheets of paper, quickly finding the one she wanted. "Here it is. The thirtieth, right?"

"That's it. To tell the truth, I'm hoping you can play it up a bit. Maybe do a little feature or something?"

"A feature?" she repeated, and Ted shook his head, making a throat-cutting gesture. "I don't think so. Ted tells me space is tight this week."

"It's a very worthy cause, you know," Roger said. "I'm chairman of the hospital's board of directors and I can assure you this addition to the ER is desperately needed. It will benefit the entire community."

"I wish I could help," said Lucy. "I did do a story about it a few months ago when you were looking for donations."

"I know, Lucy, and we certainly appreciated the coverage. It was a very positive story." Roger paused. "I'm afraid our situation has changed since then," he said. "A promised contribution, a major contribution, in fact, has been withdrawn. We need to come up with an additional hundred thousand before we can break ground."

"That's a lot of money. You certainly can't raise that at a Las Vegas night."

"Of course not. But events like the Las Vegas night draw attention to our project and help attract donors."

"I understand," said Lucy. "Perhaps I can help. I could do a story about the need to make up for the lost contribution."

"Oh, no! Don't do that!"

"Why not?" Lucy was puzzled. She was sure townsfolk would respond to a plea for contributions.

"We're after major contributors, and they won't donate unless they believe the project is viable. The first hint of trouble and they'll snap their purses shut."

"That doesn't make sense," said Lucy.

"I know, but that's the way it is. You lose one contributor and next thing you know, they're all drifting away. I could just strangle W–W–W . . ."

Lucy was on it quicker than a tick on a hound. "Weatherby? Was it VV's lawyer?"

"*Whoever*, that's what I was going to say. I could just strangle *whoever* it was who made the decision to cut this much-needed gift. But it's all off the record, anyway."

Roger was usually a calm center of rationality when the selectmen's meetings threatened to get out of hand, so she was quite surprised at his frantic tone and hurried to reassure him.

"Off the record, absolutely. I won't breathe a word of it, I promise. And I bet I can find a picture we can run. A picture's worth a thousand words, right? In fact, I'm sure we've got a file photo of you at the roulette table at last year's Las Vegas night."

"That'll be great, Lucy. Thanks."

"No problem."

Lucy had barely ended the call when Ted demanded to know what she'd promised to keep off the record. "I'll decide what's off the record," he growled.

"It's no big deal," said Lucy. "The hospital auxiliary's run into a snag, that's all. A major donor has withdrawn a promised contribution and they're scrambling to make up for it."

"That's getting to be a familiar story," said Ted. "Weatherby again?"

"Roger wouldn't say, but I think so."

"The economy must be worse than I thought if the rich aren't rich anymore," said Phyllis.

"Everything's relative, I guess," said Lucy, who was searching the computer files for the photo she'd promised Roger.

"If that hospital expansion is threatened, we have to cover it," said Ted. "The hospital is bursting at the seams. The ER is totally inadequate. The state made the expansion a condition of recertification. If it doesn't go through, we could lose our hospital."

"I didn't think of that," admitted Lucy.

"Roger's not the only one on that board," said Ted. "Why don't you call the others? See if you can get confirmation."

"But I promised Roger . . ."

"You didn't promise the others," snapped Ted. "Get on it."

A very reluctant Lucy was just starting to dial Millicent Frobisher's number when the door flew open and a flamboyant redhead blew in, wearing a mink coat so old that the silk lining was hanging down in tatters that fluttered around her ankles.

"Can I help you?" asked Phyllis.

"I have a big story," said the woman, tossing back her long wavy hair. She was wearing high-heeled black boots and had a worn crocodile bag slung over one mink-clad arm.

Phyllis glanced at Ted, who stood up. "I'm the editor," he said, holding out his right hand. "Ted Stillings."

Lucy and Phyllis watched as she took Ted's hand in one gloved hand and covered it with the other. "I'm Maxine Carey," she said, leaning forward, almost close enough to kiss him. "I'm Van Duff's ex."

"I'm very sorry for your loss," said Ted.

"Thank you," she said, still holding his hand. "That's why I'm here. I want everyone to know that Van's death was no accident. Van Vorst Duff was murdered and I have the proof right here!"

Chapter Four

This announcement didn't exactly land like the bombshell Maxine intended, but they were all interested. Definitely interested.

"That's a serious allegation," said Ted. "What proof do you have?"

"Blood tests." She pulled a much-folded sheet of paper from the crocodile purse, which was worn bare in patches, and gave it to Ted. "He had his annual checkup less than a month ago." She stepped closer to Ted and stabbed at the paper with her finger. "He was so proud he put the whole thing on Facebook. Just look. Cholesterol, way under two hundred. The good cholesterol through the roof and the bad stuff, hardly there. And he had a stress test, too, and passed with flying colors. His blood pressure was better than mine, one hundred three over seventy. Now, I ask you, does it make any sense at all that a man in the prime of health would just drop dead?" she demanded, breathing in his face.

"I'm not a doctor, I really don't know," said Ted, stepping backward and giving the paper back to Maxine.

"Well, I do know," said Maxine, carefully folding it and tucking it away. "I know that a man like Van doesn't just drop dead. He windsurfed and skied and biked and did the Ironman five times. I'm telling you, there's something fishy going on up at Pine Point!"

Ted shifted uneasily from one foot to the other, then glanced at the regulator clock on the wall. "I'm afraid I've got an appointment," he told Maxine. "But my chief reporter Lucy Stone will be happy to talk with you."

Lucy raised her hand, as if she knew the answer to seven times nine. "I'm over here, why don't you take a seat?"

Maxine plunked herself down in the wooden chair Lucy kept for visitors and Ted grabbed his jacket, making a hasty exit.

"Typical," said Phyllis with a chuckle.

"What does she mean?" asked Maxine, pulling off her gloves.

"Ted's uncomfortable with feminine drama," said Lucy, smiling. "I'm pretty sure his important appointment is at the coffee shop."

"This happens to me all the time," declared Maxine, crossing her legs and digging into her purse, extracting a tube of lip gloss. "I am so tired of these weeny milquetoasts who won't rise to the occasion. I've been battling them my entire life. 'Don't dip into capital,' they say," she said, slathering on a thick coat of bright red gloss. " 'Floss your teeth, eat lots of fiber, get eight hours of sleep every night, everything in moderation.' Well, I don't believe in moderation and neither did Van. Life's too short for moderation!"

Lucy found herself liking Maxine, even if she was a bit overwhelming. "If Van didn't die of a heart attack, what do you think killed him? And who did it? And why?"

"I wish I knew!" declared Maxine, narrowing her eyes and screwing the cap back on the tube of lip gloss. "It could have been any of them."

"Any of who?" asked Lucy.

"The Three Pigs," she said darkly. "That's what I call them, anyway."

Lucy glanced at Phyllis, who had raised her eyebrows. "Who exactly are the Three Pigs?"

"Van's sister, Vicky, and her husband, that parasite Henry, and their disgusting excuse for a lawyer, George Weatherby," said Maxine with a little nod. "That's exactly who I mean. Those three are determined to control everything at Pine Point. They won't even let me make any suggestions about the funeral . . ."

"Well, you are his ex-wife," said Lucy, playing devil's advocate.

"Not exactly. Truth is, it was a common law situation. We never actually got married. But Van acknowledged Juliette; his name is on the birth certificate and he gave her his surname." Maxine waved her large hands in front of her face; Lucy noticed she bit her nails. "We're not together anymore, not that way, if you know what I mean, but we've always been friends. Best friends. And if Van could rise up from whatever cold slab he's lying on, he'd say the same thing. And, believe me, the last thing he'd want is those three planning his funeral."

"Perhaps you could have a separate observance, a memorial service," suggested Lucy.

"That's a good idea. You know, I might do that." Maxine put her hands together and rested them on her knee. "But that doesn't change the fact that the Three Pigs are going to go for some dull old churchy thing and Van would have hated that. And, trust me, it'll be those awful peanut butter and bacon on Melba toast things for refreshments—the ones that get stuck in your throat, that you can't possibly swallow—and maybe some watered down sherry from a big economy-size jug. They won't spend a penny on anybody but themselves, you'll see!"

"There has been talk that things aren't quite what they should be up at Pine Point," said Phyllis.

"It's true!" exclaimed Maxine. "Whatever you've heard! It's awful! Poor VV, they're not taking proper care of her. She hasn't had her hair styled in months—it's all white and the nurses just chop it off."

"It was always so beautifully done," said Lucy, remembering VV's expertly tinted strawberry blond curls.

"Not anymore. And her nightgowns are in tatters. I wouldn't use them to dust with!"

"All those beautiful clothes," said Lucy.

"Just hanging in the closets, with the shoes lined up like little soldiers. It's too sad! They make her wear these ugly felt slippers—horrid big gray things—when they get her out of bed, which isn't often enough, if you ask me."

"But still she hangs on," said Lucy, thinking VV must have been declining for a very long time. It was last August, after all, when Pam was told she was too ill to see visitors.

"If you ask me, she lives for those little dogs of hers. Nanki-Poo and Yum-Yum. She adores them." Maxine rolled her eyes. "Though they're not getting proper care, either. The girl who used to walk them has been fired, the nurses won't do it, Willis won't do it. So you can imagine what happens. The place is beginning to stink."

Lucy's jaw dropped. "My word."

"The worst of it, though, is the food," continued Maxine, rolling her eyes and waving her arm in front of her. "They have a new cook, but she's not really a cook at all. She opens cans and microwaves things; she wouldn't know what to do with a fresh vegetable if it bit her. It's absolutely atrocious!"

Lucy pressed her lips together and avoided looking at Phyllis. "I understand these cuts are necessary because VV's assets have declined."

"I don't know about that. She was very, very rich and if she isn't rich anymore it's because her money has been mismanaged." Maxine pursed her glistening scarlet lips. "Or stolen. I wouldn't put it past them."

Lucy figured she might as well ask the question that was bothering her. "And you think these same three are responsible for Van's death?"

Maxine's eyes widened and she nodded her head. "Absolutely. They were all there, you see, for a family conference."

"How can you be so sure?" asked Lucy. "There doesn't seem to be any evidence of foul play."

Maxine got to her feet. "I just know it, that's all. I feel it here." She clenched her hand into a fist and pressed it to her heart. "I've never been more certain of anything and I'm going to prove it, if it's the last thing I do!"

And with that, she stalked across the room and out the door, leaving the bell jangling furiously behind her.

"Well," said Lucy, exhaling.

"Well," agreed Phyllis. "What are you going to do?"

"I guess I'm going to follow up. These are serious accusations."

"And if it's true, it's a heck of a story," said Phyllis.

"That, too," said Lucy. She put in a call to Doc Ryder but he wasn't available, so she left a message and got busy with the listings. She was trying to make sense of a confusing Easter service schedule the Episcopalians had submitted when her phone rang. It was Elizabeth calling from Florida.

"How are you doing?" asked Lucy. "I haven't heard from you for a while."

"I've been busy, Mom. You know how it is."

Lucy was used to hearing this excuse. "So how come you've suddenly found time in your busy schedule to call me?"

"I don't feel good, Mom."

Lucy's maternal antennae were suddenly picking up ominous vibrations. "Really? What's the matter?"

"I've got these awful cramps. Honestly, Mom, I thought I was going to die last night."

A second light on Lucy's phone lit up, probably Doc Ryder returning her call. She needed to wrap this up quickly because she knew from experience that he wouldn't try a second time.

"Do you think it could be your period? You've had bad cramps before. What time of the month is it?" she asked as the phone began ringing.

"It's a little early . . ."

"Better early than late," quipped Lucy. "Honey, I really have to go. I've got another call."

"Okay, Mom. Thanks."

Lucy didn't reply. She was already hitting that blinking button. As she suspected, it was Doc Ryder. "Thanks," she said, "I know you're busy."

"You don't know the half of it. People can't afford health insurance so they wait until they're desperate and then they show up at the ER. Already today I've had a late-stage melanoma, a diabetic coma, and a kid with measles—these people should all be getting regular medical care."

It was a familiar refrain, and Lucy had written several stories about the need for improved medical care in the region. "You should send them over the border to Canada," she said.

"I wish I could," said Doc Ryder. "But you didn't call

me about the need for a national health system, or did you?"

"No. Actually, we just had a visit from Van Vorst Duff's ex-girlfriend and she claims he'd just had a physical and passed with flying colors. She thinks he was murdered."

"I examined his body and I can assure you I didn't find any bullet wounds, bruises or stab wounds. He wasn't strangled, garroted or hanged and there were no signs of poisoning. I determined that his death was due to natural causes and no autopsy is required."

"She says he had no cholesterol problems to speak of and low blood pressure."

"It happens, Lucy. What can I tell you? A seemingly healthy person drops dead. Everybody thinks that if they exercise and don't smoke they'll live forever but, trust me, it doesn't happen. Everybody dies sooner or later. It just happened sooner for him. Remember that kid from Gilead, the basketball player? Seventeen with a scholarship to Bates? He fell down dead in the middle of a game."

Lucy remembered. The tragic death had stunned the entire region and terrified every parent whose child played in school sports. "That kid had an aneurysm, right? Is that what happened to Van?"

"It could have been. To tell you the truth, I only did an external exam, enough to satisfy myself that death was due to natural causes."

"I thought there were always autopsies after an unattended death," said Lucy.

"Well, his death wasn't unattended. He died in the ambulance, on route to the hospital. And, he smelled of alcohol. That could've been a factor."

Lucy remembered Van staggering as he grabbed the metal grille to push it open, and how he'd stumbled as he'd approached the children, spilling eggs from his basket.

"Look, if I had my way, I'd request a complete autopsy on everybody who dies. It's good science, we learn a lot from autopsies. But families resist. They don't want their loved ones cut open and dissected. And even when there's some question about a death, and I'm not saying there was in this instance, funding is extremely limited. I don't have the time or the money to do what I'd like to do as the town doctor. We were lucky to be able to get enough flu vaccine for the seniors last fall."

"I know," said Lucy. "But you're satisfied Van's death was natural? Nobody conked him on the head or anything?"

"Lucy, as I understand it, he was wearing a giant padded bunny head."

"So I guess that means blunt trauma is out of the question?"

He laughed. "I'd say so."

"Well, thanks for your time. It was nice chatting with you."

"Right. Oh, and Lucy, Bill is due for a blood pressure check."

Lucy was flooded with a sense of guilt. She knew he'd cancelled an appointment and she hadn't reminded him to reschedule. "I'll get right on it," she promised, hanging up and writing a reminder to herself.

"So what's the story?" asked Phyllis. The fax machine began to spew out a sheet of paper.

"Doc Ryder has no reason to suspect foul play in Van's death," said Lucy, walking across the office to the fax machine.

"Well, Maxine does seem to have a flair for the dramatic," said Phyllis.

"You can say that again," said Lucy, scanning the fax, which had just come from the local funeral home.

> *VAN VORST DUFF, of Boston, age 46, died unexpectedly on April 3.*
>
> *Van was born in Milton, Massachusetts, where he attended Milton Country Day School. He graduated from Lawrence Academy in Groton, Massachusetts and attended Colgate University in Hamilton, New York.*
>
> *A keen sportsman and nature lover, Van volunteered his time and energy to numerous organizations devoted to conserving the world's natural resources and preserving wildlife.*
>
> *He is survived by a daughter, Juliette Duff of New York City; his mother, Vivian Duff of Nantucket, Massachusetts; his father, Andrew Duff of Brookline, Massachusetts; his sister, Victoria (Duff) Allen, and her husband, Henry Chatsworth Allen of Boston; and his grandmother, Vivian Van Vorst of Tinker's Cove.*
>
> *Burial will be private.*
>
> *Memorial gifts may be made to the International Wildlife Consortium, 12 Water St., Suite 2, Milford, MA 01757.*

"What's so interesting?" asked Phyllis. "The lunch menu from the Hot Pot?"

"It's Van's obituary," said Lucy, giving her the sheet of paper. "It sure doesn't say much."

"*Burial will be private*," read Phyllis with a snort. "Figures. They wouldn't want a bunch of curious gawkers there."

"Or the press," said Lucy.

"I guess he never had a job," observed Phyllis.

"He probably didn't need the money," said Lucy. "He volunteered."

"That's like working here," said Phyllis. "Considering how little Ted pays us, we're practically volunteers."

Lucy laughed. "Did you notice who isn't mentioned?"

Phyllis nodded. "Maxine."

"Pretty interesting, if you ask me," said Lucy, tapping her finger on her chin. "I wonder if she's on to something."

Chapter Five

"I could have a chat with Elfrida," offered Phyllis.

"Would you?" asked Lucy eagerly.

Phyllis shrugged. "Sure. I'll put her on speakerphone so you can hear, too."

Lucy listened to the rings, which sounded very loud. Elfrida was in no hurry to answer, but finally they heard her breathy Marilyn Monroe voice. "Pine Point, this is the kitchen," she whispered.

"It's your aunt Phyllis. I'm just calling to see how you're holding up, what with Van's death and all."

"It's awfully sad. I liked Van. I mean, I didn't really know him very well, but he was nice. A real gentleman." Lucy wasn't sure how to take this—Elfrida was a notoriously poor judge of men.

"I suppose VV is very upset," said Phyllis.

"I'm sure she is, but those nurses, Lupe and Sylvia, don't exactly confide in me. They want this, they want that, they're constantly demanding rice pudding and chicken broth and when I tell them to help themselves, they get all huffy and nasty. Like I have to open the refrigerator and hand them the plastic package—like they can't find the packs of rice pudding themselves? Now they want me to order some fancy Belgian beer for VV, something about B vitamins, I don't know. What I do know is if I start buying expensive stuff like that, Mr. Weatherby will have a fit! He goes over all the bills with a fine tooth comb, believe me."

Lucy was having a hard time keeping a straight face—she could just imagine Elfrida telling the nurses off—but Phyllis was clucking her tongue sympathetically. "I'm sure you've got a lot to do, getting ready for the funeral."

"Tell me about it," moaned Elfrida in her soft voice. "Willis was just in, giving me a list of foods to prepare. It all has to be done by Thursday and I don't know where to begin. What are tea sandwiches? You can't make sandwiches out of tea, can you? And he wants dozens and dozens. And tea cakes! I never heard of them. What are they?"

"Like pound cake, I think," offered Phyllis. "The sort of thing people can pick up in their fingers. No messy icing."

"I'm not very good at cakes. I've only used mixes. I usually buy the kids' birthday cakes at the IGA, all decorated," said Elfrida. "I don't know what I'm going to do." There was a small silence. "And, you know what? They're not using paper plates! VV has hundreds of dishes and cups and saucers and glasses and I'm supposed to wash them all by hand, because they're very fragile."

"You're going to need extra help," said Phyllis.

"Exactly. That's what I told Willis. I'm a cook, not a scullery maid!"

"What did he say?" asked Phyllis.

There was a little pause before Elfrida answered and Lucy wondered if Willis had made some disparaging remark about Elfrida's cooking—she had certainly left herself open to it. "He's going to check with Mr. Weatherby about hiring some temporary help."

At this point, Lucy couldn't resist joining the conversation. "You know, my friend Sue and I would be happy to help. Nobody makes a better tea sandwich than Sue!"

For the first time in the conversation, Elfrida seemed to perk up. "Really? What about those pound cakes?"

"No one better than Sue. And I'm one heck of a dishwasher."

"Well, thanks for offering. I have to get approval from Willis, he's the butler, but I'm pretty sure I can get him on board."

Lucy knew that when Elfrida wanted to wind a man around her little finger, she usually succeeded. "Well, I'm here at the office. Let me know, okay?"

Phyllis switched off the speakerphone but continued her leisurely chat with her niece, inquiring about all of Elfrida's children and their various problems. Like many childless people, Phyllis never hesitated to offer advice on discipline, dealing with school administrators, and even how to get the little ones to bed. Lucy, meanwhile, called her best friend, Sue Finch.

"I need to ask a big favor," she began when Sue answered.

"Uh-oh," replied Sue with a chuckle.

"I've gotten a tip that Van's death was suspicious and I want to go undercover at Pine Point, and I need you to help."

Sue was suspicious. "How exactly do you think I can help?"

"Well, we're going to be kitchen help. Elfrida needs help with the food for the funeral."

"You want me to be a sous-chef?" Sue considered herself a bit of a gourmet.

"Nothing that fancy. Just tea sandwiches and cakes."

"No way, not with my back," said Sue, who had recently retired from the classroom at Little Prodigies, the child care center she owned with Chris Cashman. "I can't stand for hours on end, not anymore. All those years in the classroom did me in."

"You can sit," said Lucy. "You don't have to stand to mix up cakes and cut sandwiches."

Sue was doubtful. "Maybe. But answer me this: How are you going to investigate this hot tip when you're stuck in the kitchen?"

"Details, details," said Lucy, who hadn't quite worked that out herself. "We'll cross that bridge when we get to it." She crossed her fingers and took a deep breath. "So, will you help?"

"Maybe," said Sue, who enjoyed bargaining. "If the price is right."

"I'll get back to you."

The deadline for the *Pennysaver* was at noon Wednesday and at five minutes past, Lucy pulled up in front of Sue's house and honked. A minute or two later, Sue appeared at the door, carrying a roomy tote bag. "What have you got there?" asked Lucy, as Sue seated herself in the car.

"My knives, of course," said Sue, holding the bag so Lucy could peek inside.

"We're making sandwiches, not butchering a pig," said Lucy, eyeing the formidable *batterie de cuisine*.

"You never know," said Sue placidly. "It's better to be prepared. So how much are we getting paid for this gig?"

This was the question Lucy had been dreading. "Mmmmm . . . ," she began, braking suddenly as a large garbage truck pulled out in front of them. "Did you see that?"

"Hard to miss," said Sue, "but don't change the subject. How much?"

"Minimum wage."

"I haven't worked for minimum wage since I graduated from college!" exclaimed Sue. Indeed, even though she was going to spend the afternoon up to her elbows in egg salad and cake batter, she was impeccably dressed in a wool pants suit and a cashmere sweater and had applied her usual flawless makeup. Her glossy black hair was styled in a neat pageboy and her nails were freshly manicured.

"Look, you can take my pay, too," offered Lucy, dressed as usual in jeans and running shoes, topped with a machine-washable acrylic sweater beneath a tired parka. Her short haircut was also of the wash-and-wear variety. "I'm doing this because it's the only way I can get into the house for the funeral."

"That's not necessary," mumbled Sue. "But, why do you think Van's death was suspicious, apart from your suspicious nature, that is?"

"I saw Van collapse," admitted Lucy, "and I assumed it was a heart attack or a stroke or something like that. But his ex-girlfriend came to the *Pennysaver* office on Monday, and she insists his death was no accident. Furthermore, she says Van's sister Vicky and her husband and their lawyer are all in cahoots, trying to get control of VV's money."

Sue knit her brows together. "Sounds to me like you've got us walking into a hornet's nest."

Lucy grinned. "The trick is not to get stung."

When they reached the mansion, Sue was all for marching right up to the front door but Lucy restrained her. "We're the help, remember? Back door."

Sue gave her a withering glance. "You're kidding, right?"

Lucy shook her head and her curls bounced. "No. Elfrida warned me. Back door."

It was really sort of interesting, thought Lucy, as they

trudged along the oyster shell drive to the rear of the house. Up until now, she'd only seen the mansion from the point of view of a visitor and, as the architect clearly intended, had been impressed by the grandeur of the place. Now, as a worker, she was discovering the necessary service area that was cleverly concealed by a stone balustrade and leafy shrubs. Descending a rather shady, dank staircase, they found themselves in front of a locked door. A doorbell was marked with a neatly painted sign, PLEASE RING.

Lucy rang.

Nothing happened.

She rang again, and nothing happened.

Sue was just about to press the button one more time when the door opened and they were confronted with the imposing figure of Willis the butler. As always, he was dressed in a single-breasted black suit, with a white shirt and somber gray and black striped tie. His face had a well-tended look, clean shaven and pink cheeked, but his hawklike nose gave him a formidable aspect. "Yes?" he inquired, looking down at them.

"We're the temporary kitchen help," said Lucy. "I'm Lucy Stone and this is Sue Finch."

Willis looked them over. "I guess you'll do," he said with a sniff.

"We'll more than *do*," said Sue. "You're lucky to have us. I'm a top-notch cook—and Lucy is, too."

Lucy blushed at this surprising praise from Sue.

"I recently won a prize for my blueberry cheesecake," said Lucy, who had been the unexpected winner at a Valentine's Day dessert contest.

"No need to rub it in," whispered Sue, who was still a bit miffed that her fabulous brownies didn't take the prize.

The two women followed Willis down a rather dim

hallway, where every other light fixture was turned off. "Why the gloom?" she asked, raising her voice.

"We're saving energy," said Willis, opening a door and standing aside for them to enter.

They found themselves in a businesslike office, where Willis had the necessary paperwork waiting, for their social security numbers and signatures. "As day workers, you are considered independent contractors so no payroll taxes will be deducted from your compensation. I believe we have already agreed on the hourly wage."

"Lucy may have, but I don't believe I have," said Sue, lifting her chin. "My rate is fifteen dollars an hour."

Willis's eyes widened and he pressed his lips together. "Then I'm afraid we will not need your services," he said, picking up Sue's paperwork and preparing to rip it up.

"She's just kidding," said Lucy, glaring at her friend.

"Can't blame me for trying," muttered Sue, taking the papers from Willis and scrawling her signature in the highlighted space. "This is how the rich get richer and . . ."

Lucy delivered a gentle kick to Sue's shin. "Where's the kitchen?" she asked brightly.

"Follow me," said Willis, as if he were a docent leading a museum tour.

The kitchen was at the end of the hallway and looked to Lucy as if it had come straight out of a PBS period drama. Windows placed high on the walls allowed plenty of light, which revealed rather grimy, grease-stained walls and ceiling. An enormous black coal stove dominated the room, but a small electric stove stood next to it. A large wooden table in the center of the kitchen was the primary work space; an old-fashioned white porcelain sink with exposed plumbing beneath hung from a wall. Another wall was occupied by several refrigerators and wire racks that held provisions as well as pots and pans.

There was no sign of Elfrida.

"Where is that damned woman?" muttered Willis. "Never here when you want her."

"Looking for me?" Elfrida appeared in one of the numerous doorways leading off the kitchen, wiping her hands on a dishtowel. "I was just washing up the lunch things."

You had to hand it to the woman, thought Lucy. Even in a stained white apron and an ill-fitting pastel green uniform, she looked spectacular. It didn't hurt, of course, that the uniform was too tight across her bounteous breasts, and the requisite hairnet barely contained her wavy blond hair, which escaped in wisps that curled charmingly around her heart-shaped face. Even with her feet shod in rubber kitchen clogs, her amazing legs were, well, amazing.

"These ladies are here to help with preparations for tomorrow's reception," said Willis. Something in his tone made Lucy feel as if she should curtsy.

"Oh, I know Lucy and Sue," said Elfrida, giving them each a hug. "Now let me get you girls some aprons. Who's washing and who's baking?"

"Lucy will be washing," said Sue in her teacher's voice.

"That's right," said Lucy, resigned to her fate.

Elfrida took her hand and led her to a room off the kitchen—which Lucy supposed was the scullery—where a lonely, aged dishwasher stood among stacks of plates, cups, and saucers, and row upon row of crystal glassware. Lucy had never seen anything like it, except perhaps at the china shop at the outlet mall. "Do you have any rubber gloves?" she asked.

Several hours later, Lucy dried the last crystal sherry glass and placed it on a tray, among dozens of others neatly lined up like soldiers on parade. The gold-rimmed plates were neatly stacked, ready to be carried upstairs, as were the cups and saucers. Lucy shook out the dishtowel she'd been using and hung it with several others on a wooden rack to dry. Then she went into the kitchen to see if Sue needed help.

"How's it going?" she asked.

Sue turned off the electric mixer. "What did you say?"

"Do you need any help?"

"Sure do. The oven is full, but you could get started on those sandwiches. I've boiled up a couple dozen eggs—you could make egg salad. There's also tuna, a tiny bit of smoked salmon—oh, and there's radishes that need to be scrubbed."

Lucy had been to enough receptions at the Quissett Yacht Club to be familiar with radish and butter sandwiches, a true WASP delicacy. "So I shouldn't bother looking for the caviar?"

Sue laughed. "No caviar. This is the economy buffet."

Lucy was shelling the eggs, sniffing at the unpleasant sulfur smell, when one of the nurses popped in. "Whew!" she exclaimed, speaking with a slight Spanish accent. "What a stink!"

"Eggs," said Lucy, going on to introduce herself and Sue. "We're helping out for the funeral."

"I'm Sylvia Vargas," said the nurse, a plump woman in her late twenties, dressed in blue scrubs and white clogs. "I take care of Mrs. Van Vorst." She looked around. "Where's that cook?"

"I think she stepped outside for some fresh air," offered Sue, who was pouring batter into a cake tin.

"Fresh air! She's smoking!" Sylvia shook her head. "A cook who smokes! Can you believe it?" She stalked over to the outside door and yanked it open, then stepped through, leaving it ajar. "Elfrida! Don't you know smoking is bad for you? You'll get cancer!"

Lucy and Sue could hear the conversation clearly; their eyes met, and they both smiled.

"You didn't come all the way down here to warn me about smoking," said Elfrida.

"No. I want to know why you switched brands on Mrs. V's nutrition drink. This new one tastes terrible."

"Mr. Weatherby said the other stuff was too expensive," said Elfrida. "He said to get the generic stuff."

"I should make him drink it," said Sylvia, coming back inside. She opened the refrigerator and extracted a can of the stuff, then left the kitchen. A moment or two later, they heard her arguing with Willis in the hallway.

"No way!" Sylvia was saying, in no uncertain terms. "I'm a nurse, not a cleaning lady! And, by the way, this nutrition drink is expired. It's past the sell-by date."

There was a low male murmur; Lucy and Sue couldn't quite make it out. Determined to hear the conversation, Lucy went over to the swinging door and pushed it open a tiny bit with her foot.

"Perhaps you could consider it a favor to Mrs. Van Vorst," Willis was saying. "She certainly wouldn't want visitors to see the house at less than its best. She would fret. It might even be bad for her health."

Sylvia was laughing. "Good try, but once again, may I remind you that I am a professional, highly educated, registered nurse. Cleaning is simply not part of my job description. If you want the house cleaned, you'll have to hire more cleaners. Tracy can't do it all herself."

"I wish I could," said Willis. "You know the situation as well as I do. Mr. Weatherby will not approve another penny for this funeral. I had a hard enough time convincing him to let me hire those two kitchen helpers."

Lucy looked at Sue, who raised her eyebrows.

"I don't want to hear it, Willis. That's your problem. All I do is take care of Mrs. V. Meds, temps, blood pressure, that's my job. Oh, and by the way, Yum-Yum peed on the carpet again, and as I've told you before, cleaning up dog messes is not my job!"

"*Not my job, not my job*," muttered Willis, and Lucy hopped back to the sink and her eggs. She was peeling one when he entered the kitchen and grabbed a bottle of cleaning liquid and a roll of paper towels.

"Oh, Mr. Willis," she said in a bright voice. "I've finished washing the plates and glasses—would you like me to carry them upstairs?"

Willis stared at her, mouth open in surprise. "That would be a great help," he said. "Follow me."

Lucy did, scurrying behind him as he zoomed down the long hall and began climbing up a scuffed back stairway and down yet another dimly lit hallway. He finally opened a door and Lucy found herself stepping into the dining room. The large central table had been moved to the side of the room and other smaller tables had been placed in a row in front of the French doors; folded damask tablecloths were lying on each table. Beyond, through the open double doors, she glimpsed an elegantly decorated room, where piles of chairs were stacked here and there. "The drawing room," he said. "That is where the service will take place."

Lucy nodded, taking in the dining room's arrangement. "Cakes and sandwiches on the big table, beverage service on the smaller ones?" asked Lucy.

Willis's eyebrows shot up. He seemed surprised at Lucy's competence and it took him a moment to respond. Finally, he nodded. He made an odd figure, dressed in his formal outfit and clutching the cleaning equipment, and

Lucy saw he was not the imperturbable butler she had thought he was, but a man who was struggling to do the best job he could in difficult circumstances.

"I'll get started," she said, shaking out a tablecloth and spreading it on one of the smaller tables.

Willis cleared his throat. "You and your friend seem to be very capable," he said. "Would you be interested in working tomorrow, serving and cleaning up?"

Lucy jumped at the opportunity, but she wasn't at all sure about Sue. "No problem," she said, crossing her fingers. "We'll be here."

Willis nodded and departed to clean up after Yum-Yum, and after a moment's hesitation, Lucy went to the doorway, watching as he climbed the carpeted staircase. When he was out of sight she quickly followed, tiptoeing across the tiled hall where the center table was bare, without the valuable Karl Klaus sculpture. Lucy wondered if *Jelly Beans* was normally kept in storage between events, as she continued up the carpeted stairs. Reaching the spacious hallway upstairs, she noticed one of the many paneled doors was slightly ajar and went over to it.

As she stepped closer, she was aware of a stale, rank scent emanating from the room, as if the windows hadn't been opened in a long time. Peeking through the slight gap into the dimly lit room, she had a glimpse of VV's head, propped on a pile of pillows. Her hair, now white, seemed flat and heavy, and her cheeks were sunken. Her nose jutted out sharply and was her most prominent feature. One scrawny hand, like a claw, rested on the bedcovers.

It was a shocking sight and Lucy withdrew, hurrying back down the stairs. She didn't know what she'd expected. She'd heard VV was not doing well, but she hadn't expected to see this corpselike creature. The image was still fresh in her mind as she continued down the service stairs to the kitchen, intending to start bringing up the clean crockery and glassware.

"Goodness," said Sue, looking up from her mixing bowl. "You look like you've seen a ghost."

"Almost," said Lucy, slipping into a chair. "I saw VV."

"Was it bad?" Sue was pouring cake batter into a loaf pan.

Lucy nodded. "Really bad. This isn't right."

"What do you mean?" asked Sue, scraping out the last globs of batter from the bowl.

"I only got a glimpse, but she looked like a skeleton. Her hair was nasty—looked like it hasn't been washed in weeks." Lucy swallowed. "Her room stinks."

"That doesn't make sense." Sue shoved the pan into the oven and shut the door. "That nurse, Sylvia, seems competent enough."

"She was arguing with Willis. You heard them. There's not enough help to keep the place clean, they're skimping on VV's nutrition, it's crazy. I don't see how you go from being a millionaire to having to drink expired cans of nutrition drink in just a few years. She can't have lost all her money."

Sue was already creaming butter and sugar together with the electric mixer. "If you ask me," she said, raising her voice over the hum of the motor, "I don't think she's lost her money at all. After all, the stock market is the one thing that's recovered in this recession. I think somebody else wants it and has decided it's time for VV to go."

"That's absolutely horrible," said Lucy, picking up a tray of crystal stemware and beginning the long trek to the dining room upstairs.

When she got there, she found a middle-aged woman pushing a vacuum back and forth on the Persian rug. Seeing Lucy awkwardly negotiating through the doorway with the heavy tray, the woman switched off the vacuum and went to help.

"Here you go," she said, holding the door for her.

"Thanks," said Lucy, setting the tray down on the nearest table. "That stuff is heavy, and I've only got about ten more trays to go."

The woman smiled. "I'm Tracy," she said. "You must be new here."

"Lucy Stone. I'm helping out for the funeral."

Tracy's eyebrows shot up in surprise. "Really? Extra help? I can't believe that cheapskate Weatherby okayed spending the money."

"Not much money," grumbled Lucy, whose back was already beginning to bother her. "Oh, well, back to the mines . . ."

"Hold on," said Tracy. "There's a dumbwaiter."

"A what?" asked Lucy.

"One of those mini-elevators. I'll show you." Tracy led the way to a small room off the dining room. "This is the butler's pantry, and this," she said, opening a cabinet door, "is the dumbwaiter." She pushed a button on a control panel and the shelved unit sank out of sight, revealing an empty shaft. "It goes down to the kitchen."

"Elfrida never told me," exclaimed Lucy.

"She probably doesn't know. It goes upstairs, too, to the master bedroom."

"How handy," said Lucy.

"It is handy, but they don't use it much, now that VV doesn't entertain anymore. The dining room hasn't been used for ages."

"Do the nurses use it?" asked Lucy.

Tracy shook her head. "They'd rather go down to the kitchen themselves. It makes a change, you know? Otherwise, they'd be stuck in that room all day."

"Well, thanks," said Lucy. "This will make my job a lot easier."

She turned to go back down to the kitchen to load the dumbwaiter when one of the French doors opened and a thirtyish woman entered, carrying a potted orchid, and stepped carefully around the temporary tables. She was dressed for outdoor work, in jeans and a barn jacket, with sturdy duck boots on her feet.

"Hi, Tracy," she said, smiling over the nodding pink blooms. Her brown hair was pulled back in a ponytail, and her cheeks were pink. She carried with her a scent that Lucy, a keen gardener, recognized. It was the scent of newly turned earth and green leaves, fresh air and sunshine. "Where do you want these?"

"I don't know. You better ask Lucy, here. She's in charge of the arrangements for the collation."

Lucy laughed, introducing herself. "I don't think I'm in charge of anything. I'm just helping out for a day or two."

"I'm Izzy Scannell. I'm supposed to be the head gardener, but I'm down to one helper, which means I'm more of a yard worker. Lately, I've been cleaning out the beds and weeding; pretty soon I'll be mowing. It's just maintenance now, no more experiments with the perennial bed, no more additions to the water garden."

"That's a beautiful orchid," said Lucy.

"It's a good thing orchids are tougher than they look—they're about all I've been able to keep going in the greenhouse. Now they're earning their keep, as we won't have to order expensive arrangements from a florist."

"That should please Mr. Weatherby," said Lucy.

Izzy shot her a questioning glance. "What do you know about Mr. Weatherby?"

Lucy smiled. "I've only been here a few hours, but I've heard plenty about how cheap he is."

"You can say that again," said Izzy. "He's made me lower the temperature in the greenhouse and he's been, as he says, 'concerned' about the cost."

Tracy chuckled. "Sounds like you're in trouble," she said, unplugging the vacuum and pushing it into the next room.

Izzy twisted her lips into a sardonic grin. "She's right. Expressing 'concern' is the first step around here. I think it's time for me to look for a new job before I'm fired."

Lucy was spreading another tablecloth. "Perhaps he'll be so taken with your orchids that he'll reevaluate."

"I'm not holding my breath," said Izzy, nodding at a wheelbarrow full of blooms that was on the terrace, just outside the French doors. "So where do you want me to put them?"

Lucy asked her to set the plants on the floor, planning to add them as a final touch after she'd arranged the plates, silver, and glassware. Then she went back downstairs for another load of tableware, wondering exactly how she was going to convince Sue to agree to work a second day at Pine Point.

Chapter Six

The *Pennysaver* with Lucy's photo of the EMTs working over the collapsed figure of Van Duff was lying on the table in Jake's Donut Shop. The rescue workers' bodies blocked his head; all that could be seen of Van were his plush-covered legs and feet. TRAGEDY AT EGG HUNT, read the headline.

"It *is* a tragedy," said Rachel Goodman, shaking her head. Her long black hair was caught in a loose bun that wobbled and her big brown eyes were mournful. "Some of those children are going to be scarred for life. They saw the Easter Bunny, an iconic figure, collapse right in front of them. Talk about trauma!" Rachel was a psych major in college, and had never gotten over it. She was one of the four friends who gathered at Jake's, where the coffee was strong and the conversation even stronger, every Thursday morning for breakfast.

"Oh, I don't know," countered Sue with a chuckle, tucking a lock of her expensively cut hair behind her ear with a perfectly manicured finger. "I bet a Cadbury cream egg would go a long way toward restoring any kid's mental health." Sue was a dedicated dieter and limited herself to black coffee.

"Those things are disgusting," protested Pam Stillings, who was a fan of whole grains and natural foods and always had the yogurt and granola bowl. She was married to Lucy's boss, Ted.

"I didn't want Ted to use that photo on the front page," said Lucy, her fork poised over the hash and eggs combo plate. "It was worse, if you can imagine such a thing. The head of the bunny costume was here," she said, pointing with her fork to the white margin outside the photo. "It looked like the Easter Bunny had been decapitated."

Rachel was horrified. "Oh, dear."

"I got him to crop it out, it was just too . . ." Lucy speared a chunk of hash with her fork and dipped it in the egg yolk.

"Graphic," said Sue. "That's the word you want."

"Inappropriate," said Lucy, swallowing. "That's what I told Ted. The *Pennysaver* is a family newspaper, though I don't know if kids really read newspapers these days."

"I don't think anybody reads newspapers," said Pam with a grim expression. "Circulation's down."

"Well, Lucy," said Sue, lifting her cup and sipping her coffee, "if Ted lays you off, you can always go into catering."

"That reminds me," said Lucy. "Don't forget we agreed to work at Pine Point this afternoon." Sue had done no such thing, but Lucy was hoping to finesse that point.

"I don't remember agreeing to that," said Sue. "I was planning on cleaning out my closet and putting the winter things in storage."

"Please," said Lucy in a small voice. "I really need you. This is my only chance to get in the house again . . ."

"Are you going undercover?" asked Rachel, leaning forward and whispering.

"Why? What are you investigating?" asked Pam.

"Nancy Drew here thinks there's something suspicious going on at Pine Point," said Sue with a sniff. "If you ask me, the only suspicious thing is why they ever hired Elfrida as a cook! She can't even make a simple pound cake. Lucy had me cooking up cakes and sandwiches for after the funeral all yesterday afternoon and now she wants me to be a server while she goes sniffing around."

Rachel broke off a piece of her Sunshine muffin. "Lucy might be on to something. I know Bob is concerned about VV," she said, popping the bit of muffin in her mouth. Rachel's husband, Bob, was a lawyer.

"How so?" Lucy asked.

"Well, he represented VV for years, but last summer he got a letter from another lawyer saying VV no longer required his services. He called the house to check, but was told VV was too weak to speak to him. Willis, however, confirmed the change, saying this new guy, Weatherby, was handling everything. Bob told Willis that he would continue to represent VV unless he got something in writing and a day or two later he got a brief note, very terse, typed, with VV's signature on the bottom. Bob said it didn't seem like VV's way of writing—her notes were always handwritten and full of dashes and exclamation points—and the signature was dubious. He's been trying to decide what to do. He feels responsible for her, but she has every right to hire whomever she wants to represent her. It's awkward."

"I don't know if this is relevant," said Lucy, "but there does seem to be some sort of economy drive going on at Pine Point. The staff has been reduced, they're cutting spending every way they can. Even Van's funeral . . ."

"Egg salad sandwiches!" exclaimed Sue. "And sherry from a jug!"

Pam nodded in agreement. "They only gave twenty-five

dollars to the Hat and Mitten Fund last year. I think VV really got slammed in the recession."

Rachel knit her brows together. "I don't think so. The stock market has recovered, it's jobs and housing that are still depressed. And I happen to know that VV is doing just fine, at least she was last summer." Her hand flew to her mouth. "I'm actually not supposed to know that—forget I said it."

"I'll forget in a minute," said Lucy. "First tell me what you know and how you know it. Off the record, of course."

"Well," said Rachel, as they all leaned in closer, "Bob was very upset when he learned that VV no longer wanted him to be her lawyer and he mentioned that considering how much money she had, he should have demanded a retainer. He said here she was with hundreds of millions of dollars and he only charged her his usual hourly rate, the same rate he charges clients with a lot less money." Her cheeks grew pink with embarrassment and she hurried to defend her husband. "That's not really like him, he's not greedy, it was just that he was so upset. He'd represented her for years and years."

They all nodded in agreement, aware that Bob's fees were extremely moderate and he did a great deal of work *pro bono*.

Rachel looked at Lucy. "Now, remember, you're forgetting I ever said anything about this."

"Right," said Lucy, waggling her fingers. "It's gone. What was it you said?" But she knew, they all knew, that it's very hard to forget hundreds of millions of dollars.

About a hundred specially invited guests were seated in the drawing room where the funeral service for Van Duff was underway; Lucy and Sue were busy in the dining room with last minute preparations. They could hear bits and pieces of the service as they laid out the platters of sandwiches and sliced cake and made sure there was cream—Sue pointed out that it was actually milk—in the creamers and sugar in the sugar bowls.

"He was always up for a good time," they heard a male voice saying. "Whether it was a last-minute trip to catch the waves at Baja or a round of golf at the National, he was your man. I don't think I ever heard him say the word no. Van was never too busy to help out a friend. I remember when I got stranded in Bali, after the tsunami. I don't know how he even knew I was there, but a couple of days after the disaster, I'm out there on this beach, trying to help these people whose village was completely destroyed—I mean absolutely nothing was left standing—and what do I see but a huge catamaran that comes right up on to the beach and who's at the wheel but Van. He gives me a wave and then he starts unloading boxes of food and clothing and bottled water. He saved the entire village. I don't think they would have made it without his help; they had nothing." There was a long pause and then they heard him continue, his voice tight with emotion, "I'm gonna miss you, bro."

Other speakers continued in the same vein: Van was terrific at golf, a keen competitor on the tennis court, a sailor who loved to take risks, a generous friend to those in need, a lover of wilderness and a defender of endangered species. It was the last speaker, however, who they found most moving.

"Van was my father," she began, in a voice so soft they had to strain to hear her. Crossing the dining room and peeking through the double doors, they saw a beautiful young woman standing at the podium. Tall and whippet thin, she was dressed simply in black which made a stunning contrast to her buttery blond hair and creamy complexion.

"In addition to everything else, Van had terrific genes," said Sue. "You know, I've seen her before. I can't remember where."

"Shh," hissed Lucy. "I want to hear."

"He wasn't the sort of father who read bedtime stories and tucked you in at night, he wasn't the sort of father who made you eat broccoli," she said, getting a laugh. "In fact, there were long periods when he wasn't around—but that didn't matter, because it made it so special when he was.

"I have one memory I want to share with you. It was when I was very little, maybe four or five years old. It's one of my first memories. We had a snowstorm, a big storm that kept us indoors all day. Daddy blew in just as the sun was coming out the next morning and he had Mom bundle me up in my boots and snowsuit. We started out walking but the snow was too deep for me so he picked me up and set me on his shoulders and carried me up to the top of our road, Pickering Avenue. It was early in the morning and no cars were out, but the road had been plowed, leaving just a couple of inches of packed snow, perfect for sledding. Dad set me down on this big old Flexible Flyer sled and wrapped his arms tight around me and away we went, sailing down Pickering Avenue. I've never again done anything as exciting, and I've never felt as safe as I did in my daddy's arms, flying through that cold winter morning."

Lucy's and Sue's eyes met and they both had to brush away tears. In the drawing room, someone struck a few chords on the piano and everyone shuffled to their feet to sing "Morning Has Broken." Sue adjusted the parsley garnish on a platter of sandwiches, Lucy stationed herself behind the urns of coffee and tea, and the gathered mourners sang the final amen. Willis opened the doors to the dining room and the family formed a reception line.

Lucy recognized Vicky, Van's sister, and her husband, Henry, from the photos she had seen in the society pages. Vicky's light brown hair was done in a classic pageboy complete with a black headband and she was wearing a single strand of pearls over a black and white tweed suit. Henry's hair was graying at the temples and he was impeccably dressed in a charcoal gray suit and beautiful wingtip shoes, which had been polished and buffed to a high sheen. Van's mother, Little Viv, stood next to Henry, and Lucy was shocked to see how fragile she looked. She was so thin that her knees and elbows were knobby bulges beneath the thin silvery gray silk knit pantsuit she was wearing. Her granddaughter, the beautiful Juliette, was last in line and the two made a startling contrast between youth and age. It was impossible to avoid seeing Juliette's future in Little Viv's frailty.

Soon Lucy was too busy pouring tea and coffee to keep track of the principal mourners, and the dining room was filled with the gossipy din that inevitably follows a funeral. She suspected that the survivors were so relieved to find themselves alive and kicking that they enthusiastically embraced each other in good fellowship and indulged in the enjoyment of large amounts of food and drink. The platters were emptying fast, Lucy saw, and the sherry was almost gone. She was on her way to inform Willis that more wine was needed when she encountered her dear old friend, Miss Julia Ward Howe Tilley.

Miss Tilley, now retired, had been the longtime librarian at the Broadbrooks Free Library and knew just about everything about everyone in Tinker's Cove. Her aureole of white hair gave her an angelic aspect but she was no sweet old lady, as Lucy knew only too well. Miss Tilley—no one except a diminishing number of very old friends dared call her anything else—had a sharp tongue and didn't hesitate to use it.

"What are you doing here?" Lucy asked, embracing the old woman. "I thought you avoided funerals like the plague."

"It's true, I don't much like them," said Miss Tilley, who had some years ago celebrated her ninetieth birthday, "but as funerals go, this one wasn't too bad. They skipped a lot of the religious nonsense and stuck to Van's life, which made it a lot more interesting than most."

"I heard a little bit," said Lucy. "It made me wish I'd known Van."

"Well, you know how it is at funerals," sniffed Miss Tilley. "They only say good things about the dear departed. Believe me, there was plenty that wasn't wonderful about Van. His mother, Little Viv, is my goddaughter, you know, and she spent many an afternoon crying on my shoulder about him. He was kicked out of four or five prep schools, as I remember. Oh, he led poor Little Viv a merry chase!"

"I had no idea," said Lucy.

"Oh, yes. Van was a little devil, that he was."

"I'm sure he was. What I meant was, I had no idea you were so close to the family."

"I don't know about close." Miss Tilley shrugged her bony shoulders. "I send Little Viv a handkerchief for her birthday every year, that's about it. And, of course, VV and I grew up together, we went to the same one-room school, that sort of thing, but that was many, many years ago. People drift apart." Miss Tilley turned her attention to the buffet table. "You know, I wouldn't mind a glass of sherry and something to eat. Death always gives me an appetite."

"Right," said Lucy, reminded of her duties. "I was just on my way to see about getting more sherry from Willis."

"Well, don't let me keep you from your mission," said Miss Tilley with a wave of her gnarled, blue-veined hand.

Lucy was coming back with a freshly filled decanter when she saw Miss Tilley heading up the stairs, a plate of sandwiches in her hand, only to encounter Vicky in the middle of the flight. The two exchanged words, but Lucy couldn't hear what was said, and then Vicky shook her head, a firm expression on her face.

Miss Tilley responded by attempting to continue on her way upstairs, no doubt expecting the younger woman to step aside, but Vicky remained in place. In fact, Lucy thought she glimpsed Vicky raising her hand to block Miss Tilley's progress. The abrupt gesture caused the old woman to flinch and she seemed to be losing her balance. Lucy rushed up the stairs, fearing she was about to fall, but was preceded by a tall, gray-haired man who caught Miss Tilley around the waist and steadied her.

"Whoa, that was close," he said.

"I was just taking some sandwiches to VV," said Miss Tilley, who didn't seem rattled by her near miss at all. In fact, she seemed more determined than ever to visit with her old classmate. "I've heard she's not doing well and thought she'd enjoy a visit."

"I'm afraid that's impossible," said Vicky, glaring at Miss Tilley. "She's in no condition to receive visitors." She turned to Lucy, who was standing behind Miss Tilley, clutching the sherry. "The show is over, you can get back to work."

Lucy had never been spoken to in precisely that tone before and she found her hackles rising. "I just wanted to make sure your guest was all right," she snapped, refusing to be intimidated.

"Well, this particular guest has no business on this staircase," said Vicky.

Miss Tilley's jaw dropped in astonishment. "Victoria Eugenia, I've known you your entire life. That's no way to talk to me."

The room had fallen silent as everyone watched the little drama unfolding on the stairs, and Vicky was well aware of the attention they were attracting and quickly changed her tune. "Oh, Aunt Julia, forgive me. I don't know what I was thinking. I'm just so upset about all this . . ."

She looked about the room with a helpless expression and her husband, Henry, hurried to her side. With his arm around her waist, he led her away, up the stairs. Lucy found herself on the staircase with Miss Tilley and the gentleman who had saved her from falling.

"I'm Lucy Stone," she said. "Thanks for helping my friend."

"Oh, dear me." Miss Tilley was quite pink and flustered. "I am so sorry. I should have thanked you. You saved me from a nasty fall."

"It was a pleasure," he said. "I'm Andrew Duff."

"Such a shame about Van," said Miss Tilley, as he took her arm. "It's always terrible to lose a child."

Andrew simply nodded and Lucy realized with a shock that he must be Van's father. "I'm so sorry for your loss," she said, switching the decanter to one hand and taking Miss Tilley's free arm with the other. Together she and Andrew led her safely downstairs and installed her in an armchair.

"I wouldn't mind some of that sherry," said Miss Tilley, eyeing the bottle.

"I'll be right back," promised Lucy, who hurried over to a table where a few glasses remained. She filled two and brought them back to the pair, who were chatting amiably, like old friends. Miss Tilley was seated, looking up at the younger man, who Lucy suspected was well into his seventies. For his age, he was very good-looking, tall and lean with a full head of silver hair, and Lucy thought of Sue's remarks about Van's excellent genes. "Here you go," she said, giving them each a glass.

"To Van," said Miss Tilley, raising her glass and taking a sip.

"May he rest in peace," said Andrew. "He certainly never found it in his life."

Lucy wished she could listen in on the old couple's conversation but instead had to return to her job serving refreshments. The crowd showed no sign of thinning and they were running out of clean dishes; every surface in the room was cluttered with discarded plates, glasses, cups, and saucers. Lucy made a quick sweep of the room, gathering up as many as she could carry on a tray and sent it down to the kitchen on the dumbwaiter. She waited for it to return with a supply of clean crockery but none appeared, so she went down to the kitchen to see what the problem was. There she found Elfrida bent over the steamy sink, her face flushed and damp tendrils of hair clinging to her forehead.

"Willis said I've got to go faster, but what does he know? I bet he never washed a dish in his life. This is murder. My back's killing me and I've still got to get the nurse's supper tray ready or she'll kill me," she complained.

"I never saw such a crowd," said Lucy. "You'd think they were starving."

"I thought Sue was out of her mind, making all that food, but we're down to our last platter of sandwiches. There's still a couple of pound cakes, though, and I'm keeping the tea and coffee coming."

Lucy loaded the dumbwaiter with clean crockery and sent it up, then grabbed the last enormous platter of sandwiches and headed for the stairs. This time they seemed steeper and Lucy realized she'd been on her feet for hours without a break. It was a bit of a struggle to make it up the last few steps and she found herself staggering as she pushed the service door open with her fanny, nearly bumping into a trim little man.

"Whoa, there!" he exclaimed. "Can I help you with that?"

Lucy smiled gratefully as he took the heavy platter from her and set it on a table. "Thanks," she said, finding herself a bit dizzy. "I don't know what's come over me."

"Here, sit down a minute," he urged, taking her by the elbow and leading her back to the stairs.

Her head swimming, she held on to the railing and lowered herself carefully to sit on the top step while he watched anxiously. "Lower your head," he said. "You'll feel better."

Lucy rested her head on her knees and found that it did help, a little.

"When did you last eat?"

"Breakfast," replied Lucy.

"Stay there, I'll be right back." And in a matter of minutes he returned with a piece of pound cake and a cup of tea. "Drink up. I put lots of sugar in."

Lucy felt nauseated but sipped the tea and by the time she emptied the cup she was able to nibble on the cake. "Thank you so much," she said, looking up at her rescuer. "If you hadn't grabbed that platter, we could have had a tragedy."

He laughed. "Tiny sandwiches everywhere, it would have been a fine mess."

He was a funny fellow, spry, though he must be well

into his seventies, Lucy decided, and didn't quite seem to belong in this crowd. His gray suit was rumpled and didn't fit all that well; the sleeves were too long and the shoulders too large. His shoes weren't right, either. Instead of dress oxfords, he was wearing scuffed brown sports shoes.

"I'm not used to this kind of work. I'm just here for the day," said Lucy, and then she introduced herself.

"I'm Peter Reilly," he said, taking her hand. "I guess you'd call me a friend of the family."

"I better get back to work," said Lucy, grabbing the railing and hauling herself to her feet.

"Take it easy," urged Peter. "Believe me, in the grand scheme of things, this reception is merely a blip on the universal radar."

Lucy found herself grinning. "I'm not sure Willis would agree."

"Ah, Willis." Peter tented his fingers and Lucy had the fleeting impression that he was a priest or a philosopher. "He's uptight. They all are. Money does that to people."

"It does seem to be the prevailing theme around here. They say it's running out."

"I doubt that," said Peter.

Lucy was about to push the door open but paused. "What do you mean?"

"VV is very tight with her money. I happen to know because I was married to Little Viv for a while and money was really all that VV ever talked about. She didn't like the fact that her daughter married me—I used to be a Catholic priest, you see. I'm not sure if it was because I was Catholic, or because I left the priesthood, but whatever it was, she found me unacceptable. She ranted and raved and wrote Little Viv right out of her will." He smiled. "When we got divorced, she was terribly pleased and agreed to give Little Viv a modest annual allowance." He raised his hands and made little quotation marks in the air when he said the word modest.

"Here in town we see VV as a generous benefactor," said Lucy. "I didn't know she was so manipulative."

Peter shrugged. "As she grew older and weaker, she tried to use her money to control the family. It's natural, I suppose. It doesn't always work, of course. Little Viv couldn't care less about money, she just assumes it will be there. Van was the same way." He sighed. "I'm going to miss him."

Lucy was about to go through the door when it was suddenly pushed open and Sue confronted her. "There you are! What are you doing? I'm all alone out here!" she hissed, her eyes huge and accusatory.

"Sorry. I'll empty the dumbwaiter."

"No." Sue was having none of it. "I'll get the dishes. You can face the hungry hordes."

Lucy had been put in her place. "Yes, ma'am," she said, feeling like the lowest scullery maid in a PBS costume drama.

Chapter Seven

Back at her post, Lucy quickly served the handful of mourners who were waiting to refill their cups of coffee or tea. The crowd was thinning, she noticed with relief. There was one thing to be said for limiting the refreshments—when the food started to run out, people definitely got the idea that it was time to leave. Lucy had to tilt the coffee urn to fill a cup for Juliette, who was every bit as pretty up close as she was from a distance, and very friendly, too.

"You're a lifesaver," she said, taking the cup gratefully. "I've been too busy with the guests to have anything myself. I've been having a caffeine withdrawal."

Lucy smiled, finding Juliette's sweet smile infectious. The girl was a stunner, there was no denying it, with her widely spaced hazel eyes, high cheekbones, and swanlike neck. She was graceful, too, despite the fact that she was nearly six feet tall, and she had a casual way of tossing her long hair over her shoulder that made her approachable. *Don't be put off by my beauty,* this clever bit of body language seemed to say, *I'm really a down-to-earth, fun-loving girl.*

"Is this enough?" asked Lucy, passing her the little cup

perched on a saucer. She figured Juliette was used to the large takeout cups that seemed to be a fixture in stylish girls' hands, their cell phones at the ready in the other hand. "I can run downstairs and get you more coffee, or something to eat."

But before she could answer, or even take the cup, Juliette was caught up in an embrace from her mother, Maxine. "Mom!" she exclaimed, planting kisses on both cheeks. "Where have you been? You missed the service!"

"They told me it was at four, can you believe it?" Maxine was indignant, her chin quivering and her flowing garments, which seemed to Lucy more like a collection of black scarves than a dress, fluttering about her. "They wanted me to miss the whole thing! Imagine how I felt when I arrived and saw everybody was leaving," she said, pulling a handkerchief out of her brocade handbag and dabbing at her eyes.

"Who told you it was at four?" asked Juliette. "Mr. Weatherby?"

Maxine nodded, her eyes blazing as she scanned the room, clearly ready for a fight. Her gaze landed on a silver-haired gentleman in a black suit with gray pinstripes and highly polished shoes; he could have been a clone of Vicky's husband, Henry. "Weatherby!" she shrieked, barreling across the room toward him, her assorted garments flapping in the breeze. "I know you were behind this!"

So this was Weatherby, thought Lucy, watching the confrontation. She wasn't alone, the remaining mourners were equally transfixed.

The lawyer looked down his nose at the flamboyant woman with the brassy, obviously dyed red hair. "I don't know what you're talking about."

"Telling me the funeral was at four! You didn't want me here, did you?"

"You're being ridiculous. I'm sure you mistook the time." He sniffed suspiciously. "Have you been drinking? You're making a scene."

"I'll make a scene if I want to!" exclaimed Maxine. "Van was everything to me and you kept me from his funeral!"

"I might remind you that you and Van were never married," said Weatherby. "You're not actually part of the family."

Maxine's face grew so red that Lucy feared she might explode. "Not part of the family!" she exclaimed, incredulous. "Not part of the family! I'm the mother of his child, for God's sake." She poked Weatherby in the middle of his bony chest. "I have a lot more right to be here than you do. You're nothing but a crooked shyster lawyer and I've got the evidence to prove it."

For a moment, Weatherby seemed stunned, as if he'd been slapped, but he quickly recovered. "I'm sure I don't know what you mean," he said, sticking out his chin.

The stragglers who remained were standing about the room, fascinated by this unexpected turn of events. Little Viv, white faced and looking terribly fragile, was hurrying to Maxine, a lace handkerchief in her hand. She wasn't quick enough, however. Vicky, ever alert to the slightest rip in the social fabric, had joined the group and was taking charge. "I understand how upset you are, Maxine, but it's no fault but your own that you missed the service. We made a video of everything, you know, and I'll be more than happy to send you a copy."

"Video!" Hot tears of rage were spurting from Maxine's eyes. "I want to say good-bye to Van. Where is he? Where's his body?"

Juliette wrapped her long, graceful arms around her

mother's heaving shoulders. "You know he was cremated, Mom. He's gone."

"Gone! Gone!" Maxine fell to her knees, like the heroine in a Greek tragedy, and grabbed handfuls of her long, curly hair. "I just wanted to hold him one more time!"

Vicky and Weatherby exchanged glances and Lucy knew without a doubt that Maxine was right on the money, the two had conspired to keep her away from Van's funeral. Perhaps justifiably, she thought, considering how Maxine was behaving. Or perhaps not. At the very least, it seemed a mean trick.

Judging by the sympathetic expression on her face, Lucy thought Little Viv was thinking the same thing. She was reaching out to Maxine, supported by Andrew, who was holding her elbow. He had a stern expression on his face and was clearly disgusted; Lucy wondered which side he was on in this family drama.

Maxine was rising to her feet, helped by Juliette. She narrowed her eyes and turned on Henry, who had joined the group, standing behind his wife. "You're nothing but a bloodsucker, Henry, that's what you are. A human lamprey, a parasite. You've attached yourself to Vicky because you couldn't earn an honest dollar if you tried."

"Enough. This is enough," murmured Little Viv, the lacy handkerchief fluttering in her trembling hand.

"Little Viv is right," said Andrew firmly. "This is not the place for this discussion."

"Oh, sure, you'd like me to go away, wouldn't you?" Maxine's voice was steady, accusatory. "Well, I've been trying to have this particular discussion for some time, but nobody seems to want to talk to me, so we'll do it here and now." She fixed her eyes on Vicky. "I know what you're doing. I know what you're up to, Vicky. Now that Van is gone, you're going to inherit everything, but you don't want to wait, do you? You can't let the poor old woman die in peace in her own time. Oh, no." Her restless eyes darted from Henry to Weatherby and finally settled on Vicky. "Poor VV is a prisoner in her own home and you're flaunting her wealth all over town. You should be ashamed of yourself."

Vicky's plump face crumpled. "You've got it all wrong. I loved Van, I love *grandmère*, I'm doing everything I can to take care of her." She turned to Little Viv. "Isn't that right, Mummy?"

Little Viv tightened her grip on Andrew's hand. "Of course you are. The money doesn't matter. We're family, we take care of each other."

"If only that were true," said Maxine, pleading with Little Viv. "It's up to you—you're VV's daughter. You have to stop this."

Little Viv pressed her thin lips together and turned her pale blue eyes on Maxine. "I warned Van not to marry you—thank God for once he listened to me. You're a vile common person and it's time for you to leave."

Blinking back tears, Juliette once again wrapped her arms around her mother's shoulders. "Come on, Mom, they're not worth it." She turned to Little Viv. "My mother is as much a part of this family as I am. How do you think I felt, when I realized she wasn't here? It wasn't easy to talk about my father. I needed her support." She took her mother's hand and started to leave, then whirled around to face Vicky. "I will never forgive you for this."

"Oh, Juliette," crooned Vicky in her sweetest voice. "You did such a terrific job. Your little story, ice skating with your dad, it was lovely. We were all moved."

Juliette's face hardened in cold fury. "Ice skating! It was sledding, you moron! I went sledding with my dad and if you listened, if you cared, you'd know that."

Vicky was quick to switch tactics, pulling a handkerchief out of her pocket and dabbing her eyes. "My mistake. I'm just so, well, this is all so very difficult . . ."

"Yes it is." Peter Reilly joined the group, inserting himself between the two factions. "It's been a very long day for everyone." He turned to Maxine. "This is not productive. We'll take this up another day. Now it's time to go home. Can I give you a lift?"

"I have my car," she said. "But thank you."

Vicky and Henry had withdrawn, along with Weatherby. The three were talking together in low voices.

Maxine couldn't resist delivering a parting shot. "This isn't over," she declared. "You'll pay for what you've done. If it's the last thing I do, I'll see that you pay."

Then she whirled, her garments swirling around her, grabbed Juliette by the hand, and marched out the door.

Lucy, who had been gathering up dishes and glassware as slowly as she could so as not to miss a word of this fascinating confrontation, finally picked up her tray and headed for the butler's pantry. Sue, who was collecting the few remaining tea sandwiches and putting them together on a single plate, gave her a nod. "This is not a happy family," she said.

"I think Maxine's on to something," said Lucy. "What do you think?"

"I wouldn't trust any of them with the Sunday collection plate," said Sue, hoisting a tray and following Lucy through the door.

A couple of hours later, the tables were cleared, the dishes were washed, and Sue and Lucy were on their way out the door, each with a check for ninety-seven dollars and fifty cents in her pocket.

"I can't believe that's all we got, not even a hundred dollars," complained Sue. "We worked really hard."

"Willis did round off the last hour," said Lucy, "even though we only worked forty-two minutes."

Sue's voice was sarcastic. "Yeah, but who's counting?"

"You've got to admit it was interesting," said Lucy. "Especially when Maxine arrived."

"She really knows how to liven up a party," said Sue. "Poor Juliette, she's got her hands full with a mother like that. She's quite the career girl. Elfrida told me she's a top model in New York."

They were coming up the outside stairs from the service area behind the house, rounding the large hedge that concealed this utilitarian part of the mansion. Just beyond, they could see Izzy, the gardener, trying to pull down a vine that had climbed up the thick yew bushes. In the struggle, the vine was winning.

"You want some help?" asked Lucy.

"Bittersweet," said Izzy. "It's stubborn stuff."

"But the berries are so pretty," protested Sue.

"Camouflage," grunted Izzy. "You see the berries and think it's pretty and meanwhile it's strangling the life out of your fine ornamentals. It's a thug."

Lucy stepped beside Izzy and together they grabbed the vine, pulling with all their might, loosening yards and yards of the tangled stuff, which finally fell in a huge heap at their feet.

"Thanks," said Izzy, bundling the vine together and loading it into a garden cart. "I couldn't have done it without you."

"You better burn it," said Lucy. "It's the only way to get rid of it."

"You said it," agreed Izzy, adjusting her garden gloves and watching as Vicky and Henry left the mansion and got in a waiting limousine parked near the front door. The chauffeur held the door for them, and a moment or two later they drove off. "You gotta get rid of the thugs." With that, she bent down and grabbed the handle of the cart, pushing it away in the direction of the greenhouse.

Lucy and Sue resumed their walk to the parking lot. "You know," said Sue, "I'm not sure she was talking about the bittersweet."

"Me, either," said Lucy.

That night, with the scene from the funeral fresh in her mind, Lucy decided to broach the subject of wills with Bill. She was in bed, reading, and looked up when he came upstairs; he'd been watching a hockey game on TV.

"Who won?" she asked.

"Bruins."

"That's good," she said.

"Marchand scored in the last minute," he said, pulling his sweater over his head.

Lucy smiled, watching as he changed into his pajamas. He was still fit and trim, with broad shoulders, long back, and a tight little bottom; she could have gazed at him all night.

"What are you smiling about?" he asked, a naughty gleam in his eye.

"You're a fine-looking man," she said, "even if you're not getting any younger."

"I feel good," he said, slipping into bed beside her.

Lucy put her book on the bedside table and turned to face him. She stroked his beard, barely tinged with gray. "I worry about you," she said.

"Me? I'm fine," he said, leaning in for a kiss.

"Your work is dangerous," she said, pulling away. "You're up on ladders, you use power saws. What if something happened to you?"

"Nothing's going to happen," said Bill, flopping onto his back and staring at the ceiling.

"Everybody thinks that, but things do happen. Did you know the average age women become widows is fifty-eight?"

Bill looked at her out of the corner of his eye. "Are you planning something, Lucy?"

She put her hand on his chest, stroking him. "No way. I love you every bit as much as I did the day we got married, even more. I want to have you around for a long time."

"Good," said Bill.

"But I think we should get wills."

Bill snorted. "That would be a good idea—if we had anything to leave anybody."

"When you think about it, we've got quite a lot. There's the house, that's worth quite a bit . . ."

"A lot less than it used to be worth and, besides, it's a shared tenancy. It goes to the survivor."

"What about the college fund?"

"It's a joint account, same thing."

"But what if we both died, say in a car crash?"

"Wouldn't be our problem, would it?" said Bill, turning out the light.

Chapter Eight

The view out the kitchen window on Saturday morning was uninspiring. A few patches of filthy snow still remained and the melting snow, combined with an overnight shower, had turned the yard into a muddy mess. Libby had to go out, of course, and tracked in quite a bit of mud on her paws, so Lucy had already mopped the floor once and figured she'd have to do it many more times before sunshine and warm weather eventually dried the mud. Sometime in July, she thought sourly, putting the mop away.

Hearing her daughters Sara and Zoe singing upstairs, she smiled. Mud season came and went, it was a nuisance, but it meant that warm summer days weren't far off. It would be great to be able to open the window to warm, fresh breezes and to go outside without putting on bulky jackets, hats, and gloves. Lucy was itching to work in her garden, she wanted to get the peas and lettuce planted, she was looking forward to pulling those crisp and lovely French breakfast radishes.

Her garden tended to be on the wild side, she admitted to herself. She enjoyed the planting and the picking a lot more than the weeding and cultivating. She thought of the once perfect garden at Pine Point, where perennials sprouted where they were meant to be instead of the willy-nilly way they came up in her garden, and where weeds were dealt with promptly instead of when she got around to it. For years, she had envied VV's garden, viewing it every summer when it was part of the annual garden tour benefiting the cottage hospital. She always left wishing she had the skill and energy to emulate even one of those ravishing perennial borders that bloomed gorgeously from spring right through September, but now the garden's beauty seemed pointless, with no one to appreciate it.

And when you came to think of it, the perfect garden and the gorgeous house they had all so admired was really a bit of a sham. Somehow, you assumed that a beautiful house meant the people in them lived beautiful lives, but now she knew that wasn't the case. VV's house was a showcase, her garden an inspiration, but her family was a dysfunctional mess.

Zoe thunked into the kitchen in her green and white polka-dot mud boots and opened the refrigerator door. "I need something quick," she said. "Today's the pet parade."

Sara was behind her; her boots were a jolly pink and green plaid. "Grab a couple of those yogurt drinks," she said. "We've got to get going."

"I can cook you some eggs," offered Lucy. "It won't take a minute."

"We've got to be at the shelter in fifteen minutes," said Sara. "We've got to get all the animals in their costumes and over to the nursing home by eleven."

Lucy felt a little glow of pride. Sara and Zoe had been stalwart volunteers at the Friends of Animals shelter for years, donating hundreds of hours of time and not shrinking from the unpleasant jobs, either. They were both honor-list students and Sara had received a merit scholarship to the state university where she planned to study veterinary science.

The girls were zipping up their jackets, almost ready to go, and Lucy popped into the pantry where she grabbed a couple of granola bars. "Here you go," she said. "I'll see you later at the home."

"You're coming?"

"It's an assignment. I'm covering it for the paper."

"Don't take any pictures of me, okay? I didn't do my hair," said Sara, sporting a ponytail.

"Or me," said Zoe. "I'm wearing one of Dad's hardware store sweatshirts."

"I'll just take pictures of the animals," promised Lucy. "Now, scoot. You'll be late."

The pet parade was an Easter tradition at Heritage House Retirement Center, known to everyone in Tinker's Cove as "the old folks' home" despite the owners repeated campaigns to convince people to adopt the institution's new corporate identity. It had always been "the home" and that's what it would stay, but the new owners had made a lot of improvements. The rather grim old place had been remodeled and freshened up and the staff was more professional; on the other hand, the kitchen no longer served the buttery, creamy fish chowder that had clogged so many arteries in the past.

Today, most of the residents had gathered in the dining room, where they were watched over by a covey of nurses' aides. Some were seated in wheelchairs, others were resting in an assortment of chairs: a wing chair here, a plastic dining chair there. A few seemed engaged, chatting and looking about expectantly, while others were dozing, heads drooping and chins resting on their chests.

Lucy placed herself in front of a window so the light,

what there was of it, would be at her back, and got her camera ready. Felicity Corcoran, the activities director, clapped her hands and made a brief introduction. Someone flipped a switch and the familiar strains of the *Easter Parade* song were heard. Zoe was first, leading a sleek but nervous greyhound togged out in a blue jacket and top hat. They were followed by a bouncy little terrier in a straw bonnet, a dachshund with a polka-dot ruff around its neck, and an enormous black lab in a pink tutu.

Lucy snapped photos until there was a break in the parade, when she turned to the woman seated next to her who seemed bright and alert even though she was receiving oxygen from a portable tank on wheels. "What do you think of the show?" Lucy asked.

"What did you say?" the woman asked, leaning forward and cupping a hand around her ear.

"What do you think of the show?" shouted Lucy.

"I think they'll have cupcakes," replied the woman. "Or maybe cookies."

"What's your name?" asked Lucy, pen poised.

"I used to have a dog, a cocker spaniel," said the woman. "It got hit by a car."

"Oh, dear." Lucy patted her on the shoulder and moved along to another resident, a white-haired woman who was engaged in a lively conversation with her neighbor, an old guy wearing a golf cap.

"Hi!" said Lucy, introducing herself. "What do you think of the show?"

"It's very nice," said the woman in a soft voice.

"Terrific," boomed her companion. "I like dogs. All dogs. If I wasn't stuck here, I'd have a bunch of dogs."

"Which is your favorite?" asked Lucy, as a squabble broke out between the cute terrier and a collie. Bits of straw and artificial flowers went flying as the two went for each other, growling and baring their teeth.

"I'd put my money on the terrier," said the old guy. "What do you say, Madge? A fiver?"

Madge shook her head. "Harvey, you know I don't gamble."

"She's born-again," said Harvey with a snort. "A holy roller."

Madge smiled and rolled her eyes. "He's just teasing—he knows I'm not one of those Evangelicals. I'm a Methodist."

The unruly dogs had been removed and the music was starting again when Harvey tugged on Lucy's sleeve. "Don't tell anyone," he whispered in her ear. "Madge is really a millionaire."

Madge's cheeks got even pinker. "Don't listen to him."

"It's true. You told me yourself," said Harvey. "You said that by rights you ought to be rolling in the stuff."

"Well, ought and *is* are two different things," said Madge. "If it wasn't for Medicaid, I'd be living under a bridge somewhere."

"You know that's not true." Lucy was surprised to recognize Izzy Scannell, the gardener from Pine Point. "You know I'll always have a room for you."

Madge raised her cheek for a kiss and Izzy bent down to plant one on her cheek. "This is better, dear. This way we both have our independence."

Lucy smiled at Izzy. "Is she your mother?"

"Yup." Izzy gave Madge a hug. "Mom, this is my friend Lucy Stone."

Madge held out a small, plump hand and Lucy took it. "Margaret Scannell, but everybody calls me Madge. I'm pleased to meet you."

"Same here," said Lucy. "I work for the newspaper. Can you give me a quote, your reaction to the pet parade?"

"It's adorable—but . . ."

"She'd rather have a beer!" exclaimed Harvey, slapping his knee.

"Don't be silly, Harvey," said Madge, shaking her head. "You know I don't drink."

Izzy rolled her eyes. "Tough assignment?"

"You said it," said Lucy. "I think I'll concentrate on the animals." Raising her camera, she moved closer to the open area where the animals were parading and got down on her knees, snapping some close-ups. Then she went into the hallway, where more dogs were lined up along with a few caged cats and bunnies, and took some more pictures of the pets and their handlers. She also collected some usable quotes, noting with amusement that Sara and Zoe were avoiding her.

When the parade was over and Lucy was leaving the building, she met Izzy, who was also headed to the parking lot.

"Your mom is very sweet," said Lucy.

"Yeah, it's too bad. She's sharp as ever, she does the *New York Times* crossword every Sunday, but her body is failing her. She's got a multitude of problems: heart trouble, diabetes, failing kidneys; she's a walking medical encyclopedia."

"I'm sorry," said Lucy. "She's got a wonderful attitude."

"She does," said Izzy. "She really does. And I'll tell you, when I get depressed and worried about her, I just think about VV. My mom, on Medicaid, is a hundred times better off than VV, despite her millions. She gets good food, companionship, everything she needs. VV may be a millionaire, but, believe me, Mom is living better than she is."

"You're right," said Lucy, eager to follow up on this opening. "You're absolutely right. I was shocked by what I saw at Pine Point, and I can't help worrying about VV. Have you seen her lately?"

Izzy paused, keys in hand, resting her hips against a silver VW bug. "Are you really a caterer, or were you doing a bit of investigative reporting at the funeral?"

For a moment, Lucy didn't know what to say. "Investigative reporter!" she sputtered. "Don't I wish." She smiled ruefully. "I'm just a jill-of-all-trades, I'm part time at the paper, I try to fill in with whatever comes along. You know how it is. I'm scrambling like everybody else, trying to make ends meet in this economy."

Izzy opened her car door. "I sure do," she said, settling herself behind the wheel. "Do me a favor, run a picture of my mom with that story?"

"I'll try," promised Lucy, giving Izzy a little wave as she drove off.

Easter Sunday dawned cold and crisp, but at least the sun was out. Lucy was busy in the dining room, setting the table with her best china and silver. A pot of blooming hyacinths was in the center of the table and a growing collection of adorable ceramic bunnies was arranged on the damask cloth.

Lucy had invited Toby and Molly; Patrick's place was set with a vintage Peter Rabbit plate Lucy had found at a thrift shop. She'd also invited Molly's parents, Jolene and Jim Moskowitz, making sure to put Jim as far from Bill as she could. Bill didn't like Jim, who owned a prosperous insurance agency, but Lucy was determined to maintain a positive relationship with the in-laws—not for their sakes, but to provide a supportive family for Molly and Toby and most especially, Patrick.

Lucy gave the table a final once-over, adjusting a napkin here and a fork there, and when she was satisfied everything was perfect, she went into the kitchen to baste the ham. She was bent over the oven when Bill came down the stairs.

"That smells great," he said.

Lucy shut the oven door. "I've got deviled eggs and crudités for starters; there's ham, scalloped potatoes, caesar salad, and baby peas for dinner and I made a fancy Easter basket cake for dessert. Do you think that's enough?"

"Sounds great," said Bill. "Is there beer?"

Lucy sighed. "Beer and rosé, to go with dinner."

"I'll stick with beer," said Bill. "I suppose Jim will be looking for single malt Scotch."

"Well, he's out of luck, then," said Lucy with a shrug. She studied her husband, handsome in the dress slacks and jacket he rarely wore. His hair was graying at the temples, true, but he still had plenty of it—and a twinkle in his eye. She smiled and rested her arms on his shoulders. "Can I get you to wear a tie?"

"No way," he said, as Libby started to bark, announcing Jim and Jolene's arrival. "Damn. They're here."

"Behave yourself," warned Lucy.

"I will if he will," grumbled Bill.

When she went to the door, Lucy was pleased to see that Molly and Toby were also arriving, which meant everybody focused on little Patrick. Sara and Zoe had set up a little egg hunt on the porch and everyone had a great time encouraging three-year-old Patrick as he searched for the brightly colored plastic eggs and placed them in a basket.

Then they all went inside, gathering in the living room where Sara and Zoe served the hors d'oeuvres and Lucy put the finishing touches on dinner. When they had all gathered at the table, Bill mumbled a quick grace: "Lord, for what we are about to receive, make us truly grateful, amen."

"And for the gift of thy precious Son, also," added Jim.

Lucy noticed Bill growing a little red under the collar as they all intoned another amen.

"That's an adorable Peter Rabbit plate," said Jolene brightly. "Wherever did you find it?"

"Oh, I don't quite remember," said Lucy, who knew perfectly well she'd snagged the plate for a dollar at Our Lady of the Harbor's thrift shop.

"We gave Patrick a similar one," continued Jolene. "Actually, a little set, with a bowl and mug as well as a plate. I found it at Tiffany's—we were in Boston for a weekend getaway—and couldn't resist."

"That was the least of it," said Jim, who was always eager to let everyone know he had plenty of money to spend and didn't mind spending it. "She had to have a grandmother ring, too."

Jolene blushed and held up her hand, waggling her finger. "No pressure, kids, but there's room for plenty more stones on this ring. Right now there's just this lonely little emerald."

Molly and Toby exchanged glances; they tolerated Jolene's meddling but didn't enjoy it.

Lucy was about to get a fresh beer for Bill, who had gone from a slow simmer to something close to a full boil, when Jim leaned back in his chair. "You know, Bill," he said, "a lot of folks our age don't want to spend money on themselves—they don't indulge themselves like we did with that weekend in Boston—because they want to leave a nice estate for their kids. But I tell Jolene here not to worry, you can have both. The way you do it, Bill, is with life insurance."

"Uh, Jim, I think I'm pretty well set in that department," said Bill, hoping to forestall the sales pitch he suspected was coming.

"I'm not saying you aren't. I'm sure you have adequate coverage, but the truth is you can never have too much. Take me, for example. When I go—and let's face it, Bill, statistics show that it's us men who pop off first—Jolene here will be a rich woman."

Jolene covered her husband's hand with her own. "You know nothing will replace you, Jim. I'd rather have you than any amount of money."

"Dad, I wish you wouldn't talk about these things," said Molly, who had taken Patrick out of the high chair and had set him on her knee. "We want you around for a very long time. We want to see you at Patrick's wedding."

Lucy was keeping an eye on Bill, who was using his knife to shove a few remnants of salad around on his plate. "I understand Lucy's made a special Easter dessert," he said.

"That's right." Lucy was on her feet, picking up Jim's and Jolene's plates.

"That was delicious, Lucy," said Jim. "But just let me say this, Bill. With life insurance, you can create an instant estate for your loved ones; you can die a millionaire."

"That's fine," said Bill, pulling a lottery ticket out of his pocket and displaying it. "But when it comes to gambling, I'd prefer a bet I don't have to die to win."

"Coffee?" said Lucy. "Who'd like coffee?"

Later, when the guests had left and Lucy was loading the dishwasher, she thought about what Jim had said. Bill had a modest life insurance policy, enough to cover the mortgage, but that was about it. With so many other demands on their finances, a big life insurance policy hadn't seemed like a top priority. Lucy was confident in her ability to support herself if something happened to Bill, and, as for leaving a big estate for the kids, well, it seemed to her that it would be better for them to depend on themselves. She and Bill had never inherited very much; she'd gotten some money when her parents died, but it was little more than a nice nest egg, a cushion she kept for emergencies.

As she scraped the dishes and put them in the dishwasher, her eyes fell on the Peter Rabbit plate she'd been so proud of. Well, maybe Jolene had trumped her on that one, but she wasn't going to let it bother her. She was willing to bet she'd gotten more pleasure out of finding that plate and buying it for a dollar than Jolene got out of her expensive Tiffany's purchase. The hunt and the excitement of finding a bargain always gave her a bit of a high.

She shut the door and switched the machine on, listening to it hum. No matter how you looked at it, whether you had too little or too much, money was a problem. Look at VV, she thought. She had all that money, maybe even hundreds of millions of dollars, and it wasn't bringing her—or her family—much happiness.

Little Viv, who was in her sixties, was apparently still dependent on her mother. Lucy wiped the counter down, wondering how much that "modest allowance" Peter Reilly had told her about actually was. Whatever the amount, it seemed more than ample for Little Viv's needs. But what about Vicky? She was in her forties, brought up in an atmosphere of wealth and privilege. But if VV was holding tight to her money, and if Vicky's husband wasn't wealthy in his own right, well then Vicky might well be up against it financially. It would be only natural to feel that she was entitled to some of VV's fortune. Indeed, she might be getting impatient, aware that she wasn't getting any younger.

What did Maxine call Vicky, her husband, and the lawyer? The Three Pigs? Lucy wondered if she was on to something, or if she was just the pot calling the kettle black. How much was Maxine due to inherit, she wondered, now that Van was dead?

Lucy rinsed out the sponge and put it in its place; the kitchen was tidy and ready for tomorrow morning. The coffeepot was filled and ready to go, the timer was set, and Bill would find a fresh pot waiting for him when he came downstairs in the morning; his lunch pail was packed with two hearty sandwiches, chips, and an apple. The girls' lunches were made, their field hockey uniforms were washed and ready for them. She was a good manager and prided herself on maintaining an orderly, happy home; she doubted that things were quite so well managed up at Pine Point.

Chapter Nine

Over the past few years, a handful of crocuses Lucy had planted near the porch steps had spread into a good-size patch, even popping up here and there on the lawn. Lucy admired them when she left the house on Monday morning, struck as she was every year by the fragile flowers' stubborn persistence, returning and thriving after months of brutal cold. Nothing seemed to faze them, not even the inevitable spring snowstorm that would drop a couple of inches of wet, heavy snow. They would just close their petals tight and wait for a sunny morning.

This morning was sunny, and the crocuses had opened to reveal their bright orange pollen-covered stamens and the honeybees were buzzing from bloom to bloom. Lucy could hear them, a sure sign of spring, as they went from flower to flower, their knees orange with gathered pollen.

It was reassuring, she thought as she drove to work, that this rite of spring continued uninterrupted in spite of natural disasters and climate change. The winters did seem to be getting colder due to something they called the refrigerator effect, but the summers were warmer and that wasn't such a bad thing in Maine. Lucy was looking forward to planting her garden, perhaps adding a few more tomatoes and other heat-loving plants, like peppers and eggplants.

Maybe Bill would rototill the garden for her tonight, she thought, pulling into her usual parking space behind the *Pennysaver* office. It stayed lighter longer now, and he might be able to turn over a bed or two before dinner.

She was wondering if she'd bought enough peas—were two packets enough or should she pick up a couple more?—when Phyllis greeted her with unusual exuberance.

"It's about time you got here!" she exclaimed.

Lucy was puzzled. "It's my usual time," she said, pointing to the clock on the wall. "I never get in much before nine on Mondays."

Phyllis could hardly contain herself. She had crossed her arms across her ample chest as if she had to hold herself in, and her eyes were bright as she peered over her multicolored half-glasses. "I know, I know, it's just that I've got big news."

"Okay, shoot," said Lucy, slipping off her jacket and hanging it on the coat rack.

"Elfrida called . . . ," she began.

"And . . . ?"

The words came out in a small explosion, like popcorn in the microwave. "Willis has been fired!"

Lucy whirled around, incredulous. "No!"

"Yes," she insisted, with a sharp nod that made her double chin quiver.

"But he's been there for years and years."

"Elfrida says he started there soon after Horatio died, so he's been the butler at Pine Point for something like forty years."

"VV really depends on him," said Lucy thoughtfully. "Who fired him?"

"Vicky. She's moved in, along with her husband, and they're taking charge. Elfrida says the nurses are threatening to leave; everything's crazy without Willis. Vicky and Henry are poking their noses in everywhere, giving orders right and left. Henry chewed her out because she made some chicken soup for VV. He says she's not to have anything except that canned nutrition stuff. Elfrida says she tasted it and it's absolutely disgusting. She can't see why the poor old thing can't have a little chicken broth, or some applesauce, things that have a little taste to them, but he says absolutely not. Meanwhile, he and Vicky are demanding four-course dinners, roast beef and leg of lamb . . ."

"Lamb? I saw a couple of lamb roasts at the IGA, and they were around forty dollars."

"I guess the money they're saving on Willis's salary buys a lot of groceries."

"What about Elfrida? Can she handle all this cooking?"

Phyllis shook her head. "She's got cookbooks and she calls me and asks for advice. It's one of those situations; she figures she's going to get fired and she'd like to quit, but she doesn't want to abandon VV. At this point, there's just her and the gardener girl there, and the nurses." Phyllis lowered her voice. "Elfrida thinks there's some immigration issue with them so they get them cheap."

Lucy was thoughtful as she sat down at her desk and booted up her computer. If Elfrida's report was true, and Lucy thought it must be, Vicky and Henry had also fired Tracy, the cleaner, and Izzy's helper, too. It seemed odd to her that the couple would choose this particular time to get rid of staff at Pine Point. In Lucy's experience, even families with very modest means called in extra help when they had an invalid to care for. She remembered when Marge Culpepper had her bout with breast cancer and had such a difficult time with chemotherapy. She'd told Lucy she had a hard time keeping track of the home health-care people and the visiting nurses and the friends who dropped by; she said she'd never been so busy. She'd even joked that being sick was a full-time job.

Of course, thought Lucy, the situation might be somewhat different if Vicky and Henry were up to no good, as Maxine had alleged. In that case, they would most certainly want to get rid of the faithful family retainers. They'd also want to get rid of any extra witnesses who might notice something out of order. She supposed they'd love to get rid of the nurses, too, if only they could. The next best thing would be to terrorize them, which wouldn't be difficult if their immigration status was in doubt.

Lucy stared at the screen, studying the list of stories she was working on: the selectmen's meeting, the finance committee's recommendations for the annual budget to be voted at the town meeting, the calendar of events, spring planting advice from master gardener Rebecca Wardwell. They all seemed trivial in contrast to the Gothic horror story she suspected was taking place at Pine Point.

"Hey, Phyllis, do you think I could interview Elfrida?"

Phyllis was suspicious. "For a story, you mean?"

"Just background, deep background. I wouldn't even have to mention her name."

"I'm pretty sure they'd fire her if they caught her talking to the press—she had to hang up real fast last time she called me." Phyllis's eyes widened. "She says she doesn't know how she does it, but Vicky seems to be everywhere all at once, like she's got eyes in the back of her head or ESP or something."

For the first time ever, Lucy found herself feeling sympathetic toward Elfrida. She was a free spirit, she didn't do anyone any harm. She must be wondering how she got herself into this horrible situation. Thinking of horrible situations, Lucy remembered the paperwork Willis had made her sign when she worked at Pine Point. Digging in her roomy purse, she dug out the wrinkled sheets of paper and found, scrawled on the bottom, Willis's cell phone number. "Just in case you need to reach me," he'd said. Lucy dialed the number.

When he answered, Lucy spoke quickly, fearful he'd refuse to speak with her. But Willis was too polite, too well trained, she realized, to hang up on a caller, even one from the media.

"I was sorry to hear you've been let go," she said, oozing sympathy. "And after all these years."

Willis, it turned out, was human. "Almost forty years, can you believe it?"

"No, I can't," said Lucy. "Did they give you a reason?"

"I can only assume I did not give satisfaction," said Willis in his stilted butler-speak.

"I very much doubt that—I've seen you in action. You're an excellent manager."

"Well, thank you for your concern," he said. "If you hear of any openings, I'd appreciate it if you'd keep me in mind."

Lucy couldn't help chuckling; she was hardly in a position to know anyone who required a butler. "I certainly will," she said, as her mind took a different path. "What about legal redress? Are you considering anything like that?"

"I'm sure I don't know what you mean," he replied in a clipped tone.

Lucy was thinking out loud. "Well, Bob Goodman was VV's attorney, until last summer. Vicky and Henry fired him, too. Perhaps you should call him, see if you can sue for lost wages, damaged reputation, age discrimination, even anxiety and health issues. I'm sure he can come up with something."

Willis's tone of voice changed. "I'm sorry, but I have to go—someone's at the door."

Lucy was pretty sure she'd touched a nerve. "Well, good luck. I know you'll find something."

"Thank you," he said, ending the call.

Lucy sat at her desk, staring at the computer screen. Willis was no dummy, she thought, reflecting on her recent experience at Pine Point. He was a thorough-going professional who managed to keep that huge house running on a miniscule staff and sharply reduced budget. He had also worked for VV for a very long time, decades, and it seemed more than likely that the two had developed a congenial relationship in that time. Maybe even something a bit warmer, thought Lucy. Willis might well have come to see himself as his aging and increasingly frail employer's protector. She would be amazed, she decided, if he hadn't put in a call to Bob Goodman the moment he learned he was being axed.

She stood up, picked up her bag, and grabbed her jacket off the coat rack. "I'll be back soon," she told Phyllis.

"I know that look," said Phyllis with a satisfied smile. "It's your newshound look."

Lucy was zipping up her jacket. "Do me a favor and stay in touch with Elfrida."

"I will. The poor thing needs a sympathetic ear."

With a little wave, Lucy hurried out of the office and hopped into her car. Ted hadn't authorized this little expedition and she knew she'd better make it fast; she didn't have time to walk over to Miss Tilley's little antique Cape-style house with its weathered-gray cedar shingles and white corner boards.

Rachel answered the door, holding a couple of plates and some silverware. "Hi, Lucy. Can you stay for lunch? I was just about to set the table."

Lucy inhaled the enticing scent of roast chicken and sighed. "No, I can't stay, but it sure smells great."

"Oh, well, another time." Rachel tilted her head toward the living room. "Her ladyship is in her usual place."

"Actually, I wanted to talk to you," said Lucy. "Have you got a minute?"

"Sure." Rachel led the way into the living room where Miss Tilley was in her usual spot, a Boston rocker in front of the fireplace where a bright little blaze kept the room toasty warm. Lucy gave her a hug and a kiss and took a seat on the sofa, while Rachel perched on a wing chair. Cleopatra, the Siamese cat, was sunning herself in the window.

"What brings you here?" asked Miss Tilley. "Somehow I don't think you came to chat about the spring flowers."

"Actually, my crocuses are spreading like crazy. I've got quite a display," said Lucy. "But the daffodils seem to be disappearing."

"Odd," said Miss Tilley, preening a bit. "My daffodils are bigger and better than ever. They're filling in that entire corner by the apple tree."

"They say to plant day lilies and daffs together but I find the day lilies push out the daffs," offered Rachel. She dropped her voice and added, "Day lilies can be garden thugs, very aggressive."

"Speaking of thugs, that's why I'm here," Lucy said. "I heard that Vicky and Henry fired Willis."

"So Rachel tells me," said Miss Tilley.

Rachel nodded, her eyes very large. "This is off the record, Lucy, but he was at the house most of the weekend with Bob. I don't know exactly what was going on, but there was a steady stream of people from Pine Point—the gardener, Elfrida, and several others I didn't know."

"At the house? Why not the office?"

"I think it was sort of secret and the house is a lot more private; the office is right on Main Street." Her voice rose, a trifle indignant. "He had me making pots and pots of coffee and tea and even sandwiches for these folks, but when I asked him what it was all about, he just said, 'All in good time.' He didn't even come to bed until very late, after I was asleep, and that's very unlike him. And when I went downstairs in the morning, I saw the lights were still burning in his office, as if he'd worked so late he was too tired to remember to turn them off. That was Sunday morning and I thought I'd let him sleep in a bit because he'd been up so late, but these two men showed up and insisted they had an appointment with him. He got right up, threw some clothes on, and disappeared into his office again."

"What were the men like?" asked Lucy, thinking this seemed like something from a Dickens novel.

"A very odd couple," reported Rachel. "One was tall and quite distinguished, white hair, wearing a sports coat and tie, and the other was shorter and he was dressed, well, he looked like he'd gotten his clothes in a thrift shop or something. They were worn and faded and didn't fit all that well."

"No names?" asked Lucy, thinking these descriptions would fit Little Viv's ex-husbands, Andrew Duff and Peter Reilly.

"No names, but they were there for a very long time."

"It sounds to me like the troops are rallying around VV," said Lucy.

"Or against Vicky and her husband," said Miss Tilley.

"Isn't it the same thing?" asked Lucy.

"Not at all," insisted Miss Tilley. "The question is, are they really trying to protect VV or do they just want to preserve their place at the trough, if you'll forgive my French."

"Maxine calls Vicky and Henry and their lawyer, Weatherby, the Three Pigs," said Lucy.

"They're all feeding off VV, whether they work for her or if they're hoping to inherit, she's got the money and they want it," said Miss Tilley. "They're all looking for what they think is their fair share."

"It seems a bit more complicated than that," said Lucy. "Vicky and Henry seem to be keeping VV as a virtual prisoner, denying her proper food and care."

"I'm no fan of Vicky's," declared Miss Tilley. "You saw the way she treated me at the funeral—she practically knocked me down the stairs. But I was in the wrong. I should have checked with her before attempting to visit VV. For all I know, she was too ill to receive company, maybe even sleeping. I shouldn't have intruded."

Lucy and Rachel's eyes met in astonishment; they'd rarely heard Miss Tilley suggest she might be in error.

Lucy glanced at her watch. She knew Ted would be arriving at the office soon and wouldn't be happy to see her empty desk. "But what if it's the other way around, what if Vicky and Henry are, perish the thought, trying to hasten VV's death in order to get her money?" She thought of the gaunt, frail figure in the bed she'd glimpsed from the hallway. "Don't you think somebody should intervene and protect her?"

Miss Tilley shrugged. "She's very old, older than me, and she's been awfully tight with her money all her life. It's understandable. She came from nothing, she grew up on an egg farm, so I suppose she was afraid of losing it and becoming poor again. But if you ask me, she should have settled some of that money on her family. I suppose she thought she could use it to control them but that never works, it just encourages resentment and jealousy. Little Viv danced to her tune, made a proper marriage and all, but when that didn't work out and she wasn't happy, she decided it wasn't worth it and she rebelled—briefly. Van, bless his soul, saw what happened to his mother and went his own way, helped by a trust fund from his father. Vicky has tried to be the good little girl, waiting dutifully for her inheritance, but I suspect she's getting a bit tired, and who could blame her? She's not getting any younger."

"So you think Vicky's in the right?" asked Lucy, her voice doubtful.

Miss Tilley shook her head and flapped one of her big, blue-veined hands. "I don't know who's right. I do think VV has been very foolish. You reap what you sow and she's sowed discord and envy in her family."

Once again, Lucy thought of her mother's warning: "Envy is a green-eyed monster that comes hissing hot from hell." She also had to admit her own thoughts had been similar to Miss Tilley's. Just last night, she'd smugly compared her own family to VV's unhappy situation at Pine Point. She nodded and stood up, preparing to leave, but Rachel had another question.

"So VV's money came from eggs?" she asked.

"Oh, no. The egg farm died along with VV's parents. She was an only child and she had no interest in it at all. She was always very ambitious and when World War Two broke out, she saw it as a big opportunity and went off to Washington. She said she was going to snag a rich husband there and she did. Horatio Van Vorst was friends with FDR, maybe a school buddy or something. Anyway, Horatio's family owned steel mills and profited greatly from the war. . . ." She slapped her knee and cackled wickedly. "Probably said they were just doing their patriotic duty!"

The big old grandfather clock in the corner was striking twelve and Lucy knew she couldn't dally any longer. Ted would be furious if she didn't have any copy ready for him to edit. "I've got to go," she said, giving Miss Tilley's hand a squeeze and planting a kiss on her cheek. "But this has been very interesting." She gave Rachel a parting hug. "Thanks for the inside info. Who knows, this might turn into a story."

Rachel gave her a sad smile. "Bob's working so hard on this, I don't think it's just about money. He's not like that. I think he's worried about VV."

Lucy squeezed her hand. "I think you're right."

Miss Tilley couldn't resist getting off a parting shot. "VV's money has gotten her in a fine pickle," she said, a note of triumph in her voice. "But what good's money, if you haven't got your health?"

Chapter Ten

Lucy knew she was in for trouble when she pulled into the parking lot behind the *Pennysaver* office and saw Ted's minivan in the spot marked EDITOR AND PUBLISHER. She hurried in, head bowed by a guilty conscience. She not only hadn't filed any stories yet, she hadn't even begun to write them.

Ted was at his desk, on the phone, which gave her a reprieve, and she tried desperately to come up with an excuse. She knew he wouldn't approve of her spending all that time engaged in investigative reporting of Pine Point; it only counted if he assigned it. In his view, she should have been writing up those meetings and her interview with Rebecca Wardwell. Maybe she could plead poverty, claiming that she had to moonlight to make ends meet. It really wasn't much of a stretch, considering that neither she nor Phyllis had had a raise since the recession began.

But when Ted slammed down the phone and jumped to his feet, he wasn't angry with her at all. "Lucy, have you got your camera?" he demanded.

"Sure," she said, pulling the little digital point-and-shoot model out of her bag.

"Let's go," he said, grabbing his jacket. "They found a car at the bottom of Lover's Leap."

"Whose car?" asked Phyllis.

"They don't know. They're pulling it out now and we've got to hurry if we're going to get any photos."

Ted was a true newshound and loved nothing better than a breaking story—especially one that involved sudden and violent death. Lucy rolled her eyes and shook her head as she followed him out the back door, giving Phyllis a little wave. They got in Ted's minivan and he was rolling before Lucy managed to fasten her seat belt. "Did the police call you?" asked Lucy in a skeptical voice.

"Are you kidding?" scoffed Ted. "I got a call from Milo's Crane Service. I think he wants some free publicity."

"I wondered how they were going to get a car out of there," said Lucy, hanging on to the door handle as Ted took the corner too fast. "That's a pretty high cliff. Five or six stories maybe?"

"At least," said Ted, accelerating now that he'd cleared Main Street.

"Who discovered it? The water's pretty deep there. It would cover up a car," continued Lucy. She realized she was pressing hard on the car floor with her right foot, as if she were braking. If only she could, she thought. "Do we have to go this fast?"

"I want to be there when they pull the car up. Not just for the pictures. You get more information when everybody's on the scene and before they remember the new police department policy that all information has to come from the chief. Honestly, I can get more information from our cat than I can from the chief."

Lucy nodded. She'd developed her own source for police department news—the chief's mother, Dot Kirwan, who worked at the IGA. She'd discovered that Dot was terribly proud of her son Jim and was only too happy to boast of his achievements when Lucy showed an interest. All she had to do was inquire how Jim was doing to get a concise update on department activities. The one drawback was that it was expensive; she had to buy enough groceries so that Dot didn't finish ringing up her order before she'd related all there was to tell.

Lucy's thoughts were following this line, wondering how much space she had in the freezer. Ted was now speeding along Shore Road, fast approaching the deadly curve, where a MEN AT WORK sign had already been posted. He braked hard and the van wobbled a bit, threatening to fishtail, and Lucy sent up a silent prayer. Then they saw Officer Barney Culpepper in the middle of the road, hand raised, standing in front of a huge flatbed trailer with the promised crane on board blocking the entire road.

Ted followed Barney's hand signals and pulled the van over to the side of the road, setting his emergency flashers on. Then they both got out and went over to talk to Barney.

"What's going on?" asked Ted.

"There's a car down there," said Barney, hooking his thumbs into his black leather belt. "Somebody took the curve too fast."

"Who discovered the car?" asked Lucy.

"Jogger. One of those crazy guys who has to run a marathon every morning—he lives in one of those new McMansions on Shore Road. Computer guy, I think. Anyway, he said he runs the same route every day and today he noticed the sunlight bouncing off the water in a weird way and when he looked closer, he realized there was a mirror down there. One of those side mirrors." Barney paused for effect. "It was low tide or I don't think he'd ever have seen it. Then he noticed those skid marks in the road." Barney pointed and they saw two black lines, curving ominously toward the cliff edge. "Whoever went in was flying—they didn't go through the guard rail, they went over it."

Lucy was silent, imagining the terror the driver must have felt, lifting off to certain doom.

"So what's the plan? How are they going to get it out?" asked Ted. The crane was moving slowly off the flatbed and toward the side of the road where a number of police officers and construction workers had gathered.

"They're gonna lower a couple of divers down there and they're going to rig up some straps for the crane to hook on to and then, if it all goes according to plan, they'll raise the car."

"Is anybody inside?" asked Lucy.

Barney's face softened and his jowls wobbled a bit. "Prob'ly. It didn't get down there on its own," he said in a gruff voice. He gazed off into the distance, looking across the choppy blue water to the horizon, then pulled himself together with a humph. "They will go too fast along here."

The crane was in position now and Ted and Lucy went over to the edge of the road, where two wet-suited divers were getting ready to descend. A large wire-mesh bucket had been fastened to the crane's hook and they all watched as the first diver climbed inside and gave a wave, which Lucy caught with her camera. Then he was up off the ground, and Lucy snapped as many shots as she could as the boom of the crane swung around and the diver began the drop toward the water. When he left the bucket and began swimming, it was raised to collect the second diver, who soon joined his comrade in the water.

Cautiously peering over the edge, looking down the rocky cliff face with its projecting boulders, Lucy thought she could just make out a pale shape beneath the surface of the water, something that could be the roof of a light-colored car. The divers looked quite small down there; they were treading water, adjusting their masks and breathing apparatus, and then they disappeared beneath the surface.

The tension was terrible. Lucy feared for the safety of the divers, who were in dangerous, rough waters that pounded the rocky shore, and she was also afraid that the car might contain someone she knew. Probably not, she told herself. She hadn't heard of anybody who'd gone missing, but there were plenty of people in town who lived alone and whose absence wouldn't be noticed until the mail and newspapers started piling up and somebody finally decided to investigate.

They seemed to stand there for a very long time, waiting, but finally the crane's cable went tight and a dripping, white sedan with a crumpled front end and smashed windshield came into view. Police officers moved everybody back, the crane swung around, and there was a gentle thunk as the automobile landed back on the road, where it belonged. Lucy was busy snapping pictures, peering through the camera's viewfinder, and it wasn't until Ted grabbed her by the elbow and pulled her away that she realized that the dark shape draped over the steering wheel was a person.

The mood of the bystanders suddenly changed. The chatty camaraderie of a group of individuals focused on a challenging task gave way to somber silence as the gravity of the situation overwhelmed them. Lucy could hear the waves crashing down below, she felt the chilly breeze ruffling her hair, and then there was the shriek of metal on metal as the bucket was lowered once again to begin the process of retrieving the divers.

The arrival of an unmarked car meant that State Police Detective Lieutenant Horowitz was now on the scene and a handful of officers hurried to greet him and fill him in on the situation. One uniformed officer handed him a sodden handbag, an artsy looking thing made of colorful brocade, and Lucy felt a shock of recognition. She'd seen that bag somewhere, quite recently. But where?

A couple of crime techs were covering the car with a blue tarp and a tow truck was just arriving on the scene when she suddenly remembered. It was just then that Lt. Horowitz cleared his throat, as if preparing to make an announcement. Realizing that Lucy and Ted were the only media representatives present, he approached them, bag in hand.

"We've made a preliminary identification of the deceased," he began.

"Maxine Carey?" asked Lucy.

Horowitz raised one fine, barely-there gray eyebrow in surprise. "How did you know?"

"I recognized the handbag. I saw her at Van's funeral."

Horowitz had a long upper lip and watchful eyes and he always wore a rumpled gray suit. His thin gray hair, Lucy noticed, was steadily receding. He scratched his chin thoughtfully. "So she's related to that old lady at Pine Point?"

"Vivian Van Vorst," said Ted. "Everybody calls her VV."

Lucy shook her head. "They're not related. She was the grandson Van's ex-girlfriend. They had a daughter together. She's grown now." Lucy gazed at the car, now shrouded in a blue tarp, that was being hauled onto the tow truck. "There was quite a flap at the funeral. Maxine accused some family members of abusing VV in order to get her money."

Ted's jaw dropped. "How do you know all this? That funeral was invitation only. Were you invited?"

"Not exactly. Sue and I were hired to help out with the collation afterwards."

"You never mentioned that," said Ted, looking puzzled.

"I wanted to make a little extra money," said Lucy, a defensive note in her voice.

Horowitz wasn't buying it. "What were you after?" he asked.

"I'd heard rumors that things were dodgy at the house, especially after Van died. You know, the guy in the Easter Bunny suit."

"I heard about that," said Horowitz. "The local doctor didn't find anything suspicious, right?"

"That's right," said Lucy. "But Maxine thought it was definitely suspicious. She accused Van's sister, Vicky, and her husband, Henry, of getting rid of Van in order to inherit all of VV's money. They've been pleading poverty, firing staff and cutting corners, but Maxine believed they just want to get control of the house and of VV."

"So she was angry when she left the funeral?" asked Horowitz.

"Really angry," said Lucy. "Furious."

"And I suppose she had a few sherries, or even something stronger?"

"We ran out of sherry," said Lucy. "But I don't know how much Maxine drank."

"When people are angry, they tend to drive too fast," said Horowitz, his gaze following the departing tow truck. "Sometimes with tragic results."

Ted was writing it all down in his reporter's notebook, a thin, spiral-bound pad of paper. Horowitz noticed and cleared his throat. "As I said earlier, this investigation is in a very preliminary stage and I'm not ready to make a statement as to the identity of the victim or the circumstances of her death."

"But you are going to investigate?" asked Lucy. "You're going to check the car for tampering?"

Horowitz sighed. "We will follow the appropriate procedures," he said.

"I think the state crime lab should take a real close look at the brakes," said Lucy.

Horowitz sighed. "We'll be taking this one step at a time, and we'll use the crime lab if necessary, but I'd like to remind you that the state is having a budget crisis and there have been cutbacks at every level. Quite frankly, the lab has more work than it can handle and we will not request their services unless there is a compelling reason to consider this death suspicious rather than the tragic accident it most likely is."

Ted had left them. He was hurrying across the tarmac to interview one of the divers, who was stripping off his wet suit.

Taking advantage of the fact that she was alone with Horowitz, Lucy spoke right up. "Something's rotten up at Pine Point," she said, tilting her head in the direction of the estate. "The butler's been fired. He and some other employees got together with Bob Goodman over the weekend. I'm sure they want to counteract Vicky and Henry's influence but I'm not sure what they're planning. There's a crooked lawyer, too, named Weatherby, who's working with Vicky and Henry. Maxine was threatening to reveal something about him."

Horowitz's eyes widened. "You've been busy, haven't you, sticking your nose in where it's not wanted?"

Lucy felt she had to defend herself. "It's not just me. A lot of folks here in town have been worried about VV."

"She's a millionaire," said Horowitz, scowling.

"That doesn't mean she isn't a victim of elder abuse," said Lucy.

Horowitz's expression hardened. "Elder abuse! I'll tell you about elder abuse. Just last week, I arrested a fourteen-year-old kid who beat his grandmother to death because he wanted her TV so he could sell it and get himself some Oxy. That's elder abuse."

He turned on his heel and returned to his vehicle, executing a neat turn and rolling off down the road. Lucy joined Ted and snapped a photo of the diver, a handsome young guy.

"It was pretty challenging down there," he was saying. "The wave surge and the current made for less-than-ideal conditions. The water temperature was definitely a challenge, but we were able to successfully complete our mission and recover the car." His face clouded. "It was too bad about the lady," he said, zipping up his official state police warm-up jacket.

Lucy couldn't forget his words as she got back in the van with Ted. *It was too bad about the lady*. Maxine was pretty outspoken, she was definitely on the edge, thought Lucy, but she didn't deserve to end up like this.

She remembered the day Maxine had stopped by at the *Pennysaver* office, claiming Van's death was no accident. Now she was dead, too, and it made you wonder. Two unexpected deaths involving the same family in just a few days seemed unlikely, and when you added in VV's many millions of dollars, those deaths seemed pretty suspicious. If a kid would beat his grandmother to death for a TV, what would a resentful, impatient heiress do for hundreds of millions?

"You're awfully quiet," said Ted, driving the speed limit for once in his life. Lucy wondered if the sight of Maxine's crumpled car had made him more cautious.

"Just thinking," said Lucy. "We met her, you know. Maxine. She came to the office. She was very vibrant, very alive."

"Not anymore," said Ted. After a bit, he asked, "Does she have any kids?"

"A daughter," said Lucy, envisioning Juliette. The two, mother and daughter, had seemed close. Now the poor girl had lost both her parents. She would be devastated. "Grown. Sue says she's a model. She lives in New York City. Why?"

"I was just thinking about the obit," said Ted. "Maybe you could give her a call."

Lucy's temper flared. "In a day or two, okay? She's lost her father and now her mother. Can't we give her some space, some time to deal with her loss?"

Ted braked at a stop sign and flipped on his turn signal. "Sure. You don't have to do it today. But remember, deadline is noon Wednesday."

Lucy glared at him. "I'm beginning to understand why people kill," she said.

It went right over Ted's head. "You know, I don't understand. I never have." He made the turn, picking up a little speed. "I don't like war, capital punishment, murder, any of it. Live and let live, that's my motto." He patted the steering wheel and chuckled. "Besides, there's always the editorial page. The pen is mightier than the sword, it really is."

Lucy found herself smiling. He was incorrigible. Newspapers across the country were in trouble, readership was dwindling, circulation figures dropping, and here he was proclaiming the power of the pen. Ink apparently did run in his veins.

"Make that the Internet," she said. "The Internet is mightier than the sword."

He swung into the parking lot, turned neatly into his

marked space, and braked. "You're right," he said. "I could kill. I could kill whoever invented the Internet."

"Get him on Twitter," said Lucy.

"Twitter? What's that?" asked Ted, following her into the office.

Chapter Eleven

Phyllis was waving a piece of paper when they entered the office. "This fax just came," she was saying. "From Bob Goodman. He's holding a press conference tomorrow."

Ted shrugged. "Big deal. He's taking on a partner? Remodeling his office?"

"I don't think so, Ted," said Lucy, grabbing the paper and quickly scanning it for details. "It's just as I thought," she said, stabbing at the paper with her finger. "Look here: 'Filing suit against Victoria Duff Allen, Henry Chatsworth Allen, and George M. Weatherby on behalf of James Willis for wrongful dismissal' and—ohmigosh, it's right here—'demanding an investigation into alleged instances of elder abuse and fraud.' " She plunked down in her desk chair. "I expected this."

Ted looked at her, puzzled. "You did?"

She gave a self-satisfied nod. "You see a lot when you're passing the canapés," she said. "And, of course, I had inside information from Elfrida."

Phyllis was beaming in her corner behind the reception counter. "You could say Elfrida broke the story."

Ted's expression was skeptical. "Well, let's hope Elfrida

doesn't get fired." He turned to Lucy. "And the same goes for you. I haven't seen any copy yet and if I don't get those stories I need, you're going to be *here* tomorrow morning instead of sitting in the first row at Bob's press conference." He paused. "And don't forget the listings."

"Right, Ted." Lucy twirled her chair around to face her computer. Soon she was clicking away on her keyboard, transcribing her notes from the finance committee meeting. It was all very predictable; sometimes she felt she was writing the same story week after week. The town manager presented a budget and the finance committee members tore it apart, demanding to know why the highway department was spending so much on office supplies or why the school board was buying grass seed. The town manager's response was always the same: "I'll look into it and get back to you." And so it went, week after week, leaving her mind free to roam.

And roam it did. She couldn't stop thinking about Maxine and how indignant she'd been the day she came into the *Pennysaver* office with her accusations against the Three Pigs, as she'd called them. It was easy then to dismiss her as slightly cracked or even self-interested, but now it seemed she was on to something. The same went for the scene at the funeral. Miss Manners might well term her behavior inappropriate, but Lucy believed Maxine's accusations came from deep conviction. She'd believed that something was not right at Pine Point and she wanted to fix it, and that was an impulse that Lucy understood and even shared.

Abandoning the finance committee story, she did a quick computer search and found Juliette's website. It had been professionally produced and featured lots of photos which drifted across the screen in a seemingly endless slide show. After gazing at those enormous eyes, that perfect nose, and those gorgeous cheekbones for a few minutes, Lucy clicked on CONTACT JULIETTE, getting a modeling agency. Lucy doubted very much they would provide her with Juliette's phone number, but she hoped they might pass along a message, so she called them.

"John Gale Agency," announced a female voice with a distinct New York accent.

"I'm Lucy Stone with the *Pennysaver* newspaper in Tinker's Cove, Maine. I'm trying to reach Juliette Duff."

"What's this in regard to?" demanded the voice.

"I'm looking for information about her mother—for her obituary."

"Did you say obituary?"

"Yes. Juliette's mother, Maxine Carey, was in an automobile accident. Her body was found this morning."

"My God!"

Lucy's heart was sinking, realizing she'd gotten ahead of herself. Horowitz had found Maxine's purse, complete with driver's license, but that wasn't enough for an official identification. It was possible, indeed likely, that Juliette didn't know about her mother's death. She certainly didn't want to be the one to tell her. "I can leave a number and she can call me when she's ready," suggested Lucy, hoping to buy some time.

"I'm afraid that's impossible. She's on a photo shoot somewhere in Peru. Really remote, up in the mountains. No phones, no cell phones, no Internet, nothing."

Lucy let out a long sigh of relief. "For how long?"

"Hard to say. Wim Wilson is the photographer and he's, well, an *artiste*. He'll go to hell and back to get the right shot, and take everybody with him." She sighed. "Poor Juliette. She left right after her father's funeral and now her mother is gone, too? It's not going to be a very nice homecoming, is it?"

"No, I'm afraid not," said Lucy, finding the receptionist surprisingly talkative and fishing for more information. . "Have the police called? Juliette is her mother's next of kin."

"Just before you," said the receptionist. "They didn't say what it was about and I figured it was a traffic ticket, something like that. Juliette drives like a maniac. I told them the same as I told you, she's in Peru, in the mountains."

For a moment, Lucy pictured Horowitz trudging up a rock-strewn path panting as he chased Juliette through thin air in a treeless landscape. "There must be some way they can reach her," she said.

"Well, if there is, I don't know it," said the receptionist. "Have a nice day."

Ted was on it before Lucy could replace the phone in its cradle. "Is there a problem?"

"I can't reach Juliette. She's in Peru, on a photo shoot."

Phyllis's penciled eyebrows rose in surprise. "Peru!"

Ted knit his brows together. "When will she be back?"

"Not until the photographer is satisfied."

For once, Ted was speechless. "Humph," was all he could manage.

Bob Goodman had hired a function room at the Best Western out by the interstate for his press conference and had even provided several vats of coffee and a mountain of Danish, but he could have saved the expense. Only a handful of reporters showed up on Tuesday morning and Lucy recognized them all when she and Ted arrived. There was Pete Withers from the *Portland Press*, Bob Mayes who was a stringer for the *Boston Globe,* and Deb Hildreth from the local Gilead Enterprise. The TV stations had all passed, but there was a kid from the radio station at the community college, a good-looking kid with a shaved head, fiddling with a fancy recording setup.

Ted went straight to the refreshment table where he got busy talking shop with Mayes and Withers. Lucy took a seat in the front row, next to Deb, where she was soon joined by Rachel. "Wow, this is disappointing," Rachel said. "You'd think there'd be more interest in the mistreatment of one of the country's wealthiest women."

"Don't despair," said Lucy. "The editors haven't put two and two together. They don't realize it's about VV."

"It said 'elder abuse' right in the press release," said Rachel.

"Yeah," agreed Deb. "But it led with the wrongful dismissal suit. I bet they didn't read past that."

"Really?" asked Rachel, raising her eyebrows.

"Really," said Lucy. "But never fear—when we break this story, all hell is going to break loose. Trust me. *Inside Edition* will be calling before you've had your first cup of coffee tomorrow morning, and Nancy Grace will, too."

"I hope so," said Rachel.

Lucy patted her hand, pretty sure that this was one of those instances where getting what you wished for turned out to be more than you'd bargained for. Rachel and Bob were not prepared for the media storm that Lucy sensed was coming, as surely as she knew when a hurricane was brewing. "My advice is turn off your phone when you go to bed. Unplug it or you won't be getting any sleep."

Rachel looked doubtful and Lucy added a knowing nod for emphasis and pulled her notebook out of her purse. Opening the notebook, she jotted down the time and place, then glanced around the room, waiting for the show to begin.

A long table with a number of microphones was set up in the front of the room and promptly at nine-thirty Bob

Goodman along with Willis, Andrew Duff, and Peter Reilly filed in and sat down. Bob looked as if he'd been burning the candle at both ends; he had puffy circles under his eyes and he was hunched forward, which made his suit jacket seem too big. He glanced nervously at Rachel, receiving a big smile and a thumbs up, and then he straightened his shoulders. Then he tapped the mike a few times. The reporters who'd been standing by the refreshment table quickly took their seats, and he proceeded to introduce the others.

"As I stated in the press release, the purpose of this conference is to announce a civil suit by James Willis against Victoria and Henry Allen and their attorney, George Weatherby. Mr. Willis alleges he was wrongfully dismissed from his position as butler to Vivian Van Vorst, who resides at Pine Point in Tinker's Cove. Mr. Willis states he has served his employer, known as VV, faithfully for some thirty-seven years.

"Mr. Willis claims he was dismissed, against Mrs. Van Vorst's wishes by Mr. and Mrs. Allen because he interfered with their efforts to take control of Mrs. Van Vorst's fortune, estimated to be well over a hundred million dollars."

It was that phrase, *hundred million dollars*, that got their attention. Suddenly, coffee cups and Danish were set aside in favor of tape recorders and notepads as the reporters sensed a really big story. Lucy had experienced it before in press conferences when the humdrum and routine suddenly became a riveting story. You could feel it in the air, which suddenly became electric; you could see it in the body language of the reporters, who were leaning forward, hanging on every word.

"Mr. Willis also alleges that the Allens, abetted by their attorney George Weatherby, continually harassed Mrs. Van Vorst, a frail ninety-two-year-old widow, demanding that she sign numerous documents that were against her interests. The Allens have in this way seized control of various properties, including Mrs. Van Vorst's Beacon Hill townhouse, as well as various trusts and investments.

"In addition, the Allens have stripped Pine Point of numerous works of art, including Mrs. Van Vorst's prized sculpture, *Jelly Beans*, by the modern master Karl Klaus. Some of these works were subsequently auctioned and the proceeds claimed by the Allens. *Jelly Beans,* which Mrs. Van Vorst always intended to give to the Museum of Fine Arts, is now in Saudi Arabia, sold in a private sale negotiated by George Weatherby, who retained the proceeds.

"Furthermore, Mr. Willis, along with Mr. Peter Reilly and Mr. Andrew Duff, have all witnessed a deterioration in Mrs. Van Vorst's living arrangements and standard of care. Staff at Pine Point has been reduced to the point where the house is not properly maintained. Deliveries of flowers have been discontinued, meals are substandard, even laundry and trash removal have been reduced in frequency."

Bob's voice rose as he declared: "Vivian Van Vorst, who was formerly one of the region's most generous benefactors and who gave unstinting support to numerous charitable organizations, is now confined to a filthy bed, denied fresh linens and nightclothes, is subsisting on an inadequate diet completely devoid of fresh food, and is even refused the company and consolation of her beloved pet dogs, Yum-Yum and Nanki-Poo.

"This is an intolerable situation and we are demanding that the district attorney immediately begin an investigation of these allegations of financial misconduct and elder abuse by the three individuals named: Victoria Allen, Henry Allen, and George Weatherby. We are confident that an investigation will result in criminal charges and will hopefully restore Mrs. Van Vorst to an acceptable level of comfort and care. Thank you. Now we will take questions."

"Who exactly are these Allens?" asked Pete Withers from the *Portland Press*.

"Mrs. Allen is Mrs. Van Vorst's granddaughter, and she is the daughter of Mr. Duff, who is present here today, and his ex-wife, also named Vivian, who is Mrs. Van Vorst's daughter."

"This question is for Mr. Duff. Is it true you're alleging your own daughter is abusing her grandmother?" asked Withers.

"I'm afraid so," said Andrew Duff slowly, his cheeks reddening. "It is not something I want to do, but I find that I must. I cannot sit idly by and allow this situation to continue. I am very fond of VV and her present living conditions are intolerable."

"So how much was VV paying Mr. Willis?" asked Bob Mayes, the *Globe* stringer. Lucy knew he always got down to business, asking the tough questions.

"I earned seventy-eight thousand a year, plus room and board," said Willis.

"No wonder you're suing," said Mayes, who earned much less, along with most everyone in Maine.

Bob was ready to defend his client. "I might remind you that a trained butler like Mr. Willis could expect to earn much more; according to the most recent figures I could find, the going rate for a top-notch butler is well over six figures annually. Mr. Willis was content to earn less because of his affection for VV and their long-standing relationship."

"Am I hearing this right? Mr. Willis and VV had a relationship?" asked Deb Hildreth.

"An employer-employee relationship. Nothing improper, I assure you," said Bob.

"What's with the jelly beans?" asked the kid from the community college. "They don't cost much, they're reduced now. You can get a bag for twenty-five cents."

Bob was smiling. "*Jelly Beans* is a sculpture that graced Mrs. Van Vorst's foyer for many years; it is a work by the acclaimed sculptor Karl Klaus. Mrs. Van Vorst was one of the first to recognize Klaus's genius. His works now go for millions of dollars. The work was promised to the Museum of Fine Arts, but we believe it was sold to a Saudi citizen instead. That's one reason why we're asking the DA to investigate."

"What is Mr. Reilly's relationship to Mrs. Van Vorst?" asked Ted.

"I am a former son-in-law," he said, smiling genially. "I was also married to Little Viv."

"The same Vivian as him?" asked Withers, rudely pointing to Andrew Duff.

Peter was unfazed, still smiling. "The very same."

"And how much is the old lady worth? Can you tell me again?" asked Mayes, once again going straight to the heart of the matter.

"Something in the neighborhood of a hundred million dollars," said Bob.

"And they won't give her clean sheets?" asked Deb, struggling to understand.

"Only once a week," said Willis. "And then the top sheet goes on the bottom. She gets one clean sheet and one clean pillowcase a week."

"Well, it is better for the environment," said Deb. "Less laundry, less nitrogen in the water."

"I don't believe the environment is a concern here," said Willis, in a voice so dry Lucy expected it to crack.

Lucy raised her hand. "What do you hope to achieve? What would be the best possible outcome?"

Bob gave her a grateful smile. "The best outcome would

be that Mr. Willis goes back to Pine Point and takes complete control of the house and provides a proper and appropriate standard of care for Mrs. Van Vorst. As for the criminal allegations, we expect a full investigation. It's up to the DA to decide what steps to take after that, but we expect charges will ultimately be brought against the Allens and Weatherby. If that happens, we expect the court to dismiss the Allens as Mrs. Van Vorst's legal guardians and to name a new guardian."

"Who would that be?" asked Lucy.

"That would be up to the court," said Bob. He looked around and saw no more raised hands. "Thank you all for coming," he said. "And, please, take some of those Danish."

When Ted and Lucy got back to the *Pennysaver,* the expected media storm was already brewing. The phones were ringing constantly, e-mails were streaming in, and the fax machine was spewing out sheet after sheet. Phyllis was doing her best to keep up with it all, but she was clearly overwhelmed.

Ted quickly assessed the situation. "Phyllis, you handle the fax and anybody who comes in; Lucy, you keep an eye on the e-mails and don't forget those stories I need. I'll handle the phones." He sat down and reached for the phone, then slapped his hand to his forehead. "We've got to get something on our website."

"I'll do it," said Lucy. "I'll write something up quick."

The *Pennysaver* office was usually pretty quiet, so Lucy found it exhilarating to be in the center of a breaking story. She pounded out her version of the press conference and posted it, then turned to the e-mails. She could hear Ted taking the calls, dismissing inquiries from other news outlets as politely as he could and chatting up the callers who had new information. From time to time, scraps of conversation penetrated her thought processes: *You were a cleaner at Pine Point and you saw Vicky kick Nanki-Poo? You recently sold Henry a Rolex watch? Your brother used to cut the grass at Pine Point but he was fired? You work at Walmart and you're sure you helped Vicky find some cheap track suits for her grandmother? When was that?*

On and on it went, with callers reporting large and small instances of bad behavior by Vicky and Henry. They may have thought they were insulated and protected in their chauffeur-driven limousine or behind the gates at Pine Point; they may have thought they were anonymous on the streets of Beacon Hill; they may have thought the townhouse was private and secure. But they were mistaken. Now it seemed everyone from the Merry Maids who cleaned the townhouse to the bank teller who cashed their checks to a shoe salesman at Neiman Marcus had tales to tell. Even a few members of the boards at the Museum of Fine Arts and the Boston Ballet were eager to dish about Vicky's bad manners.

Only Weatherby leaped to their defense.

"Wow, that was fast," said Lucy, firing up the printer. "Weatherby has already issued a response." She handed Ted a copy.

"Figures," snorted Ted. "He says the sale of *Jelly Beans* was entirely necessary to enable VV to stay in the comfort and familiar surroundings of her own beloved home in light of recent stock market losses. He claims Mr. and Mrs. Allen have no motive other than preserving and protecting VV's assets so she may enjoy a peaceful and pleasant environment in her final days."

"Good luck with that," said Lucy, who had followed a tip to check out YouTube. There she found a video of

Vicky, clad in a leopard-skin coat, arguing with a waiter on one side of a split screen. The other side showed a frail VV, clad in the same coat, getting out of a limousine. "This video makes it look like Vicky's actually snatched the leopard coat off poor VV's aged back."

Phyllis leaned over her shoulder, studying the computer screen. "Talk about nerve," she fumed.

"It might've been a gift," said Lucy, clicking the mouse. "Oh, here we go. A tiara!"

"Check out those earrings," said Phyllis, who loved bling. "I think VV was wearing them with the leopard coat."

A few clicks and they were watching VV get out of the limo once again, wearing a fabulous pair of diamond and pearl earrings that Lucy recognized. "She wore those a lot. I've seen her wear them at the Easter egg hunt."

"Not anymore," said Phyllis. "Now Vicky wears them."

"How much do you think they're worth?" asked Lucy, deferring to Phyllis's expertise.

"Depends," said Phyllis, zooming in for a close-up. "Those are some pretty hunky diamonds; 'course, they might not be top quality. It's hard to tell from the photo, but conservatively speaking, I'd say a couple hundred thousand, minimum."

"Interesting," mused Lucy, who was flipping through her notebook, looking for the notes she'd taken at the finance committee meeting. "One pair of earrings would cover the entire middle school budget shortfall. If they can't find the money, they're going to fire an art teacher, a couple of teacher's aides, and one part-time maintenance man." She sighed. "Puts it all in perspective, doesn't it?"

"Yeah," agreed Phyllis. "Especially since that shop at the outlet mall does some pretty good fakes for seven ninety-nine; three pairs for nineteen ninety-nine." She shook her head, showing off a pair of sparkly bangles.

* * *

The *Pennysaver* was going to press at noon Wednesday, much to the relief of the exhausted staff members. All three had been hard at work until eleven o'clock the night before, scrambling to get their normal work done despite the constant interruptions, and had come in early that morning. They might be at the epicenter of a breaking story of national interest, but *Pennysaver* readers would still want to know about the free movie at the library on Friday evening and the latest developments in the annual budget battle.

Ted had edited the last story and was ready to send the final copy to the printer electronically when the fax machine whirred into action.

Lucy and Ted froze at their desks and Phyllis went over to the machine. "Stop the presses," she said with a sigh.

"Really?" Lucy was hoping it was a joke.

"Really. The DA is bringing charges of elder abuse, fraud and embezzlement against Vicky and Henry," she said, handing the paper to Ted.

"Call Aucoin!" ordered Ted, naming the district attorney. "What about Weatherby? No charges against him?"

Lucy crossed her fingers and dialed. She was sure the DA would not be available. She tapped her foot nervously, listening to the rings, and much to her amazement heard Phil Aucoin's voice on the line.

"Lucy Stone at the *Pennysaver*," she said. "I gotta be quick, I promise. We're on deadline."

Aucoin laughed. "Go ahead, Lucy."

"First, what's the basis for the charges against the Allens?"

"We received information that we determined to be credible, and that was supported by Weatherby."

"That was my next question. Why no charges against Weatherby?"

"He's cooperating with the investigation."

"He's gone state's evidence?" asked Lucy.

"Yup."

Lucy had a mental image of the rats leaving a sinking ship. "Self-preservation?"

"Of a sort. He'll certainly be disbarred, but he may be able to avoid jail time. Judges don't look kindly on lawyers who abuse their clients and I'm sure he's aware of that. It was really his only option."

"One last question. Are you looking at the deaths of Maxine Carey and Van Duff?"

Aucoin sighed. "At the moment, I have no evidence that the deaths are suspicious, but I'm open to the possibility. I'd be only too happy to nail those two with murder," he said. "That's off the record, by the way."

"Got it," said Lucy, clicking away on the keyboard. "Thanks."

"Good work, Lucy," said Ted, reading her quick recap of the conversation. "I just stuck it on top of the lead story. We're done."

"Don't kid yourself," said Phyllis with a wry grin. "This thing is just beginning."

Chapter Twelve

Once the paper was finally sent to the printer, Lucy had the afternoon to herself. The *Pennysaver* was a weekly and there was no sense writing stories that would be old news by the time the next issue came out. She usually spent Wednesday afternoons catching up with grocery shopping and other errands, but today she had an appointment to get her car inspected. Much to her surprise, she found Barney sprawled in one of the recliners in the waiting room at Al's Auto Care, watching a Red Sox game on the TV provided for customers' entertainment.

"A hundred forty million and the guy is zero for five," fumed Barney, as she took the chair next to him.

"The Sox are not getting off to a good start this year," she said, flipping the lever and raising the foot rest. "Bill's pretty disgusted. He didn't even watch the end of the game last night."

"Me, either." Barney's chin sank into his jowls, making him look a bit like a tired old basset hound. "Looking on the bright side, there's still a hundred and fifty games to go." He groaned as the batter struck out on a high fly, ending the inning. "He coulda bunted and got on base—what was he thinking?"

Lucy shrugged. "I guess a hundred and forty million doesn't buy brains." She turned and looked at him curiously. "So what are you doing here, wasting the taxpayers' money?"

"We've got to get the cruiser inspected, just like everybody else, and it needs new tires."

"They couldn't have dropped it off so you could do something else?" she asked, playing devil's advocate.

"I guess the chief didn't think of that," he said, wincing as the Toronto batter sent the ball flying toward the Green Monster. "You got anything particular in mind that I should be doing?"

"Well," began Lucy, "I was wondering about Maxine's car. The one that went over the cliff? I just wondered if anybody's taken a look at it."

"Not as far as I know," said Barney, smacking his fist down on the arm of the chair and pounding it as two Toronto runners made it to home plate. "A fumble? He fumbled a high fly that my wife could catch."

"How is Marge?" asked Lucy. "And Eddie? How's he like the community college?"

"Marge is fine. She's turning the house upside down with spring cleaning. Eddie's looking for a job, something with flexible hours that won't interfere with his classes." His face brightened with pride. "He got all A's on his midterms."

"That's great," said Lucy, who knew that Eddie, a vet, had struggled with drug addiction after his return from tours of duty in Iraq and Afghanistan. "He's a smart kid."

"Yeah, but he's got a long row to hoe if he's going to be a physical therapist."

"He'll make it," said Lucy. "I'm sure of it."

"Well, it's been nice," said Barney, getting the high sign from the service manager and standing up. "Looks like the cruiser's ready to roll."

Lucy caught his sleeve. "Just a quick question—off the record. Do you think they're going to check out Maxine's car? Horowitz said something about staff cuts at the crime lab."

He stood there, twirling his cap on his finger. "I really don't know. It's in the impound lot around back . . ."

"You mean it's right here?" asked Lucy.

He nodded. "Yeah, the town's got an arrangement with Al. It's easiest, 'cause he does the towing. But don't you get any ideas about asking one of the guys here to take a look at it," he said, catching her eyes in a level gaze. "I'm warning you, Lucy. That would be tampering with evidence."

"I'd never dream of doing any such thing," said Lucy, who had of course been planning to do just that.

"Better not," he said, hitching up his belt and settling his cap on his head. She watched him through the plate glass windows as he drove off in the cruiser, then turned back to the TV. The game had ended, the Sox had lost fourteen to three, and a trio of talking heads were analyzing the game.

"The Red Sox are not performing up to expectations," one was saying.

"That's right, they were favored for the World Series when the season began," said another.

"It's hard to say whether the defense or offense is worse," said the third, as Lucy finally spotted the remote lying on a chair. She quickly changed the channel, checking out the latest news on NECN. It was odd to see the county courthouse in Gilead on TV, but there it was, with a reporter standing front and center.

"Victoria and Henry Allen were seen entering the courthouse a little over an hour ago," the perky blonde in a lime green suit was saying. "They have been sequestered in the chambers of Family Court Judge Marian Foster since their arrival, along with their former attorney, George Weatherby."

A film clip ran, showing the well-dressed, perfectly groomed couple making their way through a crowd of reporters. Henry, looking ever the gentleman, in his gray suit, was trying to shield his wife from the crush of reporters thrusting microphones in her face. Even though Vicky was facing serious charges, she managed to look as if she was on her way to a garden party rather than entering a courthouse, dressed in a pale green suit complete with matching headband and pearls. There was an awkward moment when George Weatherby held the door for them; the two glared at him before rushing into the building.

"Attorney Bob Goodman, who is bringing suit against the Allens on behalf of Vivian Van Vorst's former butler, James Willis, is also at the meeting in the judge's chambers, along with several other family members."

The screen switched from the reporter to the news desk, where the anchor posed a question. "What can we expect from this meeting, Jessica?"

"That's not really clear, Ed, but courthouse sources say it is likely that Judge Foster is reviewing the guardianship arrangements for Vivian Van Vorst. Victoria Allen is presently the aged millionaire's guardian and the judge may want to change that considering the charges of elder abuse, embezzlement and fraud that have been leveled against the Allens."

"And when will they be arraigned on those charges?" asked Ed.

"Tomorrow," replied Jessica, who was nearly knocked off her feet as the courthouse door opened and the Allens were once again surrounded by a scrum of reporters. "No comment, no comment," was all Henry had to say, and Vicky wasn't talking at all.

* * *

The two maintained their silence at the arraignment, too, where they answered the district attorney's long list of charges against them with two words: "Not guilty."

Lucy, who was standing in the back of the packed courtroom, didn't believe them and neither did the judge. Superior Court Judge Anthony Featherstone set bail at a quarter of a million dollars for each of the defendants and ordered them to surrender their passports, citing the possibility that they might flee the country. Further, acting on the advice of Family Court Judge Marian Foster, he stripped Victoria Allen of her guardianship and named Bob Goodman as VV's temporary guardian, responsible for her care. The cameras rolled as the two were led from the courtroom in handcuffs for a brief stay in the holding cells until bail could be arranged. Lucy thought that Vicky's and Henry's expressions probably resembled Marie Antoinette's, when she faced the mob and was dragged from Versailles.

Outside the courtroom, Bob was making an announcement in the lobby. "As you know, I've been appointed Vivian Van Vorst's temporary guardian and my first piece of business will be to rehire James Willis to his former position as butler. Mr. Willis has assured me he will take immediate steps to improve Mrs. Van Vorst's living conditions and to maximize her comfort. Judge Foster has also ordered a complete medical evaluation of Mrs. Van Vorst's health and that will be undertaken immediately." He chewed his lip, gathering his thoughts. "I think that's all for now. Thank you."

"What about the money?" asked one reporter.

"That's up to the DA," said Bob. "I understand he's already began an audit, but you'd have to ask him." Then he was shouldering his way through the crowd and was gone before Lucy could ask the question that was on the tip of her tongue: "Are you demanding an investigation into the deaths of Maxine Carey and Van Duff?"

Back at the office, Lucy tried calling Bob, but couldn't get through. She was trying for the fifth time when she heard her cell phone go off in her purse and scrabbled frantically, tossing wallet and cosmetic bag and keys on her desk until she finally found it. It was too late, of course; the call had gone to voice mail.

The caller's voice was unfamiliar; she identified herself as a nurse calling from a hospital in Palm Beach. "I'm calling for your daughter Elizabeth. She's just come out of surgery, she's doing fine . . ."

Surgery? What on earth? Lucy could barely wait for the message to end so she could reply to the call. Heart pounding, she waited while the phone rang and rang and was finally answered.

"I just got a call about my daughter, Elizabeth Stone," she began.

"That's right. Elizabeth is here and she's doing fine, she's just coming out of the anesthesia."

"What happened?"

"I'm not at liberty to discuss a patient's treatment. We take patient confidentiality very seriously . . ."

"But I'm her mother!" wailed Lucy.

The voice became very low. "It was an emergency appendectomy." Then the voice was louder. "You'll be able to talk to her in a couple of hours," she said. "Or I can refer you to the doctor."

Lucy considered. "I don't suppose the doctor will be able to tell me much . . ."

"Not without a signed consent from the patient," said the voice.

"I understand," said Lucy, who was already making plans to get the next flight to Florida.

* * *

It was early the next morning when she got to the hospital in Florida, and rushed into Elizabeth's room. Elizabeth was asleep and almost as pale as the white hospital sheets; if it wasn't for her dark, spiky hair Lucy wouldn't have recognized her vital, lively daughter. She took her hand in her own and stroked her hair and Elizabeth's eyes opened.

"Mom!" Her voice was weak and scratchy, but her smile was genuine Elizabeth.

"How do you feel?"

"Horrible. Like I was run over by a truck."

Lucy wanted to hug her daughter, but was afraid of hurting her so she contented herself with squeezing her hand, the one without the I.V. "What happened?"

"Remember those cramps I told you about . . ."

Lucy was suddenly stricken with guilt. She'd dismissed the pains when Elizabeth told her about them and had suggested they were probably menstrual cramps.

"Well," Elizabeth continued, speaking slowly, "it was appendicitis and the darn thing actually ruptured but I thought it was the flu and then I collapsed at work yesterday and they rushed me here by ambulance and apparently removed a good part of my insides."

The door opened and a plump, fresh-faced doctor who looked just about old enough to have finished high school entered, chart in hand.

"I'm Doctor Mahoney," he said, extending his hand.

"I'm Elizabeth's mom, Lucy Stone."

"Nice to meet you, Mrs. Stone. Would you mind stepping outside for a moment while I examine Elizabeth?"

"No problem," said Lucy, smarting a bit from the dismissal. It wasn't so long ago that she was in charge of Elizabeth's health. She remembered standing by the examining table in Doc Ryder's office, hugging her little one to her chest while the doctor administered inoculations or peered into her ears or down her throat. "Looks like a touch of strep," he'd say, speaking to her over the child's downy head. Now, those days were gone and she wasn't even included in discussions of Elizabeth's treatment.

The door opened. "Elizabeth asked me to get you," the doctor said. "She wants you to hear the plan."

Lucy smiled and went back to Elizabeth's side, once again taking her hand.

"This was a bit more than the usual appendectomy because the rupture went untreated for so long," said Doctor Mahoney. "Elizabeth's going to need to stay in the hospital for several days, maybe a week, until we can get her temperature down and get her back on solid food."

Lucy nodded. "And after that?"

"She's going to need quite a bit of care, at least at first. She shouldn't go back to work for at least six weeks."

"Six weeks!" Elizabeth raised a weak protest.

Lucy was trying to think of the best way of dealing with an invalid. "Can she fly? Can I take her back to Maine?"

"We'll have to wait and see how her recovery goes, but I think that will be all right. You need to wait for my okay, though, and I'd advise making arrangements with the airline for a wheelchair. She won't be able to walk long distances in the terminal."

Lucy nodded, trying to take this all in. Elizabeth was always the picture of health; whenever she visited home she ran a couple of miles every other day. Now, suddenly, she wouldn't be able to walk to the gate at the airport.

"Well, I have other patients to see," said Dr. Mahoney, nodding at Lucy. "Nice to meet you. If you have any questions, call my office."

Then he was gone and Lucy sat down in the chair next to Elizabeth's bed. "Looks like I'll be getting that Florida vacation I always wanted," she said with a wry smile.

"What about Grandma and Grandpa?" asked Elizabeth.

Lucy shook her head. Bill's parents lived in Florida but they'd taken to renting out their place and spending most of the year in Mexico, where costs were lower. "Looks like you're stuck with me."

"You can stay at my place," offered Elizabeth, her eyes drooping. "Take my keys."

"Good idea. In fact, I think I'll go freshen up and let you rest."

"Use my car . . . ," said Elizabeth, nodding off.

Lucy opened the drawer in the bedside table and found Elizabeth's purse and took her keys. When she held them up for Elizabeth to see, she found her daughter was already sleeping. "See you later, baby," said Lucy, planting a kiss on Elizabeth's forehead.

Lucy took a cab to Elizabeth's bright and tidy little apartment, which was decorated with IKEA furniture punctuated with a few antiques and estate sale finds. Lucy made herself a cup of coffee in the efficient kitchenette and carried it out to the tiny terrace overlooking the pool and garden area filled with colorful tropical plants. She sat there for a few minutes, enjoying the lush landscape, which was so different from Maine in spring, and called Bill.

"Six weeks? You're going to stay down there for six weeks?" he asked, after she'd assured him that Elizabeth was expected to make a full recovery.

"I hope not. I don't know how long I'm going to have to stay," she told him. "The plan is to bring her back home to Maine as soon as the doctor gives the okay." Lucy paused. "How are things there?"

"Oh, we're managing," he answered, grumbling. "But the sooner you get back, the better."

"I'll do my best," promised Lucy, who was thinking

that the blue water of the pool looked awfully inviting, and the sun felt lovely on her vitamin D–starved skin. She closed the flip phone and slumped down in the chair, put her feet up, and sipped her coffee. After a while, however, the heat became too much for her and she retreated inside, where she adjusted the wood blinds to block the sunshine.

She sat down on the slipcovered couch and switched on the TV, finding a morning news show. Much to her surprise, they were showing film footage of Vicky and Henry leaving the courthouse and, after giving a brief recap of the case, segued to a discussion of elder abuse in Florida. The segment gave her an idea and she called Ted at the paper.

"I don't know how long I'm going to have to stay," she told him. "It all depends on Elizabeth's recovery."

"It's awfully bad timing," he complained, "what with the Van Vorst story."

"I know," admitted Lucy. "But I could do some features for you, while I'm here. I was thinking of doing something on elder abuse in Florida and how they handle it."

"It's better than nothing, I guess," said Ted, giving his grudging approval.

"I'll get right on it," promised Lucy, who was already unzipping her suitcase and pulling out her swimsuit.

Lucy's days soon fell into a pattern. She woke up early every morning and went for a swim, then ate a quick breakfast, tidied the apartment, and went to the hospital. Elizabeth made slow but steady progress. She grew stronger every day, but continued to run a low-grade fever. The doctor explained to Lucy that the fever was an indication that the infection was lingering and said he wouldn't release her until he was satisfied it was completely gone. "I do not want to risk a relapse," he said.

So Lucy did her best to keep Elizabeth amused, bringing

her magazines, and staying with her through lunch. Then Lucy would leave to spend the afternoon working on the feature story she promised Ted, returning to the hospital in the evening for a visit and to check on Elizabeth's progress. Finally, on the fifth day, they got the okay to leave.

Bill met them at the airport, his welcoming smile turning to an expression of concern when Lucy finally appeared pushing Elizabeth in a wheelchair.

"It's just for the airport," said Elizabeth, noticing his dismay. "I'm really fine."

"She's supposed to rest as much as possible and she's not allowed to climb stairs or lift heavy objects," said Lucy. "She has an appointment with Doc Ryder tomorrow and he's going to monitor her progress. If all goes well, she can go back to work in five weeks."

Bill nodded and took the chair from Lucy, pushing it along. When they got to the exit, he left them to get the car; he was fuming about the parking fee when he pulled up. Then, leaving the chair on the curb, they loaded Elizabeth and the luggage and drove off, headed to Tinker's Cove and home.

Next morning, leaving Elizabeth in the care of her younger sisters, Lucy returned to work. Driving the familiar route, she noticed the white satellite trucks from the TV networks were no longer parked in front of the police station. Stories ebbed and flowed like the tide and with no new developments on the immediate horizon, the media had gone fishing in deeper waters. They'd be back, she knew, when the case went to trial.

The phones were quiet when she got to the office, and there was no sign of Ted or Phyllis. A stack of unopened mail was on the reception counter and she started flipping through it, figuring she might as well get a start on the events listing. That's what she was doing when the little bell on the door jangled and Sue walked in.

"I heard you were back," she said. "How's Elizabeth?"

"She's doing okay but it's slow. I feel so guilty. She called me asking about cramps and I told her it was probably just her period. The doctor said it was a close thing. She could have died from the infection."

"But she didn't," said Sue. "And you got a week in Florida."

"It was nice," admitted Lucy. "Except for the worrying."

"Well, she's back home and on the mend. I've only got a minute," said Sue, waving a folded copy of the *New York Times*. "I'm on my way to Little Prodigies. I've got to fill in for Chris today. Her twins have upset tummies."

"She has my sympathy," said Lucy.

"I brought you this," said Sue, handing her the paper. "There's a big story in the arts section about Maxine." She pointed to the headline with a freshly manicured finger. "See here? 'Arts community says farewell to a muse.' "

Lucy quickly scanned the story that cited Maxine as an influential figure in artistic circles who was once linked romantically to the sculptor Karl Klaus. *Her daughter,* it said, *top model Juliette Duff, just back from an assignment in Peru, spoke movingly of her mother at the memorial service.*

"Interesting, hunh?"

"Yeah," agreed Lucy. "I had no idea Maxine was interested in art."

"Or artists," added Sue.

"It does explain the sculpture. I never thought VV was into modern art, you know, and I wondered why she had *Jelly Beans.*"

"It says here that Maxine was an early admirer of

Basquiat, a muse to Julian Schnabel and that she once dated Paul Simon. That must've been before Edie."

Except for Paul Simon, Lucy had no idea who Sue was talking about. "I didn't realize Juliette was so successful," offered Lucy.

"I knew I'd seen her face somewhere," said Sue, producing a *Vogue* magazine from her tote bag and flipping through it. "But look here. Juliette in jeans, Juliette in lipstick, Juliette in jewels, Juliette seemingly naked with a tiger cub and a handbag, the whole thing is full of Juliette."

Lucy squinted at the last photo, which was spread over two pages. "You'd have to pay me an awful lot to get me to cuddle up naked with a tiger, even if it is only a cub."

"You'd need a bigger handbag," said Sue.

Lucy ignored the insult. "I was wrong about Juliette, too. I underestimated her. I thought she was just a messed-up rich kid who dabbled in modeling." She took another look at the photo, noticing that Juliette was tickling the tiger cub's chin. "I think she might be a force to be reckoned with."

"I think you're right," said Sue.

Sunday dawned a perfect spring day, the sort of spring day that was so rare in Maine that it seemed a shame to spend even a minute indoors. Lucy was no exception, so after she'd seen Sara and Zoe off to the Friends of Animals shelter, where they filled in for the full-time workers on weekends, she went straight over to Molly and Toby's house on Prudence Path.

"I want to borrow Patrick," she said, scooping up the squirming little boy in a big hug. "Elizabeth and I are going to start a garden and we need a helper."

"That's great," said Toby, who was loading the breakfast dishes into the dishwasher. "Molly's got to work today at the diner and I really need to hit the books. I've got a test in business ethics on Monday."

Lucy tickled Patrick's tummy, sending him into a fit of giggles. "Business ethics, an oxymoron if I ever heard one," she said.

"You're absolutely right," he said with a rueful grin. "It's not actually about right and wrong, it's about what you can get away with, without breaking any laws."

Lucy perched on one of the kitchen stools with Patrick in her lap. "Are you sure business school is right for you?" she asked.

"Don't worry, Mom," said Toby, peering at her over the rim of his coffee mug and taking a long drink. "I have a solid sense of right and wrong despite my professor's best efforts."

"Oh, I know that," said Lucy. "I have trouble imagining you in an office all day, wearing a tie and all that. You love being outdoors, being on the water."

Toby looked out the window, studying the little clouds scudding across the blue sky and judging the way the tree branches tossed in the breeze. "Storm's coming," he said. "And I'm glad I don't have to be out there, trying to outrace a nor'easter in a leaky tub with a hold full of fish." His gaze fell on Patrick, who was mouthing a spoon. "Did you hear about Will Smollett?"

"No? What happened?"

"He was working on *Lady Liz*, he was using a portable generator and accidentally electrocuted himself."

Lucy knew that Will had two little girls and his wife was expecting another baby. "Is he okay?" she asked.

"They say he'll make it, but there'll be medical bills and he won't be able to work for a long time. They've set up a fund for his family."

"I'll make sure we run something in the paper," said Lucy, easing Patrick off her lap and standing up. "I think we'll let you study for that test. Patrick and I have seeds to plant." She gave his hand a squeeze. "Do you like gardening, Patrick? What shall we plant?"

Patrick was thoughtful, apparently considering his options.

"Lettuce, for salad? How about radishes? Or spinach? It will make you strong like Popeye."

Patrick was clearly puzzled. "Who's Popeye?" he asked.

Lucy was shocked. "You don't know about Popeye?" she asked.

"No."

She turned to Toby. "Kids today," she muttered, leading her grandson out to the garden.

Chapter Thirteen

Six weeks later, Doc Ryder gave the okay for Elizabeth to return to Florida and her job at the hotel, but advised she go back to work on a Thursday or Friday, so she would only have to work a few days before having the weekend to recover. That was fine with Lucy, who figured she could take her to the airport on Wednesday afternoon, after deadline.

She was just leaving, after seeing Elizabeth pass through security, when her cell phone rang. It was Rachel.

"I'm sick," she whispered in a hoarse voice. "I've got a sore throat and sniffles. I think maybe I'm running a fever."

"Have you been to the doctor?"

"No." Rachel coughed. "It's just a head cold. I'm taking fluids—lots of orange juice—and resting."

"I'm sorry for you—you sound terrible."

"I think it sounds worse than it is," said Rachel, but her brave words were contradicted by another coughing fit.

"Is there anything I can do for you? Do you need anything?"

"Actually, that's why I called. There is one thing you could do, Lucy," she said, her voice fading. "Could you look in on Miss T for me?"

This was so like Rachel, thought Lucy. She was sick as a dog but she was worried about Miss Tilley. "Sure thing. Don't give it a thought. Take care of yourself."

"I will," promised Rachel in a barely audible whisper.

Lucy promptly called Miss Tilley, whose voice was much stronger than her caregiver's. "I'm fit as a fiddle," she said. "I'm ordering pizza for supper."

"What about breakfast tomorrow?" asked Lucy. "Can I bring you something?"

"I think I can manage to make a cup of tea and pour some Raisin Bran into a bowl." She paused and Lucy could hear her dentures clicking, a sure sign the wheels were turning in her old gray head. "I will need a ride—I've been invited to Pine Point for lunch tomorrow."

Lucy wondered if the old dear was suddenly senile. "Are you sure about that?"

"I am. VV called and invited me herself."

Lucy had done her best to follow the Van Vorst case while nursing Elizabeth, but it had been a juggling act and she'd apparently dropped a ball. "Really?"

"Yes, Lucy. Really. I'm supposed to be there at one o'clock. She said there will be lobster Newburg."

Lucy remembered the skeletal figure she'd glimpsed at Pine Point and was extremely doubtful, suspecting the lunch was nothing more than a pipe dream, though she wasn't sure whether it was Miss T or VV who was doing the dreaming. Nevertheless, she thought it best to indulge the fantasy. She might even get a peek into the situation at Pine Point herself, which would come in handy now that Vicky and Henry's trial was only days away.

Following Miss T's instructions, Lucy rolled through the open gates at Pine Point at exactly one o'clock on Thursday and pulled up to the front door. It was immediately opened by Willis, who came out to help Miss Tilley out of the car.

"Mrs. Van Vorst would be pleased if you would join her for luncheon," he said, speaking to Lucy.

Lucy was flabbergasted. "Me?"

"She would be honored," he said.

Lucy was suddenly aware that she was wearing a faded pair of jeans, running shoes, and a T-shirt adorned with the logo of a paint company, a freebie that the hardware store had given to Bill.

"You can leave the car here," said Willis. "It will be fine."

"All right," said Lucy, turning off the ignition and reaching for her purse. Willis held out his arm for Miss Tilley and helped her up the steps to the door and Lucy followed, thinking this was a big improvement over the last time she'd come to Pine Point, when she'd had to use the service entrance.

Willis ushered them through the foyer and into the dining room, where VV was seated at a small table set for three by the French doors. She was in a wheelchair, and still extremely thin, but her white hair had been freshly washed and styled and she was wearing a pink tweed jacket over a matching pink blouse. A beige cashmere throw covered her legs.

"Forgive me for not getting up," she said, holding out her age-spotted hands and smiling at her old friend.

Miss Tilley grasped both of VV's hands and Lucy thought she detected the merest hint of tears filling her eyes. "It's wonderful to see you," she said. "Let me introduce my friend, Lucy Stone. She's filling in for my usual helper."

"Welcome, Lucy," said VV. "Thank you so much for

bringing Julia—it's been quite a while since we've seen each other."

"Too long," agreed Miss Tilley as Lucy held her chair for her.

Lucy took the last seat, admiring the table setting as she unfolded a starched linen napkin and spread it on her lap. The floral plates were set on a perfectly smooth white damask cloth, the silver gleamed, the crystal sparkled, and the air was redolent of lobster Newburg.

"My favorite!" exclaimed Miss Tilley as Willis set a plate in front of her.

"I know how much you love it," said VV with a wicked grin. "I hope it doesn't kill you."

"I don't believe that nonsense about cholesterol," said Miss Tilley. "Do you?"

"Not a bit," agreed VV. "And my doctor says I need to gain some weight, so I've got permission to eat these delicious things." She picked up her fork and hunched her shoulders in glee. "There's key lime pie for dessert!"

Thinking that this menu sounded rather ambitious for Elfrida, Lucy posed a question: "Have you got a new cook?"

"No." A gleam appeared in VV's eyes. "I gave my cook a cookbook!"

"This is delicious," said Miss Tilley, spearing a large chunk of claw meat.

Lucy took a bite and discovered she was right; Elfrida was becoming a wicked good cook. She turned her attention to her meal, enjoying every bite and listening to the two old women as they relived old times.

"So, Julia, you're still a spinster lady and proud of it?"

"I am," replied Miss Tilley. "I never could see what men were good for."

"Children?" suggested Lucy.

Miss Tilley rolled her eyes. "Very messy, a dreadful bother."

"Money, that's what men are good for," said VV.

"I didn't need to marry for that," said Miss Tilley.

"I did," said VV. "I didn't grow up in a big house like you, with a judge for a father. I grew up on a hardscrabble farm stinking of chickens. I couldn't wait to get away."

Lucy looked around the richly decorated room at the numerous oil paintings hanging on the walls, the glittering gilt and crystal chandelier, the antique furniture, and the probably priceless Persian rug. Glancing through the window, she could see Izzy working outside, trimming a hedge. "You've come a long way," she said.

"There's always a trade-off, when you marry for money," said VV. "I didn't love Horatio, it wasn't at all like my first love, but I made it work. I made him happy. On his deathbed, he told me so. He said he couldn't have had a better wife." She paused. "Love doesn't last. Money does."

"Who was your first love?" asked Miss Tilley. "What happened to him?"

"The love of my life," said VV wistfully. "Every woman should have one. It was intoxicating. I was head over heels with him. Of course, we were only together for less than a year—there was no time for things to turn sour—and then he was gone, off to the war." She dropped her hands in her lap and smoothed her napkin. She shook her head. "You know, Julia, I think you really have missed out, being an old maid."

Miss Tilley smacked her lips as a generous slice of key lime pie was placed in front of her. "That's rather presumptuous of you. You don't know everything about me. Perhaps I'm not the old maid you think I am."

"Oh, ho!" crowed VV, digging into her pie. "I hope not!"

Despite her good spirits, Lucy sensed that VV was beginning to tire. She only ate a few bites of dessert, then seemed to drift off, gazing out the window while Lucy and Miss Tilley chatted. Willis came in with coffee and moments after he left, one of the nurses appeared.

"I'm afraid it's time for your medicine," she said, tapping her watch.

VV raised a finger. "One moment," she said, then, beckoning, she leaned toward Miss Tilley.

Sensing that VV wished to share a private thought with Miss Tilley, Lucy excused herself and went over to the fireplace on the other side of the room, where she interested herself in the seascape that hung above the mantel. Then Sylvia arrived and wheeled VV out of the room. "Do stay and finish your dessert," she called as she was pushed through the door.

Lucy returned to the table, dying to learn what VV had whispered into Miss Tilley's ear, but determined not to show it.

Miss Tilley was equally determined not to share her friend's secret, whatever it was. She polished off her pie, drained her coffee cup, and announced she was ready to leave.

In the foyer, they encountered Sylvia, who was coming down the stairs.

"VV seems to be doing very well," said Lucy. "She was bedridden when I was here for the funeral."

"Everything's changed now that Mr. Willis is in charge," said Sylvia, with a smile. "Mrs. Van Vorst began to improve the minute she realized those three were gone. I think the only way she could deal with them was by retreating into herself."

"How terrible," said Miss Tilley. "I tried to visit but they wouldn't let me."

"I know but, hopefully, that's all in the past. She's getting good food and fresh air and I expect she'll grow stronger every day." Willis had opened the door and Sylvia looked outside at the expansive lawn and beckoning gardens. "I wish we could get her out to the Italian garden, it's so beautiful this time of year, but it's too far for us to manage. We need a strong young fellow."

Lucy turned to Willis. "Is that true? Are you looking for someone?"

"Yes, we are," said Willis. "It's just part time, mostly helping Izzy in the garden. Do you know of anyone?"

Lucy remembered Barney saying that his son Eddie was looking for part-time work. "I do know someone. He's taking courses at the community college so he needs flexible hours."

"Have him call me," urged Willis. "Maybe we can work something out."

Willis accompanied them to the car and helped Miss Tilley get settled in the front seat. She was quiet as they drove down the drive and Lucy suspected the visit might have tired her out, but when they reached the gates, she spoke up.

"VV asked me to do something and I might need help," she said.

"I'd be happy to help," said Lucy, turning onto Shore Road. "What exactly does she want you to do?"

"There's the rub," said Miss Tilley, scowling. "It's confidential. I don't want to read about it in the *Pennysaver*."

Lucy's face burned as if she had been slapped, and she tried to remember that Miss Tilley was old and outspoken, sometimes even tactless. "Well, I think you know me well enough to know that I would honor a confidence."

Miss Tilley didn't reply but kept her face turned away, supposedly looking out the window.

Oh, be like that, thought Lucy, braking and cautiously approaching the curve that had claimed Maxine's life. Keep your secret. What difference could it make?

When Lucy got back to the office that afternoon, nobody was there and the door was locked. She suspected that the barrage of inquiries from out-of-town reporters, who had returned for the trial, had gotten to be too much for Phyllis and Ted so they'd vacated the premises. After entering, she checked her voice mail and found a message from Rachel, among the many others from various news outlets. She deleted them all, wondering exactly how big an idiot these big-time reporters thought she was. News was a competitive business and they could do their own footwork, she wasn't going to make it easy for them. She also worked through her e-mails, hitting the DELETE button there, too. Then she called Rachel back.

"How did it go?" asked Rachel, her voice still husky.

"Great. They included me. I had lobster Newburg with VV and Miss T."

"Oh, dear, not lobster Newburg! She's on a low-cholesterol diet."

"It was delicious, definitely not low cholesterol. Elfrida's turning into a good cook."

"That's what Phyllis told me when I ran into her at the post office. It seems that Elfrida didn't know about cookbooks; she always just followed the directions on the box. She told Phyllis that recipes are really just as easy, except that you have to find the ingredients and measure them."

"Incredible," said Lucy.

"Elfrida is in a world of her own," said Rachel. "But she's definitely good-hearted. Phyllis says she's loving her job now that Willis is back in charge. She even got a raise."

"It's like the old days," said Lucy. "VV was out of bed, in a wheelchair, and she looked great. Her hair was done and she was wearing pretty clothes. There were fresh flowers in the foyer, the lunch table was beautiful. The two of them were so cute, they really enjoyed each other."

"That's great," said Rachel. "But it could all change if Vicky and Henry get off."

"Do you think that's a real possibility?" asked Lucy.

"Bob is worried. He says financial stuff is tricky. It's complicated and it's hard for jurors to follow. Also, the fact that there's so much money involved and the jurors will be middle class means they might be turned off. They might decide that VV is a selfish old bitch and Vicky deserved to take as much as she could. But the worst thing, the thing he's really worried about, is the fact that the whole case depends on Weatherby's testimony. It's his word against theirs and he's not exactly a trustworthy witness; it's obvious he's only interested in saving his own skin."

Lucy's spirits sank as she listened to Rachel, realizing that it was all true. Jurors who were living from paycheck to paycheck, or even subsisting on unemployment, could hardly be counted on to be sympathetic to the plight of a multimillionaire who lived in a huge mansion and had private nurses and servants. Those folks would hardly consider staff reductions and the lack of fresh flowers as hardships. They would think VV was pretty well off compared to themselves.

"That's depressing," said Lucy. "The DA's going to have to convince them that VV was a prisoner in her own home and that this is really a case of elder abuse."

"All the defense has to do is claim that VV was ga-ga and Vicky and Henry were only trying to protect her interests," said Rachel. "The jurors are most likely going to be sandwich generation folks themselves who've had to deal with aging relatives and they might very well sympathize with Vicky and Henry."

Lucy thought of Izzy, who'd remarked that her aged mother was getting better care at Heritage House than VV was getting in her own mansion. "Aucoin has to show them that VV really was abused, that she would have gotten better care as a Medicaid patient," said Lucy.

"Good luck with that," said Rachel, and Lucy realized she was right.

"You know," replied Lucy, "I'm convinced those three had something to do with Van's and Maxine's deaths. Two accidental deaths in the same family, in one week, it just seems fishy to me. I'm sure they wanted to get them out of the way. Van came home and upset the apple cart because he didn't like the way VV was being treated, and then Maxine came on the scene, claiming that Van's death wasn't an accident."

"Believe me, Bob's begged the DA to investigate, but Aucoin says there's no evidence the deaths were suspicious. The cops found a half-empty vodka bottle in Maxine's car . . ."

This was news to Lucy. "Did the medical examiner check her blood alcohol level?" she asked.

"The body was pretty far gone, it had been in the water for several days," said Rachel. "As for Van, it turns out he'd suffered from arrhythmia for some time but kept it a secret."

"Yeah," grumbled Lucy. "It's not enough to know, or suspect, what happened. You've got to be able to prove it."

"Exactly," said Rachel. "But if you can come up with some proof, Bob says it would really strengthen the prosecution's case."

"I'll work on it," said Lucy, aware that there was a huge

difference between wishing and doing. She wished she could prove that Van and Maxine were murdered but she didn't have the slightest idea how to do it.

"That would be great, Lucy," said Rachel. "By the way, Bob says they need some help at Pine Point. Do you think Toby would be interested?"

"Toby's got his hands full at the moment, but I know that Eddie Culpepper is looking for a part-time job. Willis also mentioned it to me when I was there, and told me to have Eddie call him."

"Thanks, I'll have Bob call him."

"Take care. Get better soon," said Lucy, hanging up. She'd no sooner ended the call than the phone started ringing. She checked caller ID, saw it was an out-of-state 212 area code, and ignored it. Following Phyllis's and Ted's example, she turned off her computer, switched off the lights and headed for home.

Chapter Fourteen

When Lucy got to the office on Friday morning, Ted was working on a story about a fund-raiser for Will Smollett, the fisherman who'd been electrocuted and didn't have health insurance. "So the Claws are going to play and there's going to be a silent auction?" asked Ted, tilting his head to hold the phone against his shoulder and clicking away on his keyboard. "Are you still accepting donations of goods for the auction?"

Lucy hung up her jacket and went over to the reception counter, where she rested her elbows on the scuffed Formica. "Heck of a thing," she said to Phyllis. "You'd think a guy like Will would know better than to get himself electrocuted."

"Those generators can be tricky," said Phyllis, who was wearing apple green today. Her reading glasses were green with rhinestones, her sweater was green with sequin trim, and her eye shadow and fingernails were green. Lucy was relieved to see that her lips were thickly coated in a somewhat more natural peony pink.

"I don't know much about them," admitted Lucy, leafing through the stack of press releases that Phyllis handed her. "Fishing is so darned dangerous." It occurred to her that restoration carpentry was also dangerous and she hadn't yet convinced Bill that he needed a will; she filed the thought away when Phyllis picked up the conversation.

"I don't know why they bother. They can hardly make a living at it anymore, what with the catch limits and all the other regulations."

Lucy nodded. It was a subject she'd written about many times, every time the government changed the regulations, which was often.

She had picked up the press releases and was starting to cross the room to her desk when the door opened to a jangle of the bell, and a middle-aged woman stepped into the office. With her neatly permed gray hair, tailored black pantsuit, and expensive-looking black loafers, it was obvious she wasn't from Tinker's Cove, where most women wore sweatpants or jeans. When she spoke, it was with a heavy New York accent.

"I'm looking for some information and I wonder if you could help me," she said.

Lucy eyed her warily and pointed to the stack of *Pennysavers* on the reception counter. "If you're from the media, you can buy our latest issue for seventy-five cents."

The woman reached into her stylish leather tote and produced a leopard print card case. "I'm not from the media," she said, giving Lucy a card. "I'm a private investigator. Fran Martino." She stuck out her hand. "Pleased to meet you."

Glancing at the card, Lucy recognized the 212 number she'd ignored the day before. "A real private eye?"

"From New York?" asked Phyllis.

Even Ted, who had finished his interview, was on his feet. "Ted Stillings, editor, publisher, chief reporter," he said. "What can I do for you?"

"I've been hired by Juliette Duff to look into the deaths of her parents, Van Duff and Maxine Carey. She's not convinced that the local authorities conducted a thorough investigation."

"She's right!" exclaimed Lucy. "I'm Lucy, Lucy Stone. Part-time reporter."

"And you're Phyllis," said Fran with a nod to the nameplate on the reception counter. "Nice to meet you."

"So you're a big city detective come to our little town," said Phyllis with a defensive edge to her voice.

"I'm not here to make trouble," said Fran with a reassuring smile. "My client, Juliette Duff, is a young woman who tragically lost both her parents in a short time and has a lot of questions that need answers, answers she hasn't been able to get from the authorities." Fran made eye contact with each of them. "She wants closure, that's all."

"Well, I can certainly understand that," said Ted. "We'll be happy to help in any way we can. Lucy can fill you in."

"What about the listings, Ted?" asked Phyllis rather pointedly.

"There's plenty of time for the listings," he said, waving away her concern. "Why don't you make a fresh pot of coffee? Lucy and Fran can talk in the morgue."

"Since when do I make coffee?" asked Phyllis, getting rather pink under the collar.

"Never mind," said Ted, quick to avert a feminist power play. "I'll do it. Cream? Sugar?" he asked Fran.

"Just black is fine," she said, following Lucy into the tiny, dusty morgue where the old papers were kept, beginning with the *Courier and Advertisers* published in the 1850s.

Lucy pulled out a chair for Fran, then took one opposite her at the scarred oak table. She could hardly contain her excitement—here she was, face to face with a genuine private investigator. "Is it fabulous?" she asked. "Being a private eye?"

Fran's eyes brightened and she smiled. "Sometimes it's interesting, but most of the time it's a lot of donkey work." She pulled a file out of her tote and opened it. "These are copies of the official reports," she said, pointing at the papers with her finger; her nails were neatly filed but unpolished. "They're not very informative."

Ted entered with two mugs of steaming coffee. "Budget cuts," he said. "Everybody's understaffed. And remember, these are very well-connected and powerful people. Nobody wants to stir up a hornets' nest."

Lucy wrapped her hands around the mug. "Van had a heart condition. Maxine had been drinking and was upset. That was all the explanation they needed. Of course, that was before anybody knew what Vicky and Henry and Weatherby were up to."

"Juliette says that Vicky discouraged her father from visiting Pine Point, but he insisted. He couldn't believe there wasn't going to be an Easter egg hunt . . ."

"Nobody could. There was a crowd at the gate, everybody expected it," said Lucy.

"Van was in the house, challenging Vicky's authority. He was her brother, after all. He wouldn't take any guff from her. Juliette says he loved his grandmother. He would have found her situation intolerable." Fran took a sip of coffee. "Vicky had a strong motive—a hundred million dollar motive—to get rid of him."

"I suppose she could have known about his heart condition," said Lucy.

Ted was leaning against one of the shelves holding the oversize bound volumes containing the old papers. "But how did she do it? Doc Ryder didn't find any indication . . ."

"He didn't look for any anomalies," said Fran. "There were no tests for drugs, poison, nothing."

"Maxine was very suspicious about Van's death. She came in here, making all sorts of accusations," said Lucy. "That alone would have been motive enough for the Three Pigs, as she called them."

"Juliette says her mother was furious when she learned the Karl Klaus sculpture had been sold," said Fran. "*Jelly Beans* was a gift from the sculptor, she didn't think they had any business selling it. She says Weatherby must have gotten at least a million for it."

"Another motive," said Lucy.

"There's no shortage of motives," said Ted. "We can speculate all we want, but what we need is proof."

"Well, that's what I'm here to find—proof. And I intend to get it." She set down her mug. "But I'm going to need some help, someone with local knowledge."

Lucy looked at Ted. "It'll be a great story," she said.

Ted let out a long sigh. "Okay," he finally said. "But you've still got to do those listings for Phyllis."

"I will, I promise," said Lucy eagerly. "I'll work on them at home, nights, on my own time, if I have to."

"Good," said Ted. "So where are you starting?"

Lucy didn't hesitate for a moment. "Pine Point," she said. "That's where it all began."

Fran offered to drive and Lucy didn't object; the price of gas was rising and groceries cost more, but her weekly allowance had been the same for years. She happily climbed in the passenger seat and gave Fran directions to Pine Point, but she soon discovered she didn't like the direction Fran's questions were taking.

"Can you tell me a little bit about the staff at Pine Point? I'm familiar with Willis, of course, because of the court case."

"Willis has been with VV forever—over thirty years.

He's devoted to her. Vicky and Henry made a big mistake when they fired him," said Lucy.

"That's what Juliette told me. But what about the others? Is there a cook?"

"That would be Elfrida, Phyllis's niece. She's a sweet girl, has a bunch of kids. She's not a professional cook, but she's learning."

"That's a bit odd, isn't it? How long has she been there?"

"A couple of months, maybe. She got hired just before all this started."

"Interesting," said Fran. "Do you think she's involved?"

"I think she came cheap," said Lucy, feeling she had to defend Elfrida from Fran's suspicions. "There was a fancy French chef but they let him go."

"Do you know his name?"

"Pierre or Jean or Claude, I don't know. Willis will have records, I'm sure."

"What about housekeeping staff?" asked Fran.

"There are some local women who come in to clean. Willis will have information about them."

"Who takes care of VV?"

"There are two nurses, Lupe and Sylvia. I'm not convinced they're actually . . . well, they didn't come from a local agency. They seem competent enough, but I suspect there's some sort of immigration issue. Like maybe they have foreign credentials."

"Interesting," said Fran, taking heed of the DANGEROUS CURVE sign and braking. "I assume this is the place where Maxine died?"

"Yes," said Lucy. "Lover's Leap. If you want a better look, you can pull over up ahead."

Fran pulled into the overlook and they both got out of the car and went over to the fence, where a couple of coin-operated binoculars were positioned. They didn't look out at the distant islands, however, but peered down at the rocks below and at the pounding surf. Then Fran raised her eyes and examined the roadway. "She was coming in the opposite direction, right?"

"Yup. Pine Point is just up ahead, maybe a quarter mile."

"The guard rail wasn't broken?"

"She must have sailed right over it."

"What kind of car?"

"A BMW. It was completely wrecked."

Fran shook her head. "What a waste," she said, and Lucy wasn't sure if she was talking about Maxine or the car. She took another long look at the scene of the accident, then straightened her shoulders. "Let's go."

When they turned into the drive and approached the gates, Fran let out an appreciative whistle. "This is quite the place. Who cuts all this grass?"

"There's a gardener, Izzy Scannell. She's the only one left; there used to be a crew of workers."

As they passed through the open gates, Lucy noticed Eddie Culpepper driving a little lawn tractor. Spotting her, he gave a big wave, which Lucy returned.

"Who's that?" asked Fran, who didn't miss a thing.

"Just a local kid, Eddie Culpepper," said Lucy, thinking Willis had wasted no time before acting on her recommendation. "He's a new hire, he wasn't here when Van and Maxine died." She decided there was no need to go into Eddie's history as a troubled vet and recovered addict.

Fran gave her a sideways look as she pulled up by the front door and braked. "I'm just gathering information," she said. "You don't need to get defensive."

"I'm not defensive," said Lucy. "I just think you're barking up the wrong tree. The people who work here didn't have anything to gain from Van's and Maxine's deaths; quite the contrary. They put up with a lot from Weatherby and the Allens. They were overworked and underpaid. They only stayed on because they cared about VV."

Fran gave her a half smile, which Lucy understood to be a gesture of condescension. "I like to keep an open mind," she said. "You just never know about people. They're full of surprises."

Lucy followed Fran up the three stone steps to the front door, which was answered by Willis. He was happy to co-operate, once Fran identified herself and made it clear she'd been hired by Juliette, and led the way downstairs to his office. Fran settled herself at his desk and began going through the personnel files and Lucy went on to the kitchen to chat with Elfrida.

She found her taking a pan of blueberry muffins out of the oven.

Lucy inhaled the delicious scent of sugar and cinnamon. "Those smell wonderful," she said. "And, by the way, I was here yesterday for lunch and that lobster Newburg was really, really good. And the pie was lovely."

"Thanks, Lucy." Elfrida set the pan on a cooling rack. "Have one, while they're still hot. And there's coffee and tea, too. Willis got one of those single cup machines so we can have a cup whenever we want now. It makes more sense, now that we've got more people working here and everybody's on different schedules. And I put out muffins in the morning and cookies in the afternoon."

"Isn't that a lot of work for you?" asked Lucy.

Elfrida shook her head. "I can whip up a dozen muffins in fifteen minutes; cookies, too, except for the baking." She chuckled. "I never knew cooking was so easy. I'm having a ball. You know what I'm making for lunch?"

Lucy shook her head, her mouth too full of buttery muffin to speak.

"Cream of asparagus soup. I made it myself. And ham sandwiches on homemade anadama bread."

Just thinking about such a delicious menu made Lucy feel a little weak in the knees, so she made herself a cup of coffee from the snazzy new machine. "For VV, right? What do the staff get?"

"Everybody gets the same thing; lunch is at noon sharp. Mr. Willis says it's more economical in the long run." Elfrida took a warming tile out of the oven and placed it in a basket, then she piled the muffins on top. "VV is doing much better, now that she's getting a variety of real foods."

Lucy was taking a sip of the Colombian decaf she had brewed for herself, thoroughly enjoying it, when Fran appeared in the doorway. She stuck out her hand, introducing herself to Elfrida. "I'm looking forward to talking with you later. Willis is going to set up interviews this afternoon."

"Okay," responded Elfrida. "Any time before three. I have to be home for my kids."

Fran gave a brisk nod, then turned to Lucy. "Let's go," she said. "I want to see where Van died."

"Sure," said Lucy, reluctantly setting the still-full cup in the sink. "I saw the whole thing."

Fran raised an eyebrow. "You did?"

"Yeah. I brought my grandson for the Easter egg hunt."

"Then you can show me exactly what happened," said Fran. "You can be Van."

"With one major difference," said Lucy, scowling. "I have no intention of dropping dead."

She led the way upstairs to the hall, explaining that all the townsfolk were some distance away, on the other side of the closed gates. "We saw the door open," said Lucy, performing the action as she remembered Van doing it. Then she stopped, realizing the ornamental grille was open, and closed it. "This grille was in place," she said. "Van had to push it open. Maybe it stuck or something because he seemed to have some trouble with it."

But when she lifted the latch, it opened easily, and the grille swung outward in a smooth arc.

"He was in a bunny costume, with a big basket of eggs on his left arm," continued Lucy, staggering awkwardly down the steps.

"Is that how he moved? Did he stagger?" asked Fran.

"Yup. All the way to the gates, he was spilling the plastic eggs as he went," said Lucy, picturing the scene. "He got to the gates, stopped, and collapsed, right here." She dropped to the grass.

"Interesting," said Fran, crossing the lawn and taking a close look at the door. When she'd finished with the door, she got down on her hands and knees and examined the grille.

"Do you see anything?" asked Lucy, who had followed her.

Fran didn't reply, but got to her feet and brushed off her knees. "On to the impound lot," she said. "I want to see that car."

Lucy remembered Barney warning her not to touch Maxine's car for fear of destroying possible evidence. "I think you'll need permission for that," said Lucy, seating herself back in Fran's car and fastening the seat belt. "You better check with the police chief first."

Fran looked at her. "From what I hear, that car has been out in the weather at Al's Auto Care since they pulled it out of the water more than six weeks ago and nobody has bothered to take a look at it."

"That's true," said Lucy.

"I also have rubber gloves," said Fran, pulling a pair of thin exam gloves out of her tote bag. "I know what I'm doing. Believe me, I'm not going to contaminate valuable evidence."

Lucy wasn't convinced she was doing the right thing, but she had to admit that Fran had a point. If the officials weren't going to examine the car, somebody should. Fran was confident she had the necessary skills and Lucy decided to take her word for it. She had her own suspicions about the car and was eager to learn what Fran might find.

When they got to the garage, the gate to the impound lot was open and nobody seemed to be around, though they could hear voices coming from the repair bays inside. Fran was all business, opening the trunk and taking out a tool bag and a mechanic's dolly. Lucy was impressed.

"I am not going to get my clothes dirty," said Fran with a shrug. "Which car is it?"

Lucy pointed out the white BMW, a battered but sleek and classy contrast to the bulky vans and aged pickup trucks that filled the lot.

Fran put on her gloves, then pulled a small but powerful flashlight out of her bag. She first peered inside the car, paying special attention to the steering wheel and smashed windshield. Then she turned off the light and carefully examined the extensive damage on the front end. Lucy could barely stand to look at the crumpled metal and broken glass, but Fran showed no emotion at all. Finally, she positioned herself on the little trolley and rolled under the car. Lucy watched as the beam of light from the flashlight danced here and there. Then the light went out and Fran emerged, every hair in place.

"The brake line was leaking," she announced. "It wasn't a clean cut . . ."

Lucy was overcome with a sense of dismay. "What does that mean? Did it break in the crash?"

Fran was stripping off her gloves. "Maybe, maybe not.

It could have been cut intentionally but made to look ragged. I also think that iron door grille was wired and Van was electrocuted."

"Of course," said Lucy, remembering how Van had staggered when he took hold of the ornamental ironwork.

"Whoever did it is very clever, they've covered their tracks pretty well," said Fran, bending to pick up the dolly. "And whoever it is, is a skilled mechanic. This person knows what he, or she, is doing, and was smart enough to disguise the cut in the brake line." She replaced the dolly in the trunk, along with the bag of tools. "And they're not afraid of electricity . . ."

"What about timing?" asked Lucy. "What if it hadn't been Van who opened the door, but somebody else?"

Fran was thoughtful. "The killer might have rigged a switch—or might not have cared."

They got in the car once more and Fran started the engine.

"It's so cold-blooded," said Lucy, thinking that sounded a lot like Vicky and Henry.

"And technical," said Fran, shifting into drive. "This killer, whoever it is, is a real handy person."

Lucy chewed her lip, thinking that didn't sound at all like Vicky or Henry.

Chapter Fifteen

"So who's in charge of this investigation, anyway?" asked Fran. "The local cops?"

Lucy couldn't help laughing at the idea. "The local cops mostly herd tourists on July fourth, issue parking tickets, stuff like that. The state police take over when it's a serious crime like murder, a bank robbery, or a drug investigation. As far as I can tell, there hasn't actually been any investigation into Van's and Maxine's deaths—these days it seems they look for reasons *not* to investigate further—but the DA has charged Vicky and Henry with elder abuse as well as fraud and embezzlement so I guess he must be taking a close look at them."

"And where is this DA's office?"

Lucy was surprised. "You want to see him?"

"I sure do."

"He's hard to get a hold of," said Lucy, who had often tried and failed to interview him.

"Well, I've got to try," said Fran. "As a private investigator, it's my legal duty to share information with the appropriate authorities. I took an oath."

"Turn right here," said Lucy, as they approached an intersection. "Gilead is the next town over."

Much to Lucy's amazement, Phil Aucoin was only too happy to talk to Fran. His secretary, Nancy Willard, gave Lucy the usual evil eye, but when Fran produced her business card and ID, she grudgingly agreed to show them to Phil. Moments later the door to his office flew open and he was greeting Fran with open arms.

"A real private eye," he exclaimed, taking her hand and shaking it. "From New York, no less. I bet you could write a book."

"I'm planning to," said Fran with a big smile. "When I retire."

"Well, come on in," said Aucoin with a sweep of his arm. "Tell me how I can help you."

Lucy wasn't convinced the invitation included her, but she tagged along anyway. Maybe he wouldn't notice her.

"I see you've got company," said Phil, seating himself behind the big desk, which was covered with piles of papers. Other stacks of files covered most of the floor between the desk and the window.

Fran took a seat in one of the captain's chairs provided for visitors. "Lucy is helping me, showing me around and providing background."

He nodded, inviting her to take the other chair. "Fine, fine. Just remember, Lucy, whatever you hear is off the record."

"Of course," said Lucy, sitting down and crossing her legs.

Phil leaned back in his chair, folding his hands over his belt. "So, Ms. Martino, what brings you to our fair county?"

"Fran, call me Fran," she began. "I've been hired by Juliette Duff to look into the deaths of her father, Van Duff, and her mother, Maxine Carey. Their deaths may be related to another case you're working on. Juliette is Vivian Van Vorst's great-granddaughter and Van, her father, is VV's grandson and Victoria Allen's brother."

Aucoin nodded. "I'm familiar with that family's genealogical chart, believe me." He sighed. "But I've seen the paperwork. There's no indication those deaths were suspicious. It's tragic for Juliette, no doubt about that, but these things happen."

Fran nodded in agreement. "No doubt about that, no doubt at all." She paused. "But I have to tell you, I found evidence that Maxine's car was tampered with."

"Ah," said Aucoin. "You found the broken brake line."

"I didn't know you had the car checked out!" exclaimed Lucy.

"Of course we did," said Aucoin. "But it was torn, it wasn't cut."

"So it seemed," admitted Fran. "But I think it was made to look that way. I do think it was torn on purpose."

Aucoin spread out his hands in a gesture of helplessness. "I can only work with the evidence my investigators give me," he said, "and they tell me there was no sign of tampering."

Fran wasn't done; she had another trick up her sleeve. "Then there's Van," she said. "I've had questions about his death ever since I read the witness accounts, which by the way, Lucy confirms. They all agree that he reacted physically when he opened the ornamental metal grille in front of the door. Different witnesses used different words: 'staggered,' 'shook,' even 'convulsed.' That made me suspect the grille may have been electrified in some way and when I examined it earlier today, I found scratch marks near the base, as if wires had been attached."

"Or maybe somebody attached Christmas decorations to the grille," said Aucoin. "Or one of VV's dogs was in a hurry to get out. Or maybe Willis, the butler there, dropped a silver tray when he was opening the door. There could be a lot of reasons for the paintwork to be scratched."

Lucy couldn't stand it; she'd been biting her tongue, but now she had to speak. "C'mon Phil, you told me yourself you'd be only too happy to nail Vicky and Henry with a murder charge, but you didn't have the evidence. Well, now you've got something to go on. These discoveries of Fran's need to be addressed, they need to be investigated. Vicky and Henry definitely had strong motives for getting rid of Van and Maxine—they knew the jig would be up if either one of them figured out how they were robbing VV."

Aucoin rubbed his forehead, mussing up his brown hair, which he wore combed straight back. "Motive's not enough," he said. "We've all got plenty of motives for doing away with our nearest and dearest."

Fran chuckled. "You said it—but most of us don't do it. I'm convinced Vicky and Henry did."

Aucoin sighed. "I have seen no evidence whatsoever that either one of them is capable of changing a light bulb. There is nothing in their past to indicate any sort of mechanical proficiency, nothing like the sort of knowledge you'd need to pull off an electrocution. Whoever did this . . ." Aucoin was brought up short, hearing his own words. "And I'm not saying anybody did do it, but if they did, they would have to know a lot about electricity. I couldn't do it; about all I'm good for in that department is flipping a circuit breaker. And as for the brake line, I wouldn't know how to find it—and I'm pretty sure they didn't teach that stuff at the fancy schools those two attended."

That was all they got out of Aucoin, who made it perfectly clear that he had to prepare for the trial, which was due to begin on Monday. When Lucy was back in the car with Fran, heading home to Tinker's Cove, she thought about what Aucoin had said.

"You know," she began, speaking slowly, "I was at the funeral. I saw Maxine argue with Vicky and Henry and storm off in a huff."

"Were you there the whole time?" asked Fran.

"Yes. The day before, too. I was hired to help with the food so I was there before and after."

"What about Vicky and Henry? Were they there the whole time, too?"

"I think they were," said Lucy. "I was busy serving the food. I didn't observe their every move, but I did see a lot of them. I don't think they had time to tamper with Maxine's car. They were too busy with the guests."

"They didn't have to do it themselves," said Fran. "They could have hired someone, maybe someone who worked at the house. Like that kid, Eddie. He seems like a capable sort."

"I'm sure he is, but he wasn't working there then," said Lucy.

"What about the gardener, Izzy? She seems to do more than plant stuff; she does a lot of maintenance, too."

"She might have the necessary skills," admitted Lucy, "but what motive could she possibly have? And if she was going to kill somebody, I'm pretty sure she would have knocked off the people who were causing her grief: Vicky, Henry, and Weatherby."

"What about the butler, Willis?" asked Fran. "He seems like a resourceful kind of guy."

"He is, and he's very devoted to VV. I can't see why he'd kill Van and Maxine, though. They were playing on the same team, defending VV against Vicky and Henry and Weatherby."

Fran was zipping along the country road, past old farmhouses and mobile homes, hay fields and woods. "Things are not always what they seem," she said. "And people rarely are who they seem to be, at least that's been my experience. I think we're looking at this from the wrong perspective. I don't think it's about personalities and loyalties. I suspect it's all about the money."

"But Van and Maxine didn't have much money," said Lucy.

"Everything's relative," said Fran. "It might not have seemed like much to them, but I bet their bank accounts are a lot larger than yours or mine."

"That wouldn't be hard, at least in my case," said Lucy, who had just paid the mortgage and now had a balance of one hundred and thirty-nine dollars. "But Van and Maxine probably left whatever they had to Juliette—and she's making lots of money as a top model."

"Yeah," agreed Fran. "If Juliette can afford me, she's doing pretty well." She braked, coming to a stop sign and turning onto Route 1. "Anyway, VV's got the real money in this case. She can't go on forever; she's got to die sometime, probably soon, and somebody's going to become very rich." She accelerated, picking up speed, as they passed motels and gift shops. "The question is, who?"

Lucy dug around in the big African basket she used as a purse and eventually found her cell phone. She dialed Bob's office, then crossed her fingers while she counted the rings, hoping he'd answer himself and she wouldn't have to convince his secretary to let her talk to him. The secretary, Anne, picked up on the third ring.

"Hi," Lucy said, giving her name. "Any chance I could talk to Bob?" she asked.

"Sorry, Lucy. He's awfully busy these days."

"Well, you see, with all this stuff about VV, I realized my husband and I don't have wills."

"I can make an appointment for you."

"I think it would be better if I could talk to Bob. You

see, my husband isn't all that keen and I was hoping to kind of make him think it's a social thing. I'd like to meet outside the office."

"Oh, well, you're in luck," said the secretary, a note of disapproval in her voice. "He's just come in."

"Oh, thanks," said Lucy. A moment later, she heard Bob's voice.

"What can I do for you, Lucy?"

"Bill and I need wills, but Bill doesn't agree. He says we don't have anything to leave anybody and once we're dead, it won't be our problem anyway."

Bob chuckled. "I'll drop by the house and talk to him," he said. "But right now I'm tied up with the Van Vorst thing."

"I'm sure you are," said Lucy, who knew Bob had been appointed by the family court judge to represent VV. "In fact, I was just wondering about VV's will and all. Is she leaving any money to Tinker's Cove charities?"

"Lucy! You know the terms of a will are confidential." He sighed. "Besides, at this point, there are so many versions, not to mention codicils, it's going to take forever for the court to sort it all out. And that, by the way, is strictly off the record."

"It's hardly news," said Lucy.

"Well, I don't want to read about it in the *Pennysaver*," said Bob, a warning note in his voice. "I wouldn't want to have to take legal action."

Lucy figured he was bluffing, but she wasn't about to press the point, either. "I understand," she said. "But since we're off the record, can't you give me some idea who's going to be the lucky winner when VV dies?"

"No, I can't. Have a nice day."

"You've got quite a technique," said Fran dryly. "I'm amazed you get anybody to talk."

"I mostly write puff pieces, features about the new hair salon, or the rare salamander that was spotted in the Audubon sanctuary." Lucy smiled. "I did get a photo of that cute little guy, but no quote."

She was dialing once again, this time calling Rachel, who was back on the job at Miss Tilley's. "You're sounding a lot better," she began.

"Just a little cough," she said.

"Keep up the fluids," advised Lucy. "Guess what? I'm working with a private investigator . . ."

"A real private eye!" Rachel sounded impressed.

"From New York City," said Lucy. "Juliette hired her to look into her parents' deaths. We've found some evidence that the deaths were suspicious and Fran needs some information. She wants to know who inherits when VV dies. Do you have any idea?"

"I don't, Lucy, but I couldn't tell you even if I did," said Rachel, sounding a little annoyed.

"It's completely off the record," said Lucy. "It's just for the investigation."

"You don't give up, do you?" She hardly got the words out, due to a coughing fit.

"Maybe Miss T knows?" suggested Lucy, when the coughing subsided.

Rachel sounded resigned. "I'll ask."

There was a long silence but Rachel eventually returned. "Miss T says VV told her years ago that she'd made some changes to benefit Juliette. She doesn't know if it was a small bequest or the whole kit and caboodle. She doesn't even know if she's changed her will since then. It was a very long time ago; Juliette was very young. Miss T says she was too young at the time to do anything that would have upset VV, unlike Little Viv and Van."

Lucy could just imagine Miss Tilley making a crack along those lines.

"Miss T says VV used her will to control her family. She was always making adjustments, giving one more, taking some away from another, sometimes disinheriting them entirely. She says she doesn't entirely fault Vicky, that VV brought a lot of this on herself."

"I've wondered about that myself," said Lucy.

"I sure hope the jury doesn't think like that," said Rachel, sounding indignant. "Not after all the work Bob's done, trying to sort things out."

"Don't worry—the DA's got a strong case for elder abuse. And nothing excuses Vicky's and Henry's behavior. Remind the old fright of that," said Lucy.

"She heard you," said Rachel.

"I meant her to," said Lucy, laughing.

Turning to Fran, she gave her the results of her inquiry. "The only name that came up was Juliette's and there's some doubt that even she is still in the will."

"Well, this would be a first for me," said Fran.

"What would?" asked Lucy.

"Getting hired by the guilty party."

"Actually," said Lucy, speaking slowly. "It would be a smart move, wouldn't it? If Juliette did murder her parents, what better way to divert suspicion? Maybe she's playing a role here—the grieving, distraught daughter—in hopes of casting suspicion on Vicky and Henry. She's the innocent, sweet young thing and they're the evil, conniving, greedy relations."

Fran gave her a look. "You have a mind like a sewer," she said.

"It's from living in a small town," said Lucy. "You wouldn't believe what goes on here."

"I'm getting the feeling it's a real nest of vipers," said Fran with a shudder. "And people think all the crime takes place in the big city. I'm going to be glad to get back to the city!"

As they drove along, Lucy thought about an interview she'd done for the feature story on elder abuse she wrote while she was in Florida. She'd gone to the local senior center, where she spoke with a friendly caseworker who had been only too happy to vent her frustration. Eloise Walker was in her fifties, with a mop of curly gray hair, sharp blue eyes that didn't miss a thing, and a reassuring smile.

"To state the obvious, we have a lot of retirees here in Florida," Eloise had told her. "There was quite a flood when the economy was good, back in the nineties, but now those folks who came here to play golf and watch birds are getting very old and frail. Most of them don't have any family locally and they're sitting ducks for swindlers."

"What is the state doing?" Lucy had asked.

"Oh, the legislature passes laws and the police set up special units to investigate elder abuse and we hold seminars to inform seniors, but the truth is that a lot of it is closing the barn door after the cows have gotten out. No sooner do we identify one scam—say, fake home health aides or phony reverse mortgage schemes—than the crooks come up with a new one. The latest involves going after folks who die intestate—who don't have wills."

"How does that work? Wouldn't the money go to the state?" Lucy had asked.

"Yeah, but what these crooks do is they find people who've died and have no heirs, then they produce fake birth certificates and present themselves as long lost relatives so they can claim an inheritance."

"Isn't that awfully complicated? And it must be a lot of work," Lucy had said. "And isn't it easy to check the validity of the birth certificates?"

"Not if you happen to have a girlfriend working in the county records office," Eloise had replied.

"I didn't think of that," Lucy had admitted.

"My point exactly," Eloise had said. "The crooks are way ahead of us."

Lucy was called back to the present when Fran pulled up in front of the *Pennysaver* office and braked. "You got awfully quiet there," said Fran. "Penny for your thoughts."

"Oh, sorry," said Lucy. "My mind was drifting."

"You know," said Fran, "I find that very helpful. When I get stymied on a case, I let it go and think of something else. Nine times out of ten, the answer just sort of pops up."

Lucy found herself smiling. "I don't think my boss will go for that, but it's worth trying."

"Well, thanks for your help, Lucy," said Fran, checking her watch. "I've got those interviews at Pine Point and I'm heading back to the city tonight. If you get any bright ideas, let me know."

"I will," promised Lucy. "But don't get your hopes up."

Chapter Sixteen

Over the weekend, Lucy took Fran's advice and refused to think about Van's and Maxine's deaths. Instead, she kept busy, taking the girls shopping at the outlet mall for summer clothes and working in the garden, where the weeds were threatening to get the upper hand. On Sunday evening, she admitted the experiment was a failure. Her subconscious had failed to come up with a solution, but she had made some awfully good buys at the outlet mall and the garden was free of weeds.

Dinner was over, the dishwasher was humming, and Lucy took a second cup of decaf into the family room and settled herself in front of the TV. Flipping channels, looking for something other than sports, she checked the cable news channel. There she found a favorite anchor person, Lynette Oakley, reporting that Vicky and Henry's trial was scheduled to begin on Monday.

Lucy watched as the station played a tape of District Attorney Phil Aucoin, who was outlining the charges against them, which included elder abuse, fraud, and embezzlement. This was followed by a clip of the Allens' attorney, famous defense lawyer Howard Zuzick, who had little to say except that he was confident his clients would be acquitted.

Lucy expected that would be that, and the coverage would switch to the region's other big story—the continuing saga of unreliable electric service—when Bob Goodman's familiar face filled the screen. "At the center of this upcoming trial is aged millionaire Vivian Van Vorst. How is she doing?" asked the off-screen reporter.

Bob smiled and nodded. "I'm happy to say that Mrs. Van Vorst is doing much better and her health has improved considerably now that the Allens are no longer in charge of her care."

Footage then began to roll showing VV in her wheelchair, wearing a big sun hat and sunglasses and with a blanket covering her legs, being pushed about in her garden by the beautiful Juliette, who was wearing a floaty chiffon dress. The two were accompanied by Sylvia and another nurse, as well as a couple of polite young children carrying balloons who appeared to have stepped out of a Ralph Lauren ad. Juliette parked the wheelchair in front of a particularly gorgeous rosebush and bent a bough down so VV could smell the flowers' scent. After inhaling deeply, she raised her head and smiled, waving to the camera.

Points to Bob, thought Lucy, who hadn't imagined he was this savvy about public relations. Which, she realized, he wasn't. It was Juliette, the top model, who had arranged this little vignette. Those kids probably were professional models, hired for the day. The clothes, even the blanket on VV's scrawny old legs, were all color coordinated and presented a carefully orchestrated picture of an old woman enjoying a perfect spring day in her garden. This is what VV's final days should be like, Juliette was saying, and this is what Vicky and Henry tried to take away from her. Lucy thought it was a smart move and would certainly affect public opinion; she wondered, however, if it would have any effect on the trial. The jurors who were eventually chosen might or might not have seen it, and those who had would certainly be ordered by the judge to disregard it. On the other hand, the video clip made an impression that would be difficult to forget.

The trial began, as scheduled, on Monday, in the superior courthouse in Gilead. The courtroom, which dated from 1887, had recently been restored. The walls were freshly painted in cream with dark green and maroon borders, the oak paneling had been cleaned and refinished, and the massive gas-lit chandelier that hung from an ornate plaster medallion in the center of the ceiling had been restored and electrified.

Nobody was looking at the interior decor, however. All eyes in the crowded courtroom were on Vicky and Henry Allen, seated at the defendant's table. Henry was dressed in a sober gray suit, impeccably groomed as ever, looking as if he might be in a pew at church rather than in a Maine courtroom. Vicky looked as if she'd strayed out of a ladies luncheon, in a pale blue suit with her light brown hair tied at the nape of her neck with a black grosgrain ribbon. She sat with her knees together, a ladylike purse perched on her lap. Their lawyer, Howard Zuzick, by contrast, was wearing a loud tie, printed with wild cats, and his wiry gray hair sprung out from his head in every direction. He was accompanied by a young woman lawyer who was busy arranging numerous folders stuffed with papers.

Phil Aucoin sat at the other table, along with a couple of young assistant district attorneys. They conferred together in low voices, glancing occasionally at the defendants and at the judge's vacant bench. A group of family members were seated in the first row of seats outside the bar, including Juliette, Little Viv, Andrew Duff, and Peter Reilly. Juliette was dressed in a simple but stunning sleeveless gray sheath and seemed oblivious to the media attention she was receiving. Most of the photographers in the courtroom couldn't resist focusing on her, but she was only interested in supporting her grandmother, Little Viv, who clung to her hand and was quite white with terror. Andrew, who was sitting on her other side, also offered support to his ex-wife, occasionally murmuring in her ear and patting her shoulder. Peter Reilly had the aisle seat, and, of the four, he was the calmest, seemingly at ease as he waited for the trial to begin.

Promptly at ten, the bailiff announced that Judge Anthony Featherstone was presiding and all should rise. Judge Featherstone had only been on the job a few months and Lucy had never covered one of his trials before, but he looked like a no-nonsense sort who entered the courtroom briskly and got straight to business.

Judge Featherstone soon revealed he had no tolerance for courtroom theatrics, and jury selection proceeded smoothly once he warned Attorney Zuzick that he was close to being declared in contempt of court when he accused a potential juror of reverse racism. From then on, it was smooth sailing; twelve jurors and two alternates were seated and court recessed for lunch.

Lucy was sitting next to Deb Hildreth from the Gilead Enterprise, who suggested an out-of-the-way café where they could get something to eat, avoiding the crowd. When they arrived at Pizza'n'More, they found Pete Withers from the *Portland Press* and Bob Mayes, the stringer for the *Globe*, already seated and enjoying bottles of beer and pizza slices.

"Join us!" yelled Pete, when Lucy and Deb finished ordering their salads at the counter and picked their diet teas from the cooler.

"Beer? Really?" said Deb, sliding onto the padded Leatherette bench beside Bob.

"It's a journalistic tradition," said Pete, shoving over to make room for Lucy.

"Anybody taking bets?" asked Lucy, who loved hanging out with her local press colleagues and rarely got the chance. "That's another journalistic tradition."

"Long odds," said Bob. "I'd say twenty-to-one, in favor of Aucoin."

"Yeah," agreed Deb, unscrewing the cap from her bottle of iced tea. "Vicky and Henry are going to need those stiff upper lips of theirs."

When court resumed, Phil Aucoin refrained from delivering a lengthy opening statement, limiting himself to outlining the charges against Vicky and Henry—which included embezzlement, fraud, and elder abuse—and promising the jurors he would prove each one beyond a reasonable doubt. He then called his first witness, Little Viv.

Receiving an encouraging squeeze of the hand from her granddaughter, Juliette, she rose and stepped through the gate, which the bailiff held open for her. She appeared as sweet and vague as ever; even her walk was tentative as she almost seemed to be avoiding the witness chair. When she finally reached it, she perched on the edge, then popped up and raised the wrong hand to take the oath. She blushed furiously when the bailiff corrected her, then stammered as she promised to "tell the truth, the whole truth, and nothing but the truth, so help me God." Seated once again, she leaned forward and waited for Aucoin's questions, her eyes open wide.

"Please state your name," he said, in a gentle voice.

"Vivian Van Vorst Duff," she replied in a whisper.

"And you are the mother of one of the defendants, Victoria Allen?"

"Yes."

"And the daughter of Vivian Van Vorst?"

"That's correct."

"Can you describe for me what life was like at Pine Point, when you were growing up there?"

Obviously relieved that she was not going to have to face any unpleasant truths, at least not yet, Little Viv smiled. "Oh, it was lovely. Mother was known for her gracious hospitality and her beautiful home. We were only there in the summers when I was young, but I remember the gardens were beautiful. We spent long, lovely days sailing and having picnics. There were always lots of people, lots of guests. It was like a dream, really."

"You married your first husband, Andrew Duff, in 1964. Did you spend much time at Pine Point after that?"

"Oh, yes. We'd go every summer. Well, Andrew had to work, but he came up most weekends. I brought the children, Van and Vicky. They loved it at Pine Point. There was always a lively crowd, plenty of tennis and parties. Their birthdays were in the summer and Mumsy always gave them the most wonderful parties, with pony rides and music." She sighed. "And she always gave them the most lovely gifts. One year it was a Gypsy wagon to use as a playhouse, another time it was a tiny little Chris-Craft for Van to putter around in."

"Did things change after your marriage to Andrew Duff ended?"

Little Viv pressed her lips together. "Well, Andrew didn't come anymore, but the kids and I did. It really wasn't very different for them. I had a generous settlement from Andrew and Mumsy helped out if I needed a bit more. It was important to her that the kids went to good schools. She wanted to make sure that their lifestyle didn't change."

"So your mother helped with tuition, things like that?"

"She gave me an allowance while the kids were dependents."

"Do you remember how much that was?"

"In dollars?" asked Little Viv, looking a bit affronted. She was of a generation that declined to discuss money.

"Yes. An approximate figure will do."

"I don't really remember. Mr. Harrison took care of money things for me."

"Who is Mr. Harrison?"

"At the bank. If I needed money, I called him."

"Did he ever say you didn't have enough money, that your funds were low?"

"No." She paused. "But I wasn't extravagant. We lived simply."

Aucoin went to the table, where his assistant handed him a couple of sheets of paper. "I have here your income tax statements from 1980, that would be when Vicky was twelve. It shows a gift from your mother of two hundred and fifty thousand dollars, is that about right?"

Vicky blinked a few times. "If it's on the tax form, it must be."

That caused a little laughter from the assembled company, and a few smirks from the jurors.

"Can you describe your daughter's lifestyle at this time?"

"When Vicky was twelve, we lived in Milton, near Boston. She went to Milton Country Day, of course. She had ballet lessons—she was keen on ballet—and she also took riding lessons. She was having a bit of trouble with French, so Madame Robert came to the house for tutoring and conversation."

"And much of this was possible because of the funds provided by her grandmother, Vivian Van Vorst?"

Little Viv looked uncertain. "I guess so. As I mentioned, I didn't really pay attention to the financial aspect of things. I depended on Mr. Harrison to do that."

"So, unlike most of us, who have to pay attention to our finances, perhaps living within a certain budget, you simply had to ask and Mr. Harrison provided whatever amount you needed?"

Little Viv smiled; at last her interrogator understood. "That's right."

"What if Mr. Harrison discovered you needed more money than you had on hand in your bank account? What would he do then?"

"He'd ask Mumsy," replied Little Viv as if the answer were obvious.

"Did your mother ever turn you down? Did she ever deny such a request?"

"Not that I'm aware of."

"Thank you," said Aucoin, indulging in a sharklike smile. "That's all."

Little Viv started to get up, but the judge cautioned her. "The defense may have some questions for you."

"No questions at this time," said Zuzick without expression.

Visibly relieved, Little Viv practically ran back to her seat, where Juliette embraced her in a quick hug.

Vicky, however, looked distinctly uncomfortable. She'd seen the handwriting on the wall. She understood that Aucoin had portrayed her as a privileged child who had been pampered by an indulgent grandmother. It was inevitable that VV's generosity would be compared to her own stinginess when it came time to provide care for her aged grandmother.

She was also worldly enough to know that most people, including the jurors, did not have the option of calling a Mr. Harrison whenever they needed a quarter million dollars.

As for Henry, he busied himself taking notes on a yellow legal pad, and Lucy wondered if he was pretending to himself that he had a measure of control over his fate and was not at the mercy of the twelve citizens seated in the jury box.

Willis was called next, and Lucy saw Vicky visibly sink into her seat as he took the oath.

"Mr. Willis," began Aucoin, "you were employed by Mrs. Van Vorst as her butler for over thirty years?"

"I began working for Mrs. Van Vorst in 1975," he said.

"Are you still employed by her?"

"Yes."

"So you have worked this entire period since 1975 without interruption?"

"No. I was let go by Mr. and Mrs. Allen just after Easter but I was rehired when Mr. Goodman became Mrs. Van Vorst's guardian."

"Why were you let go?"

"The official reason, as explained to me by Mr. Weatherby, was that Mrs. Van Vorst could no longer afford to pay my salary."

"Who is Mr. Weatherby? Can you identify him?"

"Yes, he's in the courtroom."

"Will you point him out?"

Willis was apparently unable to do anything as rude as pointing to Weatherby, but he gave a nod in his direction and described him as "the man in the gray suit in the second row, seated under the window."

"And what was Mr. Weatherby's role at Pine Point?"

"He was an attorney in the employ of Mr. and Mrs.

Allen. When the Allens petitioned the court and became Mrs. Van Vorst's legal guardians, he took over from Mr. Goodman, who was Mrs. Van Vorst's attorney, and began managing her legal and financial affairs."

"How did this change impact Mrs. Van Vorst?"

"It was very negative. He immediately began dismissing staff members, cutting more than a half-dozen employees. Economies were taken, there were no more fresh flowers, laundry service was cut, even food."

"That must have been very difficult for you," said Aucoin.

"I did my best to manage within these constraints so that Mrs. Van Vorst was not affected, but it became increasingly difficult. I was also aware that Mr. Weatherby was pressuring Mrs. Van Vorst to sign legal documents. She used to ask me what the papers were for, but I couldn't tell her. The Allens were also taking things from the house."

"Can you be more specific?"

"Mrs. Allen took some jewelry and furs. She said Mrs. Van Vorst wanted her to have them."

"I have here a photo of Mrs. Allen," said Aucoin, handing it to Willis at the same time it appeared on a video screen. "Can you identify the jewelry she is wearing."

"Yes, absolutely. Those are Mrs. Van Vorst's pearl and diamond earrings. They were her favorites and she wore them almost every day."

Another photo of Vicky appeared on the screen. This time, she was wearing a leopardskin coat.

"That is Mrs. Van Vorst's coat; again, a garment she wore almost daily in the winter," said Willis.

It wasn't something you could measure, but Lucy sensed an atmosphere of disapproval beginning to develop in the courtroom. People whispered to each other and their expressions were grim.

"At first, I thought that Mrs. Van Vorst gave the Allens

permission to take these things," said Willis. "That's what Mrs. Allen said when I questioned her about some paintings that she was carrying out of the house, and I accepted that explanation. It wasn't until they took *Jelly Beans* that I began to doubt that Mrs. Van Vorst had given them permission."

"What is *Jelly Beans* and why would Mrs. Van Vorst have been unlikely to have given it to them?"

"*Jelly Beans* is a sculpture by Karl Klaus and Mrs. Van Vorst was terribly fond of it. She displayed it with pride on a table in the foyer. It was a gift from the sculptor and her very favorite possession."

"What happened to *Jelly Beans*?"

"Mr. Allen took it just before Easter this year."

"You saw him do this?"

"Yes. I saw him putting it in a box and I asked him what he was doing."

"What did he say?"

"He said I should mind my own business, and then he picked up the box and carried it out to his car."

"What did you do then?"

"I called Mr. Goodman, but he said he had no legal standing in the matter since he was no longer retained by Mrs. Van Vorst. He advised me to make a memorandum of the date and time, which I did. I also began keeping a record of other things I found questionable."

"It was shortly after this that your employment was terminated?"

Willis nodded. "Van Vorst Duff, Mrs. Van Vorst's grandson, died the week before Easter. They kept me on through the funeral, but let me go the day after."

There was a little buzz in the courtroom; more than a few observers had lost their jobs in the recession and took a dim view of cost-cutting employers.

"Thank you, no further questions," said Aucoin.

The defense attorney, Zuzick, hesitated a moment, but, receiving a pointed glare from Henry Allen, got to his feet.

"I just have one question," he began. "Do you not think it possible that you were terminated for cause? That the Allens may have found your attitude to them unpleasant? Perhaps they found you unreasonable and uncooperative?"

If this was intended to upset Willis, it failed. He thought a moment, considering his answer, then spoke. "That may have been the case, but that is not what I was told. I was told that it was necessary to let me go because Mrs. Van Vorst could no longer afford to pay my salary."

"How much was your salary, by the way?"

"Seventy-eight thousand dollars per year."

"Pretty good, hunh?" Zuzick turned to the jury, his expression implying that Willis had been riding the gravy train. "Plus room and board, right?"

"A studio apartment was provided, as well as meals, because I was on call around the clock."

"You got vacations and days off, right?"

"I took a few days when my mother died. That was in 1993."

"No further questions," snapped Zuzick, hurrying back to his place at the table.

The last witness called that afternoon was Sylvia Vargas, one of VV's nurses. Aucoin got right down to business. "Are you a licensed registered nurse?" he asked.

"Not in the U.S.," she said, speaking confidently with a slight accent. "I am licensed in the Philippines, where I trained at St. Lucia Medical Center, but I do not have a valid U.S. license. I was hired as a home health aide."

"But you were actually performing the duties of a nurse?"

"I was hired with the approval of Mrs. Van Vorst's doctor."

"Are you a legal immigrant?" asked Aucoin.

"I have a green card, yes."

"When did you start working at Pine Point?"

"I was hired by Mr. Weatherby, just before Christmas."

"What did you find when you came to Pine Point?"

"Mrs. Van Vorst is very elderly and frail. At first, we used to get her up in the mornings and take her downstairs for breakfast. She enjoyed sitting in the conservatory with the plants and the sunshine. She would have her lunch there, then a nap upstairs, sometimes dinner in bed. She liked watching TV, she especially liked the old movies. The hairdresser used to come twice a week, she had a massage once a week, manicures and pedicures, too."

"Did things change over time?"

"The first big change was when they shut the conservatory and got rid of the plants. We used to change her sheets every day, now it's once a week and we have to switch the top sheet to the bottom. If the sheets are soiled, we wash them ourselves. Mrs. Allen told us no more up and down stairs, that Mrs. Van Vorst should remain in her room for meals. Then she told us the doctor says no more food, only nutrition drinks. The hairdresser, all that, she said was too draining on Mrs. Van Vorst's energy."

"Did you ask the doctor about this?"

"Mrs. Allen said we should not bother the doctor with questions, she would communicate with the doctor and tell us what he said."

"When Mrs. Allen reported the doctor's orders, did you find them consistent with good medical practice?"

"No. I trained for three years at St. Lucia hospital, the best hospital in the Philippines. There I learned that patients should not remain in bed twenty-four-seven. They need a proper diet consistent with their ability to eat, they need pleasant surroundings, and they need emotional support from family."

"You believe the standard of care declined between Christmas and Easter?"

"I would not call it care, I would call it abuse. The worst was the constant harassment, as Mr. Weatherby brought her papers to sign. She used to cry, begging me not to let the man in the suit come into her room. Sometimes she had nightmares about it. She would wake up shaking and frightened by the man in the suit."

"This man in the suit was Mr. Weatherby?"

"Yes, that's what she called him."

"Why was she afraid of him?"

"I think because he would shout at her and threaten her. I always had to leave the room when he came, but I would listen at the door. One time I heard him tell her she had to sign the paper or she would be homeless, she would have to live out in the street, under a bridge if she was lucky."

Hearing this, there was a collective gasp in the courtroom. Lucy studied the jurors' faces. She saw a few jaws drop, and she saw their eyes flicker toward Vicky and Henry, only to be quickly averted. Vicky and Henry didn't betray the slightest emotion but they must have been aware, Lucy thought, of the tide of revulsion that was building toward them in the courtroom. It was never a good sign for the defendants when the jurors refused to look at them.

Chapter Seventeen

When Lucy got home that afternoon, she took a glass of white wine into the family room and settled herself on the saggy old sectional, eager to see what the TV networks were reporting about the trial. Libby had already snuggled into position beside her, resting her chin on Lucy's lap, when Lucy grabbed the remote and flicked the TV on. She was just in time for the five o'clock news from Boston, and the trial was the lead story.

Veteran reporter Jack Hennessey was standing in front of the gray granite courthouse, mike in hand. "DA Phil Aucoin spent most of today building a foundation for his case against Victoria and Henry Allen, depicting the lifestyle of aged millionaire Vivian Van Vorst before the couple became her legal guardians. He first called Van Vorst's daughter, also named Vivian, to the stand and she described idyllic days at Pine Point, the Van Vorst summer home in Tinker's Cove, Maine."

A short clip was shown in which Little Viv recounted happy times, a beatific expression on her aged face. Then the camera returned to Jack Hennessey. "Also on the stand were James Willis, Mrs. Van Vorst's butler, and a trained nurse, Sylvia Vargas. I'll report on their testimony at five-thirty."

The anchor nodded. "Thanks, Jack. And now, Harvey Lyons has the weather. Looks like we're in for a heat wave."

Lucy flipped to NECN, the regional cable channel, just in time to catch Attorney Zuzick giving a brief interview.

"What's your reaction to DA Phil Aucoin's line of questioning today?" the reporter asked. She was a young Asian-American woman with a serious expression.

"I'm gonna say what I always say on day one. It's day one. This is just the beginning. A trial is like a story and there's two sides. Right now you're hearing from the prosecution, but, believe me, we've got a terrific defense."

"Why didn't you cross-examine the witnesses?" asked the reporter.

"Strategy," said Zuzick. "The sooner we get through them, the sooner we get to tell our side of the story."

"What do you think of the jury? Eight middle-aged women, three retired men, and one child-care worker."

"Fabulous, best jury ever. I'm confident they'll come to a fair and just verdict, completely vindicating my clients."

"Well, there you have it, Sandra," said the reporter, referring to the NECN anchorwoman in her wrap up. "A confident reaction by defense attorney Zuzick on the first day of the Allen trial."

"You were there, Ngaio," said Sandra. "Do you think Zuzick's confidence is well founded?"

Ngaio looked straight into the camera. "Based on what I saw in that courtroom today, I'd say Mr. Zuzick has an uphill battle. Watching the jurors, I would have to say they seemed shocked at times by the testimony, at other times they seemed disapproving. By the end of the day they weren't even looking at the defendants, Victoria and Henry Allen."

"What can we expect tomorrow?" asked Sandra.

"Attorney Weatherby is going to testify tomorrow and that should be very interesting because he has been cooperating with the prosecution against his former clients."

"We'll look forward to that," said Sandra. "Now, the traffic report."

Next morning, traffic in the little town of Gilead was impossibly snarled. The trial was suddenly a big story and the parking lot at the courthouse was filled with satellite trucks from various TV stations, while the nearby streets were filled with cars as drivers looked in vain for parking spaces. Delivery trucks compounded the problem, double-parking as additional provisions were unloaded at the restaurants and coffee shops nearest the courthouse, which were anticipating a rush of business. Lucy joined the line of cars threading through the streets, all marked with NO PARKING signs, until she had a sudden brain wave and remembered the lot at the high school football field. It was already nearly full when she pulled in, but she did find a vacant spot at the very back. She then had to walk nearly a mile to the courthouse, worrying that she wouldn't be able to get a seat.

Her fears were confirmed when she entered the stately building's large lobby and found a line waiting at the door of the courtroom. She approached one of the court officers who was guarding the door, her press card in hand, but he shook his head. Fortunately, she saw Deb Hildreth pop up and wave to her, indicating she'd saved her a seat, and the officer let her enter.

"Thanks," said Lucy, plunking herself down beside Deb, panting from the jog to the courthouse. "You're a lifesaver. I had to park at the football field. It's crazy out there."

"I run every morning. My route takes me past the courthouse and when I saw the parking lot filling up, I went straight home to change and hurried back. I got here around seven and there were already a bunch of people ahead of me in line. I couldn't believe it."

Lucy was astonished. "You waited in line for three hours?"

"Two and a half. They opened the doors at nine-thirty. It was like a land rush in a Western movie."

"Let me buy you lunch," said Lucy.

"I figured the lunch places would be jammed so I grabbed some food, too," said Deb.

Lucy was impressed by Deb's foresight. "Well, tomorrow I'll do the early shift."

There was a little stir in the courtroom when Juliette arrived, and the news photographers lining the walls jostled for position, competing to get the best shot of the model. She was once again accompanied by Andrew Duff and Peter Reilly, but Little Viv had apparently stayed home. Spotting Bob Goodman, Lucy gave him a little wave, which he acknowledged with a nod. There was another flurry of activity when Vicky and Henry arrived, along with Zuzick, who made a point of greeting reporters he recognized from previous trials. It was a smart strategic move, thought Lucy, but even more likely was just an expression of the attorney's ebullient and friendly personality.

"I wonder why Zuzick agreed to take this case," mused Lucy aloud. "The Allens are so despicable—he's bound to lose."

"Money, my dear," said Deb. "Mucho money."

Lucy chewed her lip. "He must have found something positive about them. He must have something to build a defense on, don't you think?"

"Actually, no," said Deb, as the judge entered the room and they all stood up. "But they've got to have a lawyer, that's the way the system works, and he probably figured it might as well be him."

Judge Featherstone, as was his habit, got straight to business and Aucoin called his star witness, George Weatherby.

As he approached the witness stand, Weatherby was the very picture of a model attorney. His gray hair was clipped short and neatly combed, his complexion had the ruddy tone of a man who enjoys a glass of Scotch or two before dinner. He was wearing a neat gray suit, white shirt, and green and white striped tie. His sturdy black brogues were highly polished and, if you didn't know that this was a man who had conspired to defraud a frail old woman and had now turned on his co-conspirators, gave an impression of solidity and responsibility. Lucy, who had always considered a man's shoes a reliable indicator of his character, was insulted by his choice; in her view, he ought to have been wearing pointed-toe lizard mocs. From now on, she thought, perhaps she should only trust men like Bill, who wore white socks and tan work boots with thick Vibram soles.

Weatherby raised his arm and took the oath, then sat down and prepared himself for questioning by shooting his starched white cuffs. Lucy almost groaned out loud; it was a gesture she associated with arrogance and a show of power and which she detested. So, apparently, did Deb, who rolled her eyes.

After establishing that Weatherby was a graduate of Boston University School of Law who was a member of the bar in Maine and had practiced for more than thirty years, Aucoin moved on to his relationship with the Allens.

"Mr. Allen came to my office in Portland approximately

two years ago, asking for my assistance in recovering money he had invested with Porter Stasko."

There was a little stir in the courtroom when he pronounced the name of Stasko, known to everyone as the originator of a massive Ponzi scheme.

"Mr. Allen said he was virtually impoverished having invested his entire assets with Stasko. He was especially distressed because he had also invested his wife's trust fund and that had also been lost."

"What did you advise him to do?"

"I looked into the matter, but found there was no realistic likelihood of recovering the lost assets. In fact, the Allens had actually profited originally from the scheme—using the so-called profits to buy an apartment in New York City—and there was a definite possibility that the court would require them to sell the apartment and return that money to the court to repay others who had been swindled." He paused. "I told Mr. Allen I was terribly sorry but I could see no legal remedy to his problems."

"What was his reaction?"

"He was very upset. He said creditors were pressing him and, in fact, he didn't see how he was going to meet his next mortgage and health insurance payments. He actually broke down and cried, saying he didn't know how he was going to explain all this to his wife. He said it had all come at a terrible time. She had just become a board member of the New England Ballet and had promised to make a major donation, as is customary. It would be a terrible embarrassment, a social disaster, if she couldn't fulfill her pledge."

"And what was your response to this?"

"I asked if there were any family members who could help and he kind of laughed. He said, ironically enough—those were his words, *ironically enough*—his wife was the granddaughter of one of the richest women in America, Vivian Van Vorst."

"And I suppose you suggested he approach Mrs. Van Vorst for help."

"Exactly," agreed Weatherby, nodding and tenting his fingers. He wore a solid gold signet ring on his pinky, but no other jewelry except for a solid-looking gold watch with a simple leather band. "But he said that was no-go. His wife was the beneficiary of a trust fund, which Mrs. Van Vorst considered ample for her needs, and that was that. The old woman absolutely refused to discuss money with anyone but her attorney.

"I suggested we set up a meeting with Mrs. Van Vorst's attorney, Bob Goodman, and also advised him to inform his wife, Victoria, of the situation as soon as possible. I arranged a bridge loan for the Allens, but it was purely a temporary solution. We met with Attorney Goodman and he agreed to approach Mrs. Van Vorst on the Allens' behalf, which he did, but unfortunately the timing was bad. This was October 2008, when the stock market plunged. He reported that Mrs. Van Vorst was panicked and felt herself unable to give them the money they needed."

Lucy glanced at Bob, who was seated in front of the bar, behind the prosecution's table. His expression was grim.

"The Allens were very disappointed. Furthermore, the bank had called in the bridge loan. Things looked very bad indeed. It was after this meeting with Mr. Goodman when Mrs. Allen stated that she wondered if her grandmother was actually in her right mind. She said this panic was not characteristic and said perhaps her grandmother required a legal guardian.

"I saw that this might be a solution to their problem because a guardianship would give them control of Mrs. Van Vorst's assets. And, furthermore, it seemed that it would be in Mrs. Van Vorst's best interests to have a loving granddaughter managing her affairs, rather than a busy lawyer like Mr. Goodman, who had so many other demands on his time and attention. The court agreed and Mrs. Allen became Mrs. Van Vorst's legal guardian early in 2009."

Checking Bob's reaction, Lucy saw his face had reddened; he was clearly displeased.

"And once they had control," said Aucoin, "the Allens began to strip Mrs. Van Vorst of her assets, isn't that right? And you helped them, didn't you, by providing legal documents and forcing her to sign them?"

Weatherby hung his head. "I'm sorry to say that I did. The Allens' demands were quite modest, at first, but as time went on, they were determined to take complete control. They wanted everything. I resisted, reminding them that their immediate problems had been solved and it was only a matter of time before Mrs. Van Vorst would die and they would most likely receive a large inheritance. That did not satisfy Mrs. Allen, who felt she had been given short shrift by her grandmother and had not been able to live in the style to which she was entitled. She said I had better do as she wanted or she would report me to the bar and I would lose my license."

All eyes were on Vicky, but she didn't react; she didn't blush or even squirm in her chair. She sat there, impassive as ever, her eyes fixed on a spot on the wall above the judge's head.

"I presume you were rewarded financially for the work you did for the Allens," said Aucoin. "How much did they pay you?"

For once, Weatherby's composure faltered and he mumbled his reply.

"Could you please speak up, Mr. Weatherby?" ordered the judge.

He raised his head, knowing he had to respond and that it would do him no good. "Something in the neighborhood of five million."

There was a collective gasp.

"Five million," repeated Aucoin. "And how much did the Allens extract from Mrs. Van Vorst?"

"Something in the neighborhood of twenty-five million, not including real estate."

The gasp grew to a murmur of disapproval.

"No further questions," said Aucoin, effectively throwing his star witness to the sharks.

Zuzick was on his feet, bouncing on his toes, eager to get his first bite.

"From your testimony, we might get the idea that you were simply helping your clients, the Allens, out of a sticky situation, but that's not exactly the truth, is it? The truth is that you advised the Allens to take control of Mrs. Van Vorst's affairs, didn't you? It was your idea."

"Yes," admitted Weatherby reluctantly. "I had the definite impression that Mrs. Van Vorst was no longer capable of managing her affairs and thought she should have responsible guardians, and the court agreed."

Hearing this, Bob seemed to be struggling to stay in his seat and Lucy suspected he would have liked to wring Weatherby's neck.

"You went further than that, though, didn't you? You began managing the staff at Pine Point, eliminating numerous positions, didn't you?"

"As her fiduciary, I took steps that were fiscally responsible," said Weatherby, his face growing very red.

"You arranged the sale of *Jelly Beans* to a Saudi billionaire, Abdullah bin Said, didn't you? Why did you do that? Mrs. Van Vorst had intended for that piece to go to the Museum of Fine Arts, didn't she?"

Weatherby bristled at that, and drew himself up in a defensive position. "*Jelly Beans* and other pieces of art were extremely valuable and I determined that Pine Point was not a secure location for them. In addition, the atmospheric conditions were not suitable for some of the older oils, especially the Corot and the Pissarro drawings."

"You didn't answer my question. What happened to the money from the sale to Mr. Bin Said?"

"I would have to check my records," said Weatherby.

"Well, don't bother. I have that information right here. The money, some two million dollars, went straight into your personal account." Zuzick paced back and forth like a caged animal in the space below the judge's bench. "The Allens turned to you with a problem, looking for legal advice, and instead of looking for solutions that were within the bounds of the law, you instructed and encouraged them to break the law. Isn't that true?"

Weatherby glared at Zuzick, refusing to answer.

"Why can't you say it?" demanded Zuzick, shoving a sheaf of papers into his hands. "It's all here, in your confession."

"I think we all know that confessions are not always accurate. Sometimes people are pressured to admit things. . . ."

"That's not exactly true in your case," said Zuzick. "You were not subjected to any sort of third degree, were you? The truth is that you volunteered this confession, you wrote it up and brought it to the prosecution on your own initiative. Nobody pressured you. So once again, I'm going to ask you, did you encourage and instruct your clients, the Allens, to break the law?"

"I did," mumbled Weatherby, breaking down and pulling a large white handkerchief from his pocket and covering his face.

Judge Featherstone checked his watch and came to a decision. "We will adjourn for lunch. Court will resume at two o'clock." A quick bang of the gavel and everyone jumped to their feet, the judge disappeared into his chambers, and everybody else began stretching and gathering up their things and rushing for the doors.

Outside, the air was hot and humid and still, beneath a white sky. The TV reporters began filming their reports, some of the women standing on little step stools in order to get a shot that included the courthouse. Other reporters and courtroom observers were streaming across the road to the nearby coffee shops and restaurants and Lucy realized that Deb was right, they would never get served in time to make the afternoon session. Her car was parked too far away for Pizza'n'More to be a practical alternative.

"I think you were smart to bring that food—what have you got?" asked Lucy.

"Nothing fancy. I just grabbed what was around," said Deb, opening her enormous tote bag and giving Lucy a glimpse of a jar of peanut butter, half a loaf of bread, and a couple of bananas. They settled themselves on the grassy lawn in front of the courthouse, beneath the statue of a Civil War soldier, and made sandwiches.

"It's muggy," said Lucy, her mouth full of peanut butter and banana. "What did you think of Weatherby?"

"I think he's a creep." Deb twisted the cap off a bottle of iced tea and handed it to Lucy. "Sorry, it's warm."

"It's delicious," said Lucy, taking a long swallow. She was watching a bee fly from one little white clover flower to another, gathering pollen. "Maxine called them the Three Pigs," she said. "Vicky, Henry, and Weatherby."

Deb leaned back against a tree, her bottle of tea in her hand. "I know they were greedy and despicable, but, well, what difference does it make? They shifted some assets, they took some money, but it's not like they robbed a bank or cheated on their taxes. It's not my money, it's nothing to do with me. The way I see it, it's a whole lot of fuss about nothing. I'll never see money like that. I'm lucky to clear four hundred dollars a week after taxes and health insurance. What do I care if some rich people screw another rich person? Screw 'em all, that's what I say. Spread the wealth around."

"I wonder if the jury will feel that way," said Lucy, thinking it was quite possible. She wanted to see Vicky and Henry go to jail not only because of the way they mistreated VV, but because she was convinced they had murdered Van and Maxine. They weren't on trial for murder, however, and they weren't going to be because there wasn't enough evidence to convict them. In her mind, this trial was simply a make-do affair, a substitute for the murder trial that should be taking place.

When court resumed in the afternoon, George Weatherby was again on the stand, reminded by Judge Featherstone that he was still under oath. He nodded, signifying that he understood. He seemed to have lost the bravado he'd exhibited earlier that day. Lucy thought he actually seemed to have shrunk somehow. He looked like a beaten man.

Zuzick resumed his questioning, which was designed to portray Weatherby as the architect and prime mover of the scheme to defraud VV, and to show that he was a crooked lawyer who led his clients astray with bad advice.

"It was your idea to transfer ownership of Pine Point to the Allens, wasn't it?" he demanded.

"From a legal standpoint, it seemed advisable," said Weatherby.

"Why was that? Why would you want to make Mrs. Van Vorst a squatter in her own home?"

A few people in the courtroom gasped, shocked at the idea.

"She was not a squatter," protested Weatherby. "She had ownership for her lifetime, but the house was deeded to the Allens to avoid conflict with other family members who might have believed they had a claim to the property." He cleared his throat. "There were also certain tax advantages."

"But this was your idea, wasn't it? You presented it to the Allens and convinced them to go along, right?"

"It didn't take much convincing," muttered Weatherby.

"No more questions," said Zuzick, deciding to cut his losses. His strategy of discrediting Weatherby wasn't succeeding; it was only making his own clients look bad, too.

Weatherby was finally free to leave the courtroom, which he did without delay. Lucy knew that he was not facing charges himself, but he had been disbarred and would no longer be able to practice as an attorney.

Aucoin's next witness was Vicky Allen, but Judge Featherstone decided to postpone her testimony until the next morning in light of the stifling conditions in the packed courtroom. The aged air-conditioning system had failed, overwhelmed by the hot weather combined with the large number of people, and the temperature inside was over eighty degrees. Court was adjourned until the next day when, hopefully, the system would be up and running.

Lucy was in line next morning with her travel mug of coffee in hand at seven o'clock, and she wasn't alone. She counted fifteen people ahead of her, and the line behind was already snaking down the hall. She had gotten up at five-thirty and packed a picnic in a soft plastic cooler, cutting up the remains of last night's chicken dinner and making chicken salad. She'd also brought potato chips, fruit, and lemonade, all an improvement over yesterday's peanut butter and banana sandwiches. Not that she wasn't grateful for Deb's foresight.

By eight o'clock, Lucy had finished her coffee and her back was beginning to bother her so she slid down the wall and sat on the floor, opening the book she'd brought with her. She tried to interest herself in the plight of a French Jewish family as World War II approached, but her mind wandered instead to VV, living in lonely splendor at Pine Point.

By eight-thirty, she gave up on the doomed French family, closed the book, and got up to stretch. It was noisy in the crowded lobby and it was also growing warm.

At nine, one of the court officers opened the front doors, letting in some badly needed fresh air. It looked as if the air conditioning hadn't been fixed.

At nine-thirty, the doors to the courtroom opened and the stampede began; Lucy was able to snag a couple of seats in the third row. She put her lunch cooler on the second seat, which she was saving for Deb, and hoped nobody would challenge her. It wasn't long, however, before a heavyset woman with a lot of heavy gold jewelry on her neck and wrists demanded that Lucy remove the cooler and give her the seat. "I'm sorry," said Lucy, showing her press card, "I'm saving it for a colleague."

"Well, there's no saving seats. What do you think this is—a middle school lunchroom?"

Lucy was not about to give up the seat. "I waited in line for nearly three hours to get these seats, and my colleague will be here any minute."

"Well, I waited in line, too," said the woman.

"I'm sorry, there aren't enough seats for everyone," said Lucy, relieved to see Deb approaching. She lifted the bag and slipped deftly into the seat, blocking off the intruder and thanking Lucy. They began to chat, pointedly ignoring the woman, and she finally drifted away.

"Whew, that was a struggle," said Lucy, fanning herself

with her reporter's notebook. "She really wanted your seat."

"I wish I could let her have it—I can think of a lot better ways of spending a June day than sitting in this oven."

"Here we go," said Lucy as the judge entered the courtroom.

Like Deb, she was prepared for a long, hot morning but it was not to be. Zuzick was on his feet the moment the judge declared court was in session, saying that his clients wished to change their plea to guilty.

The announcement electrified the courtroom, which was perfectly still, except for the front row, where Juliette was sitting in her usual seat, along with Andrew Duff and Peter Reilly. The three clasped hands and seemed to let out a collective sigh, as if a long and arduous ordeal was finally over. As a member of the bar, Bob wasn't free to show emotion, but Lucy caught a brief, triumphant grin.

Even Judge Featherstone seemed shocked and quickly began questioning Vicky and Henry in turn. "Have you been pressured by anyone to make this change? Do you understand you are giving up the right of appeal? Do you realize the decision of the court is binding?"

They both answered the pro forma questions in the affirmative.

"I will take this under advisement," said the judge, "and pronounce the sentence in a timely manner." He banged the gavel. "Court dismissed."

"This couldn't be better for me," said Lucy. "I've got plenty of time to make my noon deadline."

"Me, too," said Deb.

The two followed the scrum of people rushing out of the courtroom and joined the group of reporters gathered around Phil Aucoin on the courthouse steps. Juliette and her two grandfathers stood behind him, looking pleased.

"What's your reaction to the Allens' guilty pleas?" someone was asking him.

"I guess the Allens saw the handwriting on the wall," he said.

"Were you surprised?"

"Yes, I was."

"What sentence will the judge give them?"

"The guidelines call for two to five years, so I assume it will be somewhere within those parameters."

"Is two to five years enough? In your opinion, does the punishment fit the crime?"

Aucoin grinned. "I'm a prosecutor. I'd like to send those two away for life," he declared.

Then he thanked them and broke away from the cluster of reporters and headed down the street to his office. The reporters immediately began peppering Juliette with questions, but she simply expressed gratitude to the DA's office for their hard work on her great-grandmother's behalf. Then Peter and Andrew whisked her away, tucking her into a chauffeur-driven car.

"Did you hear that?" asked Deb. "Aucoin said he wanted to put the Allens away for life. Isn't that a bit harsh?"

"Not really," said Lucy. "Not if you think they should've been tried for murder. I'd say they're getting off easy."

When Lucy got home that afternoon, she was surprised to see Bob and Bill standing together in the driveway, and figured that Bob was making good on his promise to talk to Bill about making a will.

"Hi!" she said, greeting them. She turned to Bob. "Great day in court!"

He grinned. "Sometimes justice really does prevail. Not always. But it's great when it does. It reaffirms your faith, you know?"

Lucy nodded. "Have you convinced Bill that we need to make wills?"

"No way," said Bill with a mischievous twinkle in his eye. "I'm not going to die."

"Good luck with that," said Lucy.

"Well, think over what I told you," said Bob with a smile. "Maybe you are immortal, but it's good to be prepared, just in case. The law is complicated and if you want to be sure your wishes will be carried out, you need to specify them in a will."

"Lucy and the kids will get it all, right?" asked Bill. "It's automatic."

"Not necessarily," said Bob. "What if you've got an illegitimate kid somewhere? That child could make a claim on the estate."

"I don't have any illegitimate children." Bill was firm on this point.

Bob raised an eyebrow. "Are you sure? And, these days, with identity theft, somebody could pretend."

"Good luck to them," said Bill, laughing. "Part of nothing is still nothing."

"You're being naïve," said Bob. "But I've got to get home to my good wife. You think it over and give me a call when you're ready."

"Don't wait up," said Bill.

Lucy rolled her eyes. "He's impossible."

"Come on, wife, make me supper," said Bill in a teasing voice as Bob drove off.

"Just for that," replied Lucy, slipping her arm around his waist as they walked together to the house, "you can call and order a large pizza supremo—with everything."

Chapter Eighteen

Once the trial was over, Tinker's Cove settled into its usual sleepy summer pace. Most of the town committees suspended business for the summer and town hall was quiet except for the occasional summer visitor who wanted to buy a fishing license or dump sticker. With little news to report, the *Pennysaver* turned to features and Lucy enjoyed interviewing local folks and writing up their stories.

Lucy was just leaving Hetty Greenlaw's place—Hetty's hobby was crossbreeding day lilies and she was quite excited about a striking brown-and-yellow hybrid she'd developed—when her cell phone rang. Much to her surprise, the caller was Miss Tilley.

Even odder, Miss Tilley was asking her for advice. "Lucy," she said, "I'm at my wit's end and I simply don't know what to do."

"What's the problem?" asked Lucy, resting her bottom against her car, which was parked in the shade of a big maple tree.

"It's VV. She's terrified her health will fail."

"That's too bad," said Lucy, choosing her words carefully. The woman was ancient and she couldn't go on forever, but Miss Tilley would naturally be upset at the prospect of losing a friend. "I'm very sorry to hear that."

"Well, we all have to go sometime," said Miss Tilley, brushing off her sympathy. "The thing is, I promised to do something for her, but I don't quite know how to go about it."

"Can I help?" offered Lucy.

"Of course you can help," sputtered the old woman. "Why do you think I'm calling you?"

"Okay," said Lucy. "I'll do what I can. What's the problem?"

"It's complicated. Too complicated to explain on the phone."

"Shall I come over?"

"Yes. That would be best."

"When do you want me?"

"Now!" exclaimed Miss Tilley. "I want you to come right now!"

"I'll be right there," promised Lucy, opening the car door. "Give me ten minutes."

"Five," snapped the old woman.

Lucy was still chuckling when she pulled up in front of Miss Tilley's gray-shingled Cape, where a rose of Sharon bush was in full bloom by the front door. She knocked and Rachel answered, greeting her with a big smile.

"Miss Tilley wants to speak to you privately," she said with an amused grin, "so I'm just off to the grocery store."

"Take your time," said Miss Tilley with a flap of her hand. "Why not stop at the library, too? See if they have that new Martha Grimes."

"Will do," said Rachel, closing the door behind her.

"Come on in," ordered Miss Tilley. "Don't dillydally."

Lucy obeyed, seating herself by a window where a fan provided a cooling breeze. "Now, what is this all about?" she asked.

"I'm only telling you all this in strictest secrecy,"

warned Miss Tilley. "This is not for the newspaper, or idle gossip. It's a highly confidential, personal matter."

"I understand," said Lucy, wondering what on earth could be so sensitive that it required such secrecy, especially now when presidents had sex with interns and governors sired love children with maids. "You can trust me."

Miss Tilley seemed doubtful, but continued. "The thing is, I promised to do something for VV. She's afraid she doesn't have much longer to live and, well, it really has to be done before she dies, but I don't know how to begin." She paused, then blurted out her shocking news. "Remember how she said I missed out on life because I hadn't had a lover?"

Lucy nodded.

"Well, it turns out she had a child, you see, a child that she gave up for adoption."

Lucy took the news calmly. "When was this?" she asked. "I presume it was some time ago."

Miss Tilley seemed disconcerted, as if she'd expected a bigger reaction.

"It's no big deal," said Lucy. "This sort of thing happens all the time. Didn't you ever watch *Oprah*?"

"No I didn't," snapped Miss Tilley. "And I don't approve of these modern ideas. In my day, you got married and then you had children and you didn't spare the rod when you raised them."

This gave Lucy an idea. "I presume the child was illegitimate?"

"Not at all. VV tells me she was married, briefly. Just before the war. Her husband was going overseas and she didn't feel she could care for the baby—I can't say I approve, but she was always ambitious and thought she had better things to do than mix up formula and change diapers. Anyway, the long and short of it is that she went off to Reno, that's what you did then, and got a divorce and gave the baby—it was a little girl—to some relatives of her husband's. They were infertile, apparently, and desperately wanted a child, so it all worked out for the best." Miss Tilley sniffed. "To hear her tell it, you'd think she'd done them a big favor, giving up her baby, but she really just wanted out of the whole situation."

"But now she wants to see the child before she dies, is that it?" asked Lucy.

Miss Tilley let out a great sigh. "Exactly." She paused. "And she wants me to find her."

Lucy was definitely intrigued. "Do we have a name?"

Miss Tilley got up from her rocking chair and made her way briskly across the room to her secretary, where she pulled open one of the little drawers above the writing surface and extracted a faded piece of paper which she unfolded before presenting it to Lucy. "This is her birth certificate."

Lucy read it with interest, noting that VV was named as the mother, profession, housewife. The father was listed as Michael Woods, U.S. Army Air Corps. And the child was named Margaret Saxby Woods, weighing a healthy seven pounds ten ounces and measuring nineteen inches long. She was born almost seventy years ago to the day, which gave Lucy pause. "She might not be alive," she said

"And she may have moved to Arizona, for all I know," said Miss Tilley. "Or maybe she's living right around the corner."

Stranger things have happened, thought Lucy, thinking of a pair of twins she'd read about recently who had grown up in ignorance of each other, although they lived on the same city block. "It would be a lot easier if she were a he, since boys' names don't change when they get married," she said, adding a promise, "but I'll do the best I can." She scratched her head. "What about the father? Michael Woods? Did he ever turn up?"

Miss Tilley's voice was tight with disapproval. "VV says she doesn't know."

Lucy was incredulous. "She doesn't know if her husband lived or died?"

"No." Miss Tilley shook her head. "She pranced off to Washington and met Horatio and never looked back."

Lucy knew these things happened, but she found VV's behavior shocking. "My goodness," she said. "I suppose things are different in wartime."

"Not that different," said Miss Tilley. "But I think she is feeling a certain amount of remorse as she looks back on her life. She wants to make amends, she said."

Lucy nodded. "Well, I'll do what I can to help."

"I knew I could count on you," said Miss Tilley. "Now, if you'll scoot into my bedroom, you'll find a box of Fern's Famous fudge in the bottom drawer, beneath my nightgowns."

"You're not supposed to have fudge," scolded Lucy.

"I know, that's why you have to be quick. Rachel will be back any minute!"

Lucy liked to think of herself as an investigative reporter and she had developed some considerable research skills, but she was the first to admit she didn't know much about genealogy. In truth, she could name all of her grandparents but was ignorant of three of her great-grandparents. One grandmother, who died when Lucy was eight, used to claim that her forebears were "thieves and pirates" and Lucy was never sure if she was joking or not. She had an entire drawer of old photographs that she couldn't bear to throw out, but couldn't identify, either, and odd bits of silver with unfamiliar initials that had been passed down through the family. Some day, when she had the time, she intended to do the research and fill in the blanks, but that day had not yet come. All of which meant that when she sat down at her desk and unfolded the birth certificate Miss Tilley had given her, she had no idea where to start. What had become of Margaret Saxby Woods?

For that matter, what had become of her father, Michael Woods? He had been in the service during World War II, but Lucy knew from experience that it was difficult to get information from the Department of Defense about individual soldiers. She had tried in the past and knew the department was slow to respond to requests and that many records had been lost or destroyed.

On the other hand, the *Pennysaver*'s morgue was a trove of information, containing every issue of its predecessor, the *Courier and Advertiser* which had begun publication in 1851. The problem was that none of it was cataloged, which meant she would have to go through the big old bound volumes page by page. Unfortunately, she decided, that was probably her best bet, as it would have been the local newspaper which would have reported information about the region's soldiers and sailors.

She had the office to herself. Ted was meeting with the accountant and Phyllis had taken the afternoon off to attend a funeral, so she flipped the sign on the door from OPEN to CLOSED so she wouldn't be disturbed, and closeted herself in the morgue, beginning with the volume for January–June, 1940.

Sneezing at the dust, she slowly turned the fragile yellow pages, scanning the print for anybody named Saxby or Woods. She did find a notice announcing that Michael Woods, son of Mr. and Mrs. Harold Woods, had successfully completed basic training at Fort Dix in New Jersey, but that was all. There was no birth announcement for Margaret Saxby Woods, and she saw no obituaries for any people with those names. When she checked her watch and saw it was after four o'clock, and realized she'd only gotten through the volumes for 1943, she decided she had to find a better way. On a hunch, she stopped by at the town office on her way home and had a chat with the town clerk.

Carolyn Kidd was whippet thin and full of energy. Her curly red hair seemed to explode from her head as if she'd stuck her finger in an electric socket. "What can I do for you, Lucy?" she asked with a big smile.

"I'm looking for information about a person . . ."

"What sort of information?" Carolyn leaned forward, listening intently.

"Anything, I guess. Birth, death, taxes . . ."

"What era are we talking about?" asked Carolyn.

Lucy realized the town had been settled in the late 1600s and the town records might go back for centuries. "He was a soldier in World War Two, that's all I know."

"Well, nowadays births and deaths go right into the computer and I can access them with a few keystrokes, but the older records are still on paper. His birth certificate would be in storage, down in the cellar. If he died recently, that would be in the database."

"It's worth a try," said Lucy. "I'm looking for Michael Woods, and his daughter, Margaret Saxby Woods."

Carolyn perched on a chair and started clicking away on a keyboard, tapping her foot and clicking her tongue as she peered at the screen. "I got nothing, Lucy," she finally said, shaking her head. "But, like I said, the computer only goes back to the eighties, the nineteen eighties. I'd love to get the older records in the database, but it's drudge work and I don't have the manpower."

Lucy nodded. "Well, thanks anyway. Have a good weekend."

"You, too, Lucy."

* * *

Saturday dawned chilly, gray, and rainy. Bill decided to spend the day cleaning the cellar. The girls both had summer jobs, so Lucy was free to continue her research in the morgue. She didn't mind; flipping through the old papers was interesting and gave her a picture of life in Maine during the war. There were stories about gas rationing and German U-boat sightings, drives to collect metal and paper, and the inevitable reports of local men and women killed overseas. Michael Woods wasn't among them, though, and Lucy was halfway through the fifties when she finally saw his name in bold black print.

It actually came as a bit of a shock; she'd pretty much given up, distracted by stories about new buildings at Winchester College, plans to build a war memorial on the town green, and a hilariously funny guest editorial by the Methodist pastor warning about the dangers of rock and roll music. She was still chuckling when she turned the brittle page and saw the obituary. "*Michael Woods, 36, died unexpectedly Monday evening,*" she read. His service in the U.S. Army Air Corps, in North Africa and Italy, was noted, as was a series of jobs as an insurance salesman, encyclopedia salesman, and, finally, automobile salesman. The list of surviving family members was small; there was no mention of a wife or children, but he did leave a sister, Hilda O'Dwyer, and a niece, Margaret O'Dwyer.

Unlike the obituaries she was used to writing, which went into great detail about the deceased's career, relations, hobbies, and even favorite sports teams, these few inches of print seemed wanting. It wasn't the custom in the 1950s, she realized, comparing Woods's obituary to the others on the page, which were also brief. Nevertheless, it struck her as sad that a person's entire life—loves, successes, failures—came down to nothing more than these few smudged lines. What terrors did Michael Woods face in the war? Did he have nightmares for years afterwards? Was he content with his career in sales or was he bitter that he didn't achieve more? What did he die of, at the relatively young age of thirty-six? A heart attack? Stroke? Accident? The little notice didn't say, but it did give her another lead to follow: the O'Dwyer family. But how long would it take to track them down? It had taken her the better part of two days to find any trace of Michael Woods, so how long would it take to find his sister's family? And would she have time?

On Sunday, Lucy went to Heritage House to cover the 100th birthday party of a resident, Lillian Waters. She always had mixed feelings about these celebrations. Living to the ripe old age of 100 seemed like a good thing, but all too often it really wasn't. The poor old dears rarely knew what all the fuss was about. Some were blind or deaf or senile, and their frail, misshapen bodies were covered with wrinkles and age spots. Getting old certainly wasn't for the weak, as Miss Tilley often said.

Lillian Waters was different, however. She hardly looked a year over eighty. Her abundant white hair had been freshly styled, her pink-cheeked face was remarkably smooth, and she was enjoying being the center of attention.

"All for me? You shouldn't have!" she exclaimed, bouncing into the rec room. It had been decorated with balloons and streamers in her honor, and a HAPPY BIRTHDAY LILLIAN banner was pinned up over the windows. A punch bowl filled with pink liquid was waiting on a side table, along with stacks of plates and glasses.

The celebrants were a mixed bunch that included residents and family members who were making their Sunday visits, and Lucy noticed Izzy Scannell and her mother, Madge, who was in a wheelchair and was getting oxygen through a tube fixed under her nose. Lucy was shocked at the elderly woman's sudden decline; she looked much older than Lillian, the centenarian.

Felicity Corcoran, the recreation director was calling for attention, tapping a glass with a spoon. "Welcome, everyone! Do take a seat! In honor of our birthday girl, Lillian Waters, we're going to have a short slide show depicting her amazing life."

"What about the cake?" demanded one of the partygoers, a bald man who was seated in a wheelchair.

"There will be cake," promised the director, "but first, the show. Lights, please."

The lights went out and a photo of an adorable tot in old-fashioned clothes with high-button shoes and a huge bow on her head was projected onto a screen. There were a few oohs from the audience.

The next picture was Lillian's eighth-grade graduation photo and showed a very pretty girl, on the verge of becoming a woman. That was followed by a wedding photo, the groom looking awkward and uncomfortable in a thick woolen suit with slicked down hair. Lillian looked radiant, swathed in a long lace veil and holding an enormous bouquet. Next, there were pictures of babies, a son in an army uniform, and then more babies, this time identified as grandchildren. The show ended with a group photo of Lillian's family, who were all revealed to be present when the lights went on.

"Surprise!" they all exclaimed, engulfing Lillian in hugs and kisses.

"Now do we get the cake?" demanded the old fellow again, prompting general laughter.

"Now we have cake!" declared the recreation director.

Lucy got a nice photo of Lillian cutting the cake, and another of her surrounded by her family. Then, duty done, she approached Izzy and her mother.

"Quite a party," she said. "Can I get you some cake?"

"Mom's on a restricted diet," said Izzy. "She can't have cake."

Lucy smiled down at the old woman, noticing that her head was drooping to one side and her hand was dangling beside the wheelchair. Grasping the old woman's arm, she noticed the band on her wrist, which identified her as Margaret O. Scannell.

"I'm sorry to see your mother isn't feeling better," said Lucy, struck by the woman's first name and middle initial. Could it be?

"I'm hoping she'll rally," said Izzy, whose cheerful tone belied her anxious expression. "It's happened before."

"I'm sure she will," said Lucy. "Do you mind telling me what the O stands for? I can't help being curious. I had an aunt Odette. She was my favorite aunt."

Lucy had crossed her fingers, which meant she wasn't really telling a fib.

"Nothing as fancy as Odette, I'm afraid," laughed Izzy. "It's her maiden name, O'Dwyer."

Lucy could hardly believe her ears. After days of searching, poring through dusty old newspapers, suddenly, *coincidentally*, she'd stumbled upon VV's long-lost daughter, Margaret Saxby Woods O'Dwyer Scannell. At least she thought she had. But looking at the dozing, ill old woman, she wondered if it was too late.

"Could I have a word with you?" asked Lucy, leaning close to Izzy. "Privately?"

Izzy looked startled, then agreed. "Let's go into the hallway," she said.

Once they were alone, Lucy began her explanation. "I don't quite know how to tell you, but I think your mother is actually VV's long-lost daughter, who she gave up for adoption."

Izzy didn't react to the news in the way Lucy expected.

Her body stiffened and she became defensive, challenging Lucy. "That's ridiculous. Whatever gave you that idea? And why are you investigating my family anyway?"

Puzzled at Izzy's reaction, Lucy hastened to explain herself. "VV asked me to find her daughter, a child she had with her first husband, Michael Woods. She realizes she doesn't have a lot of time left and she wants to make amends. She gave the child up for adoption, you see. The child was adopted by Michael Woods's sister, whose married name was Hilda O'Dwyer." Lucy paused, thinking maybe she had it wrong. "Does any of this ring a bell?" she asked. "Is Hilda O'Dwyer your grandmother?"

"There are a lot of O'Dwyers," said Izzy.

A vague memory took form in Lucy's head. "But they were saying something at the Easter pet parade, like she ought to be a millionaire; something like that."

"These old people say things; they get dreams and reality all mixed up," said Izzy. "Look, I really need to get back to her."

Lucy nodded. "Is there any chance she could meet with VV?"

Izzy's face reddened. "Are you crazy? You saw her condition! She's in and out of consciousness! I don't know if she's going to make it through the night." She turned to go back to the rec room, then whirled around. "Don't say a word about this, I'm warning you. Just leave my mother in peace! Okay?"

"Okay," said Lucy, stunned by Izzy's vehemence.

Chapter Nineteen

Lucy was still mulling over Izzy's strange reaction on the drive home, and on impulse decided to pay a visit to Miss Tilley.

"I'm not absolutely certain, but I'm pretty sure I've found VV's daughter," she said, perching on the sofa. The windows were open and the white muslin curtains with their ball fringes were lifting slightly in the muggy breeze; a copper lustre vase filled with orange, red, and yellow zinnias had pride of place in the center of the mantel.

Miss Tilley listened intently, rubbing the swollen arthritic knuckles on one knobby hand with the other, as Lucy explained how she may have stumbled upon the daughter VV gave up for adoption some seventy years before. Mindful of her promise to Izzy, she was careful not to reveal Margaret's identity.

"And you say she's living right here in town?" asked Miss Tilley.

"Yes. In fact, she has a bit of a reputation as the child of a millionaire."

Miss Tilley's expression was skeptical. "But she's never approached VV?"

"Maybe her folks never told her exactly who her mother

was," said Lucy. "They might have been reluctant to do that, especially since VV spent at least part of the year right here in town." She paused, glancing around the cozy room, with its white plastered walls, pine woodwork, and antique furniture. "It might even have been part of the adoption agreement. Remember, adoption was much different back then. People didn't talk about it and adopted children were not encouraged to know their birth parents. The records were sealed."

"But they told her that her mother was a millionaire?"

"Maybe she overheard her parents talking. Her mother might have been gossiping to a friend or relation. Maybe it was just a bit of family lore, presented as a tall tale . . ."

Miss Tilley nodded slowly. "Is there any chance of a meeting?"

"The daughter says no. Her mother's health is very poor."

"I don't understand. Wouldn't you think they'd make an effort, considering all that money?"

"Frankly, I'm flummoxed. I don't understand it at all." Lucy didn't say it, but she couldn't figure out why Izzy didn't make her identity known to VV, especially since she was working for the millionaire. Why not arrange a happy family reunion? Especially if it meant a likely bequest in VV's will?

"It may be that she's angry and doesn't want to give VV the satisfaction of apologizing."

Lucy nodded, amazed once again at her old friend's perception. "I can see that. Money can't buy affection, or even forgiveness."

Miss Tilley folded her hands in her lap and nodded. "Well, there it is. You can't get everything you want, even if you're a millionaire. VV didn't behave very well, if you ask me. I can't imagine why she married this Woods fellow if she was only going to divorce him a month or two later . . ."

"I imagine she was pregnant," said Lucy. "That's probably why they got married."

Miss Tilley's jaw dropped. "Of course!"

"It must have seemed a good solution at the time. She gave birth as a respectable married woman, arranged for the child to be adopted by her husband's family, got divorced, and went on her merry way. Problem solved."

"She made a mockery of the marriage ceremony—she never meant the promises she made. I believe it goes something like *to love, honor, and cherish 'til death do us part.*" Miss Tilley's expression hardened. "I've known VV for most of my life, and I've always accepted the fact that she's self-centered, but I never dreamed she would have done anything like this."

"But perhaps this is why she's always been so generous to folks in town. Perhaps she was making up for what she did. Maybe she gave gifts to all the children to make amends for abandoning her own infant."

Miss Tilley scowled. "This is so unlike you, Lucy," she said, in a disapproving tone. "When did you start thinking well of other people's motives?"

Lucy couldn't help laughing, and she was still chuckling to herself when she got in the car and headed for home. What a waste of time, she thought ruefully. She'd been carried away by a sentimental notion and had spent much too much time on research that she couldn't even use for a story. She was hoping her efforts would lead to a warm and fuzzy family reunion, but instead she'd encountered resentment and anger.

She was just turning into her driveway, where Libby the lab was wagging her tail in greeting, when her cell phone rang, so she remained in the car to take the call. Much to her surprise, it was Fran Martino, the private detective, calling from New York.

"I just wanted to give you a heads-up," she said. "Juliette's in the hospital."

"What happened?" Libby was at the car door, smiling and wiggling in ecstasy.

"She was attacked in the parking garage of her apartment. The super found her this morning, curled up in the back seat of her car, barely alive. She'd apparently crawled there after she was mugged; her purse was gone, and she'd been knocked on the head." Fran paused. "They think she was there for some time, maybe since Friday. That was the last time the super checked the garage. He had Saturday off. He said that if Juliette wasn't off on some assignment she usually left town on Friday afternoons. She has a place in Dutchess County where she likes to spend weekends."

"That's terrible," said Lucy, noticing that Libby was losing interest in the greeting business. "Nobody noticed her?"

"It's a small building, very upscale. At any given time, only a handful of tenants are actually in residence, and hardly anybody's there on the weekends."

"Is she going to be all right?" Libby was rooting around in the day lilies.

"They don't know." Fran sighed. "Time will tell, that's what the doctors say."

"All we can do is hope for the best," said Lucy, watching as Libby unearthed a very dirty tennis ball.

"I'm doing more than that," declared Fran. "I'm putting twenty-four-hour protection in place."

"You don't think it was a mugging? You think someone tried to kill her?" Libby was back, ball in mouth, tail wagging.

"Let's just say I'd rather err on the side of caution. Her mother and father were murdered, maybe she's next in line. Maybe somebody wants to wipe out the whole family."

Libby was growing impatient, standing on her hind legs, with her face in the open car window. Enough with the phone, she seemed to be saying. Let's play ball!

Lucy's mind was divided, trying to handle the dog at the same time she was listening to Fran. She didn't want the dog to scratch the door so she got out and threw the ball. "But Vicky and Henry are in jail . . ."

"Right. Which means somebody else has it in for Juliette. That's why I'm calling. I want you to keep an eye out, let me know if you notice anything suspicious."

Libby was back with the ball; she could play this game for hours. "I will," promised Lucy, hurling the ball as far as she could throw it.

The dog hightailed across the lawn and Lucy ran up the porch steps, escaping into the house just as the dog bounded back with the ball. Lucy closed the door firmly and Libby settled down on the mat, resting her chin on the ball.

Lucy dropped her phone into her bag and set it down on the table, then went into the powder room to pee. She was washing her hands, staring at her face in the mirror over the sink, thinking about VV's family tree, which was dropping leaves faster than a silverleaf poplar in August. Vicky was most certainly out of the will by now, which meant Juliette was probably VV's single heir. If Juliette died before VV, and if Izzy could establish her mother as VV's daughter, she might have a legitimate claim on VV's fortune. In fact, she thought, recalling something Bob Goodman had said, she might even think she would automatically inherit, though that was not necessarily the case.

Returning to the kitchen, Lucy opened a bag of potato chips and ate one, then poured herself a glass of white wine. Sitting at the table, she sipped and nibbled and thought about Izzy's reaction when she had suggested her mother was VV's daughter. Was it feigned? Did Izzy know all along? Had she been systematically wiping out VV's heirs in hopes of inheriting the entire Van Vorst fortune?

So much for Miss Tilley's suggestion that she was starting to think well of people's motives, thought Lucy, draining her glass. Here she was practically accusing a hardworking gardener and devoted daughter of the most cold-blooded scheme! It was preposterous, and besides, it was highly doubtful that Izzy would leave Tinker's Cove and travel to New York when her mother's health was failing and she might die at any moment.

Nevertheless, Lucy couldn't quite rid herself of that unsettling suspicion—it lingered through the next few days and seemed to follow her like a gray cloud, keeping her from enjoying the beautiful sunny days that arrived, one after another, making this the sunniest and warmest July on record. The girls spent every spare minute at the beach, Bill watered the garden every evening, and Lucy pored through her cookbooks looking for new ways to serve salad for supper.

She was just coming out of the IGA on Thursday afternoon with a bag full of the anchovies, eggs, olives, and tuna she needed for salade niçoise—she'd had a bumper crop of green beans in her garden as well as some late shade-grown lettuce and a few Early Girl tomatoes—when she bumped into Barney. He was out of uniform, but perspiring heavily in a polo shirt and shorts.

"Hi, Lucy," he said, pulling an enormous white handkerchief out of his pocket and mopping his forehead. "Some weather we're having."

"I wish it would rain," grumbled Lucy. "We need a good soaker."

"Aw, don't say that, Lucy. This weather's good for business; everybody's coming to the coast to cool off—they say it's near a hundred in Boston, you know."

"That does put things in perspective," said Lucy. "I guess eighty-five isn't so bad after all."

"Practically frigid," said Barney, as fresh beads of sweat popped out on his forehead. "Say, you know, your suspicions about Van's death might not be so crazy after all. You'll never guess what Eddie found in the garden shed at Pine Point—a portable generator."

Lucy was impatient, she wanted to get home before the ice cream melted—it was on special, buy one, get one free and she had used a dollar-off coupon. "How's that suspicious?" she asked, grumbling. "A lot of people have them in case the power goes out."

"I thought you and that big city private eye had a theory that Van was electrocuted when he grabbed the grille, something along those lines." He hooked his hands in his belt. "Eddie says there was also a tangle of wires, stuffed behind some bags of fertilizer."

Lucy was suddenly interested. "You mean the generator could've been used to electrify the grille?"

"It sure coulda been," said Barney.

"Are they checking it for fingerprints?" asked Lucy.

He shook his head. "The case is closed and, besides, a shed like that's not a secure location. Lots of people could've been in there."

"But the shed is really under the gardener's control, isn't it?" asked Lucy. "She would have the keys."

"They've got a bunch of helpers, now. There's Eddie and a bunch of others."

Lucy felt a surge of indignation. "So it's all just water under the bridge? Nobody's interested in justice anymore? You just ignore evidence?"

"I'm sorry I told you," he said, looking hurt. "I thought you'd want to know. I didn't think it would upset you. It's not like it's definite proof or anything, it just kinda struck me as interesting. I should've kept my mouth shut." He shrugged. "Must be the heat."

Lucy smiled. "I'm sorry. I shouldn't have reacted like that. It is the heat. I'm really glad you told me."

"Well, gotta go. Stay cool, Lucy."

"You, too," said Lucy, hurrying across the parking lot to her car. Heat was radiating from the black asphalt surface, and the car was an oven when she opened the door. She switched the AC onto high and waited to feel the cooling effect, aware that sweat was dripping down her back.

She didn't like the way things were shaping up at all, she thought, shifting into REVERSE and looking over her shoulder to back out of her parking space. In DRIVE, headed for the exit, she suddenly felt uneasy. Izzy had a motive for eliminating VV's heirs, and she had the mechanical ability to arrange Van's and Maxine's deaths.

Lucy couldn't make up her mind. She had suspicions—dark suspicions—about Izzy, but that's all they were. She could hardly accuse the woman, she might well be completely innocent. Lucy went back and forth in her mind as she drove the familiar route home, and it was only when she reached her driveway that she decided what to do.

Once inside the house, she stowed the ice cream in the freezer and then dug her cell phone out of her purse, checking recent calls for Fran Martino's number. Finding one with the 212 area code, she hit SEND, but all she got was voice mail. So she left a message, trying to be concise, telling her about the discovery of the generator and wires in Izzy's garden shed. But she was careful to add that it was simply circumstantial evidence, that she happened to know Izzy's mother was ill and it was most unlikely that she would have left her and gone to New York. She didn't mention Madge's possible relationship to VV; it seemed too complicated for a short message.

She was picking beans in the garden when her cell phone rang; it was Fran returning her call.

"Thanks for your call," she said. "Look, what I need you to find out is whether this gardener was in Tinker's Cove the day Juliette was attacked, or if she could've been here in the city. Can you find out?"

"I was hoping *you* could find out if she was in New York. Don't they have CCTV in the garage?"

"They didn't have it, but they're getting it now." She snorted. "Figures, doesn't it? Close the barn door after the cows have gotten out." She paused. "I really think you'd have a better chance on your end. After all, there are eight million people in New York; it's easy for someone to get lost in the crowd."

"I can try." Lucy bit her lip. "How's Juliette?"

"She's holding her own. Little Viv is staying with her at the hospital, so she's safe, too, for the time being. I'm not taking any chances."

Lucy's next call was to Willis, but once again she got voice mail. Doesn't anyone answer their phone anymore? she wondered, leaving a message requesting that he call her as soon as possible.

She was plunging the cooked green beans into an ice water bath when Willis called her back. "This might not be appropriate, but I really need to know the answer: Has Izzy Scannell taken any time off lately?"

"I'm afraid that is rather inappropriate," he replied. "Employment records here at Pine Point are confidential. I don't share that information with anyone. Why do you want to know?"

Lucy was flummoxed; she could hardly tell Willis she suspected Izzy of murder, even if she did. She had a basic understanding of the laws of slander and it wouldn't do to make unproven accusations about the woman to her supervisor. "Well," she began, trying to think of a plausible excuse for her question. "It's like this. My girls do volunteer work at Heritage House and they're very worried about her mother, and I just wanted to be able to reassure them that Izzy has been able to spend time with her."

"Oh." To be honest, Lucy didn't think Willis would buy her ridiculous excuse and there was a long silence before he spoke. "I think I can tell you that your fears are unfounded. Miz Scannell is well aware of her mother's condition. She's actually been working a reduced schedule for the past few weeks so she can be with her during her final days."

Lucy was shocked. She had no idea her wild guess was so close to the truth. "Final days? It's as serious as that?"

"I'm afraid so," said Willis. "She called Friday, from the nursing home, and said she didn't think it would be very long. I told her to take as much time as she needs."

"Well, thank you," said Lucy. "My girls will feel much better knowing she's with her."

"I understand," said Willis. "And I must congratulate you on rearing such compassionate young women. You don't often see that level of concern for others among today's young people."

"Uh, thanks," said Lucy, feeling like a complete hypocrite. Even worse, she was going to have to maintain this charade if she was going to find out if Izzy was actually at the nursing home the previous Friday. As Lucy knew only too well, having done it herself, you could make a call from anywhere and say you were someplace else.

Chapter Twenty

Lucy felt like a rat, an absolute rat, but she had to know. Izzy seemed like a really nice person, but that didn't actually mean much. Every time you read about a serial killer in the paper or watched a report on the TV news, the neighbors always seemed to describe the killer as "nice enough but kept to himself," dismissing even the terrible smells emanating from the back yard. "Well, of course we noticed it," they'd say, "but we thought it was something to do with his taxidermy hobby." Or a gas leak. Or a failed septic system. Anything, except what it really was. Some truths were too difficult to accept, so the mind manufactured excuses as a way of denying what it already knew.

But she didn't know, Lucy reminded herself, as she drove over to Heritage House on Friday morning. She had her suspicions, but she didn't know. And even if she did manage to pry the information she was seeking out of a nurse or resident, it wouldn't be conclusive proof that Izzy was a murderer. A piece of the puzzle, but not proof.

But if Izzy was with her mother last Friday, the day Juliette was attacked, it would prove that she couldn't have been the attacker. Once she realized that, Lucy felt much better about her inquiry. She wasn't trying to prove Izzy was a killer, she told herself, she was trying to reassure herself that Izzy was innocent.

And with that thought firmly in mind, she parked the car under a tree and crossed the blast furnace that was the Heritage House parking lot and stepped inside the air-conditioned lobby. She was intending to ask the receptionist for directions to the activity director's office when the elevator doors opened and Izzy stepped out, accompanied by a woman in green scrubs, probably a nurse. Intrigued, Lucy feigned interest in the sign announcing the day's activities and watched.

Izzy, she saw, was wiping her eyes and the nurse was hovering in a concerned manner. "Why didn't you call me?" asked Izzy, her voice thick with tears. "It isn't right, you should have called me."

"She slipped away, between checks . . . ," said the nurse, speaking in a soothing voice.

Izzy turned on the woman. "You mean she was all alone?" she demanded in an accusatory tone.

"She drifted off in her sleep," said the nurse, refusing to be ruffled. "It was very peaceful."

"There's no excuse for this," insisted Izzy. "If I'd known she was that close, I would have stayed with her. Nobody told me. She was all alone when she died. I should have been there."

"I understand how you feel," said the nurse. "But it's really up to God. We can't predict with certainty when a soul will be called."

"Oh, now you're trying to fob me off with religious nonsense!" Izzy was furious, and for a moment Lucy thought she was going to assault the nurse.

The receptionist must have thought so, too, because a muscular male orderly suddenly appeared and was crossing the lobby in Izzy's direction. Seeing him, she suddenly bolted for the door. "This isn't the last of this!" she yelled. "I'm going to report you to the state authorities, don't think I won't!" Then she was gone, leaving the door swinging behind her.

The nurse let out a big sigh of relief. "Thanks," she told the orderly. "That was getting intense."

"No problem," he said with a grin.

The two walked off together, down a hallway, and Lucy remembered the errand that had brought her to Heritage House. She was turning toward the reception desk when she spotted a tiny, white-haired woman sitting in one of the couches beneath the over-size chandelier that seemed to be a required fixture in all nursing homes. The woman smiled at her and beckoned.

"You're from the newspaper, aren't you?" she asked when Lucy approached.

"I am," admitted Lucy.

"I saw you at the birthday party."

"That was quite a do," said Lucy.

"Sit down. Take a load off," invited the woman, patting the sofa.

"Thanks," said Lucy, perching beside her. "I'm Lucy Stone."

"I'm Dottie Pickett, but I don't want to see my name in the paper. What I'm going to tell you is strictly off the record, agreed?"

Amused, Lucy nodded. "Absolutely."

"Madge didn't die a natural death," she said, whispering. "They gave her morphine. I saw it."

"Really?" Lucy knew that morphine was often administered to terminal patients to ease their deaths.

"They didn't tell that to the daughter, did they?" Dottie nodded. "It's a conspiracy, they're killing us off. They do it when there's no family to protect us."

Lucy saw an opening here. “So Madge really died alone?”

“That’s the only way they can do it. If the daughter was here, she’d never have allowed it, would she?”

“I suppose not,” said Lucy. “Was her daughter here a lot? I know Madge wasn’t well.”

“She visited more than some, I’ll give her that,” she replied in a grudging tone.

“Was she here last Friday?” asked Lucy.

“We always have fish on Friday,” said Dottie with a big sigh. “I don’t like fish.”

“Was the daughter, Izzy, with Madge last Friday, the day you had fish?”

Dottie looked down at her hands, which were folded in her lap. “Friday. Friday is fish day. My mother used to cook fish on Friday and the house would stink until Sunday.” She wrinkled her nose. “I don’t like fish.”

Lucy figured she’d gotten all the information she was going to get from Dottie. “I don’t like it much, either,” she said, smiling and standing up. “It’s been nice talking with you.”

“Don’t forget.” Dottie raised a crooked finger. “Everything I told you is off the record.”

“Absolutely,” agreed Lucy, noticing with annoyance that the receptionist had left her post. She went up to the desk, intending to wait, but when five and then ten minutes passed, and there was no sign of her, she gave up. She’d have to do this another time, she decided, aware that Ted would be wondering where she was.

As she expected, Ted didn’t mince words when she walked through the door, setting the little bell jangling. “Where have you been?” he demanded. “And I haven’t seen any copy yet.”

“It’s coming,” she said, wondering what the fuss was all

about so early in the weekly news cycle. "I've got the finance committee meeting for you. I just need to touch it up a bit."

"Selectmen's meeting?" Ted sounded like a high school principal who'd found cigarettes in the girls' room.

"I didn't make it," admitted Lucy. "But I've got the agenda and I'll make a few calls."

"Roger Wilcox called, wondering if you were sick," said Ted, brandishing his evidence.

"Nothing happens in the summer, anyway," said Lucy.

"No, nothing much, except Horace Winters is resigning and there's going to be a special election."

"Oh," said Lucy, biting her tongue so she wouldn't say the word she wanted to say. "I'll get right on it."

She couldn't get Horace himself on the phone—he was out fishing—but his wife explained that his doctor advised him to avoid stress and being on the board of selectmen was certainly stressful and, no, he didn't have a heart condition, but his blood pressure was a bit elevated at his last checkup so they decided it was better to be safe than sorry. And they really would like to get away to Florida for at least part of the winter so they decided resigning was really the sensible thing and this way the town could just add the selectmen's race to the November ballot. There was plenty of time to get the word out and hopefully there would be some good candidates, though, of course, she thought Horace had done a spectacular job. That was the problem really, he took it all too seriously . . .

When Mrs. Winters finally paused for breath, Lucy thanked her for her time and ended the call. She was just about to dial Roger Wilcox, the board chairman, when her phone rang. Much to her surprise, it was Bob, explaining that the wills she had requested were ready.

"Thanks, Bob, I'm kind of busy today," said Lucy, wondering how she was going to break the news to Bill that she'd taken the bull by the horns and requested the wills.

"These are just the drafts," Bob reminded her. "So the sooner you and Bill look them over, the sooner I can prepare the final copies."

"Right," said Lucy. "I'll stop in on my way home."

"Great," agreed Bob. "I'm here 'til six, anyway."

Lucy did a quick edit of the fin-com story and sent it to Ted, hoping it would keep him busy while she worked on the Horace Winters story. She had just finished that when Phyllis dropped a thick stack of press releases for the "Things to Do" listings, but it was already almost five by then, so she decided to take them home and work on them over the weekend.

"I've got an appointment," she said, shutting down her computer and stuffing the press releases into her bag. "I'll have these ready by Monday morning."

Phyllis raised a skeptical eyebrow, but Ted didn't object. "Okay. I want you to stop by at the town playground tomorrow morning and get some photos . . ." Ted was rummaging through the papers spread out on his desk. "There's a clown or something."

"Will do," said Lucy. Snapping pictures of local children at the town-funded rec program was a standard summer assignment that she enjoyed, even if it meant working on Saturday.

"Not a clown. It's Family Fun Day with ice cream. Donated by Brown Cow Dairy."

"Even better," said Lucy, deciding she'd better leave before he came up with something else for her to do.

It was only a few blocks to Bob's office but she drove. It was on her way home and she knew he was going to leave soon, and she didn't want to miss him. As soon as she stepped through the door, she realized something was wrong. Bob was standing at his desk, phone in hand, an anxious expression on his face.

"What's the matter?" she asked, fearing something had happened to Rachel, or their son, Richie.

"That was Rachel," he said, replacing the handset in its cradle. "She's worried because VV was supposed to come to Miss Tilley's for afternoon tea and she hasn't shown up yet. She called Pine Point and, according to Willis, VV left hours ago."

Lucy had that sinking feeling that accompanied a premonition of trouble. "Who was driving?" she asked.

"Izzy."

It hit Lucy like a punch. "Oh, no."

"Is that a problem?"

How to begin, wondered Lucy. "It's complicated. Her mother is, make that *was*, VV's child, given up for adoption. She died last night. Izzy's really upset, I saw her at Heritage House this morning. And I think—I don't know for sure—but I think Izzy killed Van and Maxine and attacked Juliette. Juliette's in the hospital."

Bob's chin dropped. "You're telling me that Izzy's mother was really VV's child?"

"Yes. By her first husband. She gave her up for adoption."

Bob was no dummy; he saw the implications immediately. "And if she got rid of all the legitimate heirs, Izzy thinks she'll inherit VV's money . . ."

"Would she?" asked Lucy. "Even if she's not mentioned in the will?"

"It depends. She'd probably have grounds to make a claim." He sat down, shaking his head. "When I took her deposition, she seemed so helpful and concerned about VV. I can't believe she's a killer. And for what? Money?"

The question gave Lucy pause. "I think that's how it

started," she said. "But now, I think it's something else. Revenge. Getting even." She paused. "I think VV is in danger. When I saw Izzy at Heritage House, she was very angry and emotional."

"I'll call the police," said Bob.

"I'll start looking for them," said Lucy.

"Wait, leave it to the police," protested Bob, but he was too late. Lucy was already out the door and running to her car. When Bob followed, he saw her peeling out of the driveway, taking the turn so fast that her tires squealed.

As Lucy sped along, she tried to think of a plan. The obvious thing, she decided, would be to start at Pine Point, because that's where Izzy would have picked up VV. As she drove, she kept her eyes peeled, looking for any sign of VV's town car and taking note of possible hiding places. She tried to put herself in Izzy's place, but it was difficult to imagine being a distraught serial killer who had abducted a frail old woman. Was she planning to hold VV hostage? Was she going to torment her? Kill her?

She had almost reached Shore Road and was passing the Audubon sanctuary when she had a sudden hunch and turned into the drive, just to check it out. She followed the twisty dirt road for a few hundred feet until she could see the parking area, but cautiously stopped short of entering it when she spotted the silver-gray town car. She was scrabbling in her purse, searching for her phone so she could call nine-one-one, when she caught movement out the corner of her eye and spotted Izzy coming out of the woods, alone, pushing an empty wheelchair.

Acting instinctively, she ran into the parking area, confronting her. "Where's VV?" she demanded. "What have you done with her?"

"Oh, Lucy," began Izzy, smiling broadly. "I'm so glad

you're here. You can help me find Mrs. Van Vorst. She insisted we stop here. She wanted to see the osprey nest everybody's been talking about. But while I was getting the wheelchair out of the trunk she wandered off. I immediately went after her but I couldn't find her. She's simply vanished."

Lucy didn't believe a word of it, but she wasn't about to let Izzy know that. "I'll help you look," she said. "Just let me get my . . ." She was about to say *phone*, but thought better of it; she didn't want to tip off Izzy that she was planning to call for help. "Bag," said, turning to go back to her car.

As soon as her back was turned she realized she'd made a mistake. She quickly whirled around, preparing to defend herself, but the blow came immediately, stunning her and knocking her to the ground. She was barely conscious but she felt something around her neck, something that was making it hard to breathe. She was struggling, instinctively fighting for survival, trying to pull Izzy's hands away from her throat, when the pressure on her neck suddenly ceased. She turned, gasping for breath, and saw Eddie Culpepper grappling with Izzy. He'd grabbed her by the waist and was trying to bring her down but she jabbed him in the eye, slipped out of his arms, and delivered a mean kick to his crotch. Eddie crumpled to his knees, watching helplessly as Izzy escaped, running across the parking area and climbing into the Pine Point truck he had left running behind Lucy's car. She reversed madly down the drive, scraping trees and undergrowth as she went.

Still dizzy, Lucy staggered the short distance to Eddie, who had curled up in a fetal position. "Are you okay?" she asked, her voice little more than a croak.

"Yeah," he replied in a weak voice. "I just need a minute."

"I'm calling for help," she said, stumbling on the way back to her car.

After she'd made the call, she sank to the ground beside Eddie. "They should be here soon."

"We have to find Mrs. Van Vorst," said Eddie, raising himself to a sitting position. "She must be here, in the woods somewhere."

"Do you think she's alive?" asked Lucy, who had absolutely no desire to do anything more than concentrate on her next breath.

"We've gotta find out," said Eddie, rising clumsily to his feet.

"Okay," said Lucy, holding out her hand, which Eddie grabbed, helping her to her feet.

She swayed a bit when she stood up, but her vision was clear, except for a jangly fuzziness around the edges. She discovered she could manage, just barely, to put one foot in front of the other. Eddie, she noticed, was limping, but he managed an encouraging smile as he led the way down the path.

It was much cooler in the woods, where the tall pine trees shaded the path, but Lucy didn't like the tricks her vision was playing, going in and out of focus. It was an easy, well-traveled trail that led downhill, but Lucy staggered as she went, leaning here and there on a tree trunk for support. Eddie was running ahead of her and had disappeared around a curve when she heard him yelling that he'd found VV.

She was at land's end, at the very edge of a rocky promontory facing the sea. Izzy had propped her against a pine tree and tied her fast, leaving her to the elements where she would surely have died of exposure. Hurrying as best she could, Lucy thought VV looked like little more than a bundle of rags. The frail old woman had slumped forward, and would have fallen on her face except for the cruel ropes that restrained her; she was semiconscious. Her bluish eyelids flickered when Lucy spoke to her and her cracked lips moved as she emitted a faint groan.

"Help is coming. You're going to be all right," Lucy told her, as Eddie produced a knife and cut the ropes, freeing her.

Together they managed an awkward fireman's carry, cradling VV between them in their arms and carrying her up the trail. It was uphill and Lucy fought nausea with every step. Her arms and legs were burning and she didn't think she could go on without a rest when they heard a voice calling them.

They answered and minutes later the rescue squad met them in the path and took over. VV was strapped to a stretcher and carried the rest of the way. Lucy followed, assisted by a strong EMT. Eddie refused assistance, making his own way up the trail.

When they reached the parking lot, Lucy was bundled into the ambulance along with VV. She didn't protest. Her vision was still blurry and she feared she might have a concussion, but she was also concerned about VV and wanted to make sure the old woman would be all right. The EMTs had clapped an oxygen mask over VV's face and she was lying very still as the ambulance sailed over the roads to the hospital, siren wailing. When it suddenly stopped, arriving at the ER, Lucy realized she'd dozed off. Weird, she thought, as they wheeled her inside.

When she next regained consciousness, she found an I.V. had been fixed to her hand and Bill was leaning over her, looking worried.

"Am I okay?" she asked.

"Yeah," he said, stroking her cheek. "The CAT scan was clear."

"I had a CAT scan?"

He smiled, and she felt his beard against her cheek. "Take it easy. Everything's under control."

"What about VV?" she asked.

"Responding to treatment and expected to make a full recovery. She's mostly dehydrated."

"That's good," she said, wishing her head didn't hurt quite so much. At least the blurry vision was gone.

"Why'd you do such a crazy thing?" he demanded, scolding her. "You have a lot to answer for," he said.

If he only knew, thought Lucy, guiltily remembering the wills. "Can I go home?"

Bill shook his head. "They want to keep you overnight. Just a precaution, they said."

"Okay." That was fine with Lucy. She didn't really feel like going anywhere.

"I think I better get home, though. Let the kids know you're okay."

Lucy started to nod but a stab of pain caused her to reconsider. "Bye," she said.

"I'll see you tomorrow," he said, kissing her forehead. Then he was gone and she was alone in the curtained cubicle. She felt a definite lump forming in her throat and her eyes were starting to tear, when there was a sudden commotion as another patient was rushed into the adjacent cubicle. The curtain between the cubicles had been caught and pulled slightly open, and she could see the nurses leaning over the patient. There was a series of noises, electronic beeps, and routine comments from the team. Then Lucy heard a faint voice: "I just wanted what was mine."

"Shhh," said a different voice. "You're going to be okay."

"She abandoned her baby . . . my mother." The voice was weaker, but Lucy recognized it. Izzy.

Then Lucy heard Doc Ryder's familiar voice. "We're calling MedFlight," he was saying. "You're going to take a ride to Portland." Then he lowered his voice and she couldn't hear what he was saying; he was probably issuing orders to a nurse.

A couple of minutes later the curtain opened and Doc Ryder was standing by her bedside, flipping through her chart. "You took a pretty good knock on the head. How are you feeling?"

"Not so great," said Lucy.

"The neurologist wants to keep you for observation, but it's crazy here tonight," he said. "Your room's not ready and we need this space. We might have to put you in the hallway for a while."

"Just don't forget about me," she said. "What about the woman next door? The one who's waiting for a MedFlight."

Doc Ryder peered at her over his half-glasses. "I can't discuss . . ."

"It's Izzy Scannell, right? I know her."

The doctor shook his head. "It's tragic. She was in a terrible accident and there's not much we can do for her here." He was closing her chart when a nurse arrived and whispered something in his ear, then left. He stood for a moment, studying her. "The MedFlight's been delayed," he said in a low voice. "We're really short staffed, and I can't spare anybody to stay with her. Would you do it?"

"Me? What can I do?"

His voice was even lower. "She's got massive internal injuries and time is running out. She's not gonna make it unless that MedFlight helicopter gets here soon." He paused. "I wouldn't ask if I didn't think it was important. I don't like to leave a critical patient alone, and you said you're friends."

"Not exactly friends," said Lucy. She couldn't believe what she was hearing. Just hours ago Izzy had viciously attacked her and now she was being asked to comfort her. It was like one of those situations she remembered from Sunday school: What would you do if the mean girl who didn't invite you to her birthday party was roller-skating near your house and fell, scraping her knee? Lucy knew you were supposed to turn the other cheek and give her a Band-Aid. "Okay," she said, and he helped her out of the bed and into a wheelchair.

"Just hold her hand," he said, pulling the curtain aside and wheeling her next to Izzy's bed. "Use the CALL button if anything changes."

Izzy seemed very small, lying flat on her back, not at all like the hearty, strong woman Lucy remembered helping get rid of those bittersweet vines. There were numerous tubes and wires and machines, her face was puffy and bruised, and her eyes were closed. Lucy took her hand, and Izzy curled her fingers around it. Doc Ryder patted her on the shoulder and was gone.

"You're going to be okay," she said. "The helicopter's coming."

Much to Lucy's surprise, Izzy started to speak and Lucy leaned close to hear. "I did it for my mom," she whispered, her eyes still closed. "She was VV's baby. VV abandoned her. I wanted her to know . . . what that's like . . . how it feels."

Lucy remembered how upset Izzy had been at Heritage House when she learned her mother had died, alone and unattended. Lucy was no psychiatrist, but she suspected that her mother's death had sent Izzy into some sort of crisis. Izzy had somehow mixed up her mother's lonely death with VV's decision to give her up for adoption as a baby. Both times poor Madge was abandoned and left to her fate.

"Don't talk. Save your strength," said Lucy. "The helicopter will be here soon."

"No," whispered Izzy. "I need to get it . . . off my chest."

"There'll be time for that later," said Lucy.

Izzy's voice was stronger and her eyes were open now. "I don't think so."

Lucy didn't know what to do. She desperately wanted to hear Izzy's confession, but she didn't want to do anything that would compromise her chances of recovery. Where was that darn helicopter?

Izzy tugged on her hand. "I'm sorry I hit you."

Lucy's eyes met Izzy's. "It's okay. I understand. You were upset."

"Yeah." Izzy gave a lopsided smile.

Encouraged by these signs, Lucy went ahead and asked a question that had been bothering her. "Did your mom know that VV was her mother?"

"No. When Grammy O'Dwyer died, I had to clear out her things and I found Mom's birth certificate."

"Did you show your mother?"

"I tried. She wouldn't look. She didn't want to know. She said she knew who raised her and loved her and that was all that mattered."

"It mattered to you, though," said Lucy.

"I told Van but he laughed at me, said I was lying."

"Is that why you killed him?"

"He was going to fire me."

"And you needed to stay at Pine Point because you had a plan? A plan to get close to VV so she would recognize your mother?"

Izzy nodded.

"But why did you kill Maxine?"

"After Van died, people started suspecting Vicky and . . . ,"

Izzy's voice faltered, she took a long shallow breath, then continued, "the two men."

"Her husband and Weatherby?"

"Yeah. When Maxine threatened them, I thought . . ."

"You thought they would be blamed for her death?"

"Mmmm." Izzy's voice was getting weaker and Lucy hoped that helicopter was on its way.

"Why Juliette?"

"She sent that woman . . . from New York."

"The private investigator?"

Izzy nodded.

Lucy was beginning to understand. "Juliette was determined to find out who killed her parents and that made her dangerous to you."

"Not the money." Izzy's eyelids were fluttering and her grip was weakening. Lucy squeezed her hand a bit tighter. She thought she could hear the helicopter overhead. "Didn't care," sighed Izzy, and Lucy felt her hand go limp.

She was still holding Izzy's hand when the curtain was pulled aside and a nurse announced that the helicopter had arrived and it was time to go.

"I think she's already left," said Lucy, aware the alarms were suddenly going off on the machines.

Then she was shoved outside the cubicle and there was a frantic flurry of activity as they tried to shock Izzy's heart into beating once again.

After what seemed like an eternity, Lucy heard someone speak. "She's gone. Time of death, eight forty-two."

Lucy stared at the ceiling, at the white acoustic tile dotted with holes and the translucent panel for the fluorescent lights and the gray metal track for the privacy curtain. What a waste, she thought. Van and Maxine gone, Juliette injured, and for what? Margaret had died without knowing her birth mother, and now Izzy was dead, too. And

VV—what about her? She'd been abused by one granddaughter while another worked in her garden, unacknowledged and aching for recognition.

Then the curtain was pulled aside and a thirtyish guy in pale blue scrubs approached. "Ready for a little trip?" he asked. "We've got a room ready for you."

Lucy was thoughtful as she was wheeled through the ER to the elevator. When the caregiver pushed the button, she asked, "What happened to the woman who just died?"

"An accident," he said as the doors slid open and he pushed her wheelchair inside the elevator. "At Lover's Leap. She drove into the guard rail."

"On purpose?" asked Lucy.

"It's a dangerous spot," he said with a shrug. "It could have been an accident. We'll never know."

It was true, thought Lucy, as the elevator doors opened and she was pushed into the hallway. They would never know whether Izzy had intended to kill herself or whether she'd simply spun out of control. Either way, she was her own last victim.

"Well, here we are," said the nurse, deftly angling the gurney into a vacant room. Another nurse arrived and she was transferred into a bed and tucked in for the night. "The button's right here, just push if you need anything."

Lucy let out a long sigh. She was fine. She didn't need anything.

Epilogue

It was a year later. Lucy and a handful of volunteers were at Pine Point, hiding Easter eggs in preparation for the annual hunt. Lucy had emptied her box of eggs and was crossing the lawn to get a fresh box when she noticed a motorcycle in the driveway, approaching at a sedate speed. The rider was a large, bearded man with long hair that sprang out in all directions when he dismounted and removed his helmet. As she watched, he carefully unstrapped a box he had lashed to the back of the seat and carried it to the front door, where he rang the bell.

Willis opened the door, and looked the man over. "Do you have an appointment?" he asked in his butler voice.

"No, no," admitted the bearded man. "I just brought her this," he said, indicating the box. "It's from Juliette."

Willis eyed the box suspiciously. "Just leave it on the porch," he said.

The man nodded and put the box down on the brick paving, then he strode back to his motorcycle and mounted.

Lucy watched, amused, as Willis poked at the box with a black umbrella, eventually flipping the flaps open and extracting a gleaming yellow sculpture.

"It's called *Peeps*," yelled the bearded man, who Lucy

now recognized as Karl Klaus, the sculptor, whose photo she'd seen recently in the Sunday paper. He waved, revved the motorcycle, and drove off. Lucy could hear the machine advancing down the driveway as Willis disappeared inside with the glowing, golden sculpture.

Please turn the page for
some fun Easter tips
from Lucy Stone!

Hot Cross Buns

Hot cross buns are a traditional Lenten treat, but Lucy always hates the way the sugary icing melts when she warms them up in the oven. When she visited England, however, she discovered that they make the cross with a floury paste. English buns are also heartier than the American supermarket variety, and if you make them, they're a good way to use up the candied fruits left over from your Christmas pudding.

Hot Cross Buns

½ cup milk
2 cups unbleached flour
2 Tbsp. confectioner's sugar
½ tsp. each, salt and cinnamon
¼ tsp. each, mace and nutmeg
⅛ tsp. ground allspice
1½ Tbsp. cold butter, diced
1 packet rapid-rise yeast
⅓ cup each dried currants (or raisins), golden raisins, and mixed candied fruit
1 large egg, beaten

For the pastry crosses
⅓ cup all-purpose flour
1 Tbsp. butter
1 tsp. confectioner's sugar

For the glaze
2 Tbsp. milk
1½ Tbsp. granulated sugar

Warm ½ cup milk in small saucepan and set aside.

Sift flour into large bowl; stir in sugar and spices. Rub the butter into the mixture until it resembles fine crumbs. Mix in yeast, then fruit. Make a well in the center and stir in the egg and enough heated milk to form a soft dough that isn't too sticky.

Turn dough onto a lightly floured surface and knead until smooth and elastic. Return to bowl, cover with plastic wrap, and let stand in warm place until the dough has risen by a third. (This may take 3 to 5 hours.)

Lightly oil a baking sheet. Turn risen dough onto a lightly floured work surface, knead for a minute, then divide into 6 equal pieces, each shaped into a neat ball. Set on baking sheet and cover with plastic wrap. Set aside until dough is puffy, around 45 minutes.

Preheat oven to 400 degrees F.

To make the pastry crosses: Sift all-purpose flour into small bowl, rub in butter until mixture forms fine crumbs, mix in sugar, and stir in 1 Tbsp. cold water to make a firm dough. Turn the dough onto a lightly floured surface and roll into a 2 by 8 inch rectangle. Cut into 12 strips, each 4 inches long and ¼ inch wide. For each bun, brush 2 strips with a little water and arrange wet side down in a cross on top of the bun. Bake until golden brown, about 15 minutes.

To make the glaze: Combine milk and sugar in small saucepan and cook over low heat until sugar is dissolved, about 5 minutes. Raise heat to high and boil vigorously for 30 seconds until glaze becomes syrupy.

When buns are done, transfer to a wire rack set on wax paper and brush with hot glaze.

Ricotta Pie

Lasagna is a good option for meatless Lenten meals, and thrifty shoppers like Lucy know that ricotta and mozzarella often go on sale this time of year. Most lasagna recipes only call for half a quart of ricotta, which means you need to find a recipe for the other half of the container. Here it is:

Italian Easter Pie

Crust
1⅔ cups flour
2 Tbsp. sugar
½ tsp. salt
¼ tsp. baking powder
¼ cup butter
¼ cup shortening
2 eggs, beaten

Combine all ingredients except eggs in food processor and whizz until mixture resembles small crumbs. Transfer mixture to a large bowl and add the eggs, stirring until moistened, and mixture forms a ball. You might need to add a tablespoon or two of cold water. Cover and chill for one hour.

Filling

1 (15 oz.) carton of ricotta, or half of a 32 oz. carton
1 cup sugar
1 Tbsp. flour
1 tsp. grated orange peel
dash of salt
4 eggs
1 tsp. vanilla extract
⅓ cup semisweet chocolate chips
⅓ cup diced candied citron
⅛ tsp. cinnamon

Beat ricotta, sugar, and flour in a mixing bowl. Add orange peel and salt; beat until smooth. In a separate bowl, beat eggs until thick and lemon colored (about 5 minutes). Slowly fold eggs into ricotta mixture. Gently mix in remaining ingredients.

Roll out the chilled pastry on lightly floured surface, then place in a 9-inch pie pan. Pour the filling into the crust. Bake at 350 degrees F for 55 to 60 minutes, until filling is firm.

Easter Egg Hunt

Folks like Lucy who live on the New England coast are familiar with the idea of spring but don't really experience it. Easter weather is extremely variable, ranging from howling blizzards to early heat waves. For the most part, breezes from the ocean keep temperatures cool, and clouds and rain are far more likely than sunshine. That means plastic Easter eggs are the obvious choice for outdoor egg hunts, but filling them is always a bit of a problem. The kids have already gorged on candy from their Easter baskets, so Lucy doesn't like to give them more sweets. That means the weeks before Easter are spent looking for small, inexpensive items. Here are a few suggestions:

Lip balm
Finger puppets
Plastic bugs or other creatures
Matchbox cars
Money
Barrettes
Jewelry
Stickers
Temporary tattoos
Silly Putty

Special gifts can go in eggs that are marked with the recipients' names; girly tokens can go in pink eggs, those for boys in blue eggs.

Much has happened since Leslie Meier first introduced her beloved sleuth Lucy Stone with Mistletoe Murder. *Many holidays and bake sales have come and gone, Lucy's children have all grown up. But even after twenty-four books into the bestselling series, murder is never out of the picture. . . .*

As Tinker's Cove, Maine, buzzes over a town-wide silver wedding anniversary bash, Lucy is reminded of her nuptials and ponders the whereabouts of Beth Gerard, her strong-willed maid of honor. Lucy never would have made it down the aisle without Beth's help, and although the two friends lost touch over the years, she decides to reach out. It only takes one phone call for Lucy to realize that a reunion will happen sooner rather than later—at Beth's funeral.

Beth, who was in the process of finalizing her fourth divorce, had a reputation for living on the edge—but no one can believe she would jump off a penthouse terrace in New York City. The more Lucy learns about Beth's former husbands, the more she suspects one of them committed murder.

Summoning her friend's impulsive spirit, Lucy vows to scour New York from the Bronx to the Brooklyn Bridge in search of the killer. With each ex dodgier than the last, it's not long before Lucy's investigation leads her to a desperate criminal who will do anything to get away—even if it means silencing another victim. . . .

Please turn the page for an exciting sneak peek of
Leslie Meier's

SILVER ANNIVERSARY MURDER

now on sale wherever print and e-books are sold!

Chapter One

"Honestly, I'm surprised he hasn't killed her," whispered Harry Nuttall, leaning over the deli counter at the IGA in Tinker's Cove, Maine. He was speaking to one of his regular customers, Lucy Stone, who was doing her weekly grocery shopping.

Lucy was a part-time reporter for the *Pennysaver*, the local weekly newspaper, and had developed the habit of shopping after the paper's Wednesday noon deadline, taking advantage of the free afternoon, which also happened to be a time when the usually crowded supermarket had few customers.

"So is it the usual?" Harry pulled on a fresh pair of plastic gloves. "A pound of ham, sliced thin, and a half of Swiss?"

"I guess I'll live dangerously," said Lucy, turning to watch Warren Bickford, Harry's potential murderer, presenting his wife and likely murder victim, Sylvia, with his wrapped cold cuts. Then remembering the task at hand, she turned back to Harry. "Throw in a half pound of turkey breast, too."

"Do you want it sliced like the ham?" asked Harry.

Lucy's attention had returned to the Bickfords; Warren's deli purchase had clearly not satisfied Sylvia. She glared at the label on the package through heavily made-up eyes, ran her red-tipped nails through her obviously bleached blond hair, pointed at the label, then roughly thrust the packet back to Warren. "Black Forest, Warren. I told you Black Forest! Honestly, how many times do I have to repeat myself?"

Warren bent his head and seemed to offer an apology, then trotted obediently back to the deli counter.

"Same thickness as the ham?" Harry asked again, the grin on his face revealing his amusement at Lucy's fascination with the Bickfords.

Lucy considered asking him to slice the turkey a bit thicker than the ham, but aware that Warren was under the gun to deliver the correct order, changed her mind. "Same," she said, turning to give Warren a big, warm smile. It seemed the least she could do for the poor, henpecked husband. "Nice day," she said, referring to the lovely, mild, May weather that was such a treat after the bitter cold Maine winter, which this year had been followed by an especially blustery March and extremely muddy April.

"Sure is," replied Warren, unzipping his jacket. Lucy guessed he was in his early fifties, and like most middle-aged men in Tinker's Cove, he was wearing khaki pants and a sports shirt topped with a light sweater. His thinning hair was combed in the standard left-parted barbershop cut and he was developing a bit of a paunch. That growing tummy was probably the result of an occupational hazard; as owner and operator of a limo service he spent a lot of time sitting behind the wheel. "Sorry to bother you, Harry, but I got the wrong ham. I should've asked for Black Forest. I hope it's no problem."

"No problem," said Harry, placing Lucy's three packages on the counter. "It's already wrapped. I'll save it for the next customer who wants Virginia ham."

Warren let out a relieved sigh. "Thanks, Harry." It seemed he was about to say something more, perhaps a reference to his wife, but thought better of it and bit his lip instead, rocking slightly from one sturdy Timberland shoe to the other while waiting for Harry to slice his Black Forest ham.

Lucy put her packages in her cart and pushed it along, heading for the meat counter, which ran along the back wall of the supermarket. She paused at an island displaying English muffins—buy one get two free, a deal that was hard to pass up—and witnessed Warren rejoining his wife and presenting the correct ham, rather like a little girl offering flowers to the queen.

"Warren, you always do this. You don't speak up and people take advantage of you. Just look—this ham is sliced much too thick. Not that I blame Harry. He isn't going to shove that slicer back and forth any more times than he has to, if people don't speak up and ask for thin slices."

Warren stood like a statue, letting his wife's criticisms rain down on him. "Do you want me to take it back, *dear*?" he asked, with the slightest note of sarcasm in his voice.

Sylvia expelled a large sigh. "No, Warren. We don't have time. We have a big order this week." She flourished her shopping list. "Do you think you could manage a simple task like getting the coffee while I look over the meat? Beef chuck is supposed to be on sale, but I'll be amazed if they have any left this late in the week. They probably sold it all on the weekend. Not that they'll get away with it, not with me. I'll insist on a rain check."

"You do that, dear," said Warren. "Quite right. Now, do you want decaf or regular, and what brand? Or should I go for price?"

"It never ceases to amaze me, Warren. How long have we been married? Twenty-five years next month, and you don't know what brand of coffee we drink?"

"Well, it's usually the one in the red package, but sometimes it seems to me we have the blue kind."

"*The red kind? The blue kind?* Honestly, Warren, you sound like a child." She rolled her eyes. "Get the Folgers, unless Maxwell House is on sale for half price. And don't fall for that foul French roast stuff. Can you do that for me?"

"Yes, dear." Warren trotted off in the direction of the coffee aisle, and Sylvia, as promised, attacked the meat counter. Lucy, hoping to avoid witnessing any more of Warren's humiliations, slipped off into the cereal aisle. Distracted by a special on canned soups on the end cap, where she was searching for chicken noodle but only finding minestrone and vegetarian vegetable, she wasn't quick enough to miss Warren's presentation of a green can of coffee.

"Green is decaf, Warren; everybody knows that," declared Sylvia, in a voice that could probably be heard on Metinnicut Island, ten miles across the bay.

"But it's Folgers, like you said." He attempted a weak defense. "They could have changed the package, you know."

"No, Warren, they haven't changed it." Sylvia paused to sniff a cello-wrapped piece of chuck, then replaced it. "Now, take this back and get the red Folgers. And do hurry. We've got a lot to do and I'm going to have the butcher cut me a fresh piece of chuck. The nose knows—you can't fool my nose. This meat has probably been sitting out here since Sunday."

"Right, dear," said Warren, obediently hurrying back to the coffee section to complete his assignment. Watching him go, Lucy thought Harry might have a point. Some day, maybe some day soon, Warren was bound to snap.

Diverting as that thought was, Lucy had a long shopping list that demanded great concentration as she frequently consulted the weekly ad for specials, checked prices, and thumbed through her coupon file. From time to time she heard Sylvia's strident voice berating Warren for something or other, but she didn't actually encounter the Bickfords again until she reached the checkout counter.

Warren was busy bagging their order when Dot Kirwan, the cashier, announced the amount due. "A hundred and forty-seven dollars!" exclaimed Sylvia. "We don't want to buy the store, do we, Warren? We just want to eat for a week."

"Should we put this back, dear?" suggested Warren, who was holding a large bottle of expensive olive oil. "We could get a smaller one."

Sylvia shook her head. "The larger one is a better value, Warren. You ought to know that. It's cheaper per ounce. Now pay the bill and stop grumbling."

"Yes, dear," said Warren, pulling his wallet out of his back pocket and handing a credit card to Dot.

"Let me see that!" demanded Sylvia, snatching the card out of Dot's hand. "Just as I thought. It's the wrong card!"

Dot's eyes met Lucy's, and they both struggled to maintain neutral facial expressions while Warren fumbled with his wallet. The two women were of like minds and Lucy had great respect for Dot, who was the widowed matriarch of a large family. Most of her kids and grandkids worked for the town, filling positions in the fire and police departments, which made Dot a valuable source of inside knowledge for Lucy.

"Oh, give me that wallet!" demanded Sylvia, losing patience. He obliged and she flipped it open, pulling out a wad of plastic cards. "My word! What is all this? Exxon, Sears, Shell, Visa, Plenti . . . Ah, finally! This is the one that gives us rewards, Warren." She waved the colorful bit of plastic underneath his nose. "Only use this one, from now on, only this one. You don't need the rest. You might as well cut them up and throw them away."

"I'll do that, dear," said Warren, who had continued packing the groceries and was holding the disputed can of Folgers coffee.

"Just slide the card on the keypad," urged Dot, and Sylvia complied, signing with a flourish. Warren carefully placed a plastic bag containing their eggs on the child seat and pushed the cart toward the door, followed by Sylvia, who was checking the register tape as she walked.

"Thank you and have a nice day," said Dot. Unable to stifle her laughter any longer, she burst into a fit of giggles. "I call them the Bickersons," she whispered to Lucy, as the automatic door opened and the Bickfords exited the store.

Lucy felt a certain sympathy for Sylvia as Dot finished ringing up her order, which amounted to nearly two hundred dollars despite her coupon clipping. Sylvia was right about one thing, she decided, as she pushed her heavily loaded cart out to the parking lot, and that was the price of groceries. The sun this afternoon was very bright, and she paused in the shady overhang to put on her sunglasses only to find they were missing. They weren't in the usual pocket on the outside of her purse, and they weren't inside, along with her wallet, granola bar, numerous pens, phone, and reporter's notebook, either. Sighing, she gave the cart a shove and stepped into the sunlight, squinting. She'd almost finished loading everything into her trunk when it came to her: she'd pulled the sunglasses off when she got to work earlier that day and set them down on her desk. They were most likely still there, so she'd have to swing by the *Pennysaver* office to retrieve them.

Lucky for her, there was a vacant parking spot right in front of the weekly newspaper's Main Street office and Lucy swooped right in, then dashed into the office, setting the little bell on the door to jangling. Somewhat to her surprise, she was greeted not only by the receptionist, Phyllis, but also by her editor, Ted, who didn't usually stick around the office after deadline. The two were standing at the reception counter, heads bent over a press release.

"What's up?" asked Lucy. "Breaking news?" Late breaking news was a problem for a weekly, which had to wait an entire week before printing stories that by then had become stale.

"Not hardly," said Ted, chuckling. He was not only the editor, but also the publisher and chief reporter for the paper, which he'd inherited from his grandfather. That celebrated New England journalist's rolltop desk still dominated the old-fashioned newsroom and was Ted's most prized possession.

"You've got to see it to believe it," said Phyllis, laughing so hard that her sizable bosom was jiggling as she handed the press release to Lucy. Phyllis was celebrating spring's late arrival by wearing a pink bouclé sweater that matched her pink reading glasses and her hair, also dyed pink.

Lucy quickly scanned the press release, which announced in bold capitals that Sylvia and Warren Bickford were soon to celebrate their twenty-fifth wedding anniversary in June by renewing their vows, that joyous ceremony to be followed by a reception to which the whole town would be invited. And that was not all, promised the press release, which went on to invite all the ladies of the town to participate in a fashion show of wedding gowns from the past by modeling their own dresses. All those interested should contact Sylvia at her shop, Orange Blossom Bridal.

"This is so funny," said Lucy, when she'd finished reading. "I just saw the Bickfords, who Dot Kirwan calls the Bickersons, at the IGA. She picked on him mercilessly; the poor guy couldn't do anything right. Harry, the deli guy, said he was surprised Warren hasn't murdered Sylvia. A divorce would be more appropriate than renewing their vows. The whole town is going to be laughing at them."

"It's pretty smart, if you ask me," said Ted. "It's great publicity for her bridal boutique, and also for his limo company."

"It could backfire," said Lucy. "Everybody knows it's an unhappy marriage. Nobody'd be surprised if Warren bailed out, or worse."

"Oh, I don't know," said Phyllis, in a thoughtful tone. She was a bit of a romantic, having found her great love, Wilf Lundgren, rather late in life. "There must be something that keeps them together, despite outward appearances. I think it's kind of sweet."

Lucy spotted her sunglasses, exactly where she had left them, and grabbed them, perching them on top of her head in Jackie Kennedy style. "Speaking of sweets, I gotta run before my ice cream melts—see ya tomorrow!"

Lucy thought about marriage as she drove the familiar route through town, down Main Street, and out to Route 1, then turning onto Red Top Road and up the hill to the handyman's special she and Bill had restored and in which they'd raised their four children. Sometimes the glue held, even for couples like the Bickersons, who didn't seem terribly happy, and sometimes that glue dried up and crumbled, like the stuff she'd spent hours scraping off the back of an antique picture frame she'd recently picked up at an estate sale. There had been rough spots in her marriage to Bill—she remembered fights but not exactly what caused them—but she'd never seriously considered divorce. Maybe, she admitted to herself, that was because she was far too practical to attempt to raise four children by herself, especially considering the mostly low-wage jobs available to women like her in coastal Maine. She didn't want to spend her summers juggling a couple of jobs, chambermaiding by day and waitressing by night as many local women did.

That wasn't quite fair to Bill, she thought with a smile, pulling into the driveway. She loved him. She'd been distant at first, when he began chatting her up in college, but through sheer persistence he'd gradually won her over. Now, after the house and the kids and grandson Patrick, he was so much a part of her that she couldn't imagine life without him.

Though, she admitted to herself as she began toting the heavy recyclable bags of groceries into the house, she could use a little help from him right now. What was it her mother used to say, when her father was nowhere to be found? Something about wishing she could put on her hat and walk out the door, though that didn't quite take into account the fact that Dad was just going to work. She knew that Bill, who was a restoration carpenter, was hard at work on a big project, transforming an old, abandoned church into a vacation home for a successful Portland restauranteur and his family.

Still, it was a big job, toting all the groceries that would feed herself and Bill, and their two daughters who hadn't yet flown the nest. The fact that Sara, now a graduate student at nearby Winchester College, was a vegetarian, and

Zoe, an undergraduate at the same institution, was avoiding gluten, didn't make things any easier. Her grocery list was now filled with the special foods the girls demanded: quinoa, kale, organic yogurt, free-range eggs, hormone-free milk, on and on it went. She dropped two heavy bags on the kitchen table and went out for more, eventually making three trips to get everything inside. And then there was the unloading, the sorting and the storing.

When she'd finally folded the last bag and tucked it away with the others in her bag of bags, she sat down at the round, golden oak kitchen table and considered making herself a cup of tea. Entirely too much work, she decided, opting instead for a glass of water. She sipped it thoughtfully, thinking of Sylvia's challenge: could she possibly fit into her wedding dress? Setting down her glass, she decided she had to find out.

The dress, shrouded in a garment bag, hung in the back of her closet. She hadn't looked at it in years, had almost forgotten about it. Like most mothers, she had a vague hope that one of her daughters might wear it for her wedding, but so far that hadn't happened. Even Elizabeth, her oldest, who worked for the tony Cavendish Hotel chain and was currently living in Paris, hadn't shown any interest in marriage, much less in wearing her mother's dress. It probably wouldn't suit her, thought Lucy, climbing the steep, back stairway that led from the kitchen to the bedrooms on the second floor. She would surely want something more high fashion.

Entering the bedroom she shared with Bill, Lucy opened the bifold closet doors, which stuck a bit and which Bill kept meaning to fix. She slid the clothes along the rod until she came to the long garment bag, which she pulled out and laid on the bed, then unzipped it to reveal the white dress.

It was a simple design with short sleeves and a jewel neckline. The bodice was made of Alençon lace, ending in a slightly raised waist. The full skirt was heavy satin ending in the slightest suggestion of a train, and fastened with a wide ribbon sash at the waist. It was slightly crushed from hanging in the closet all these years, and the veiled headpiece, which she had tucked into the bottom of the garment bag, was flattened.

She took it out, reshaping it with her hands, and set it on her head, fluffing out the white tulle veil, and looked in the mirror. She was much older now, but if she brought the veil forward, over her face, she almost looked like the young woman in the wedding picture that stood on Bill's dresser. But not quite, she decided, snatching the coif off and tossing it on the bed.

Picking up the dress, she held it at arm's length and studied it. It was a pretty dress but nothing like the strapless sheaths the girls wore these days, and not like the heavily beaded and hugely skirted cream puffs that had been fashionable for a while. Turning to the full-length mirror on the back of the bedroom door, she held the gown against her body and sighed. It was obvious, without even trying it on, that she could never fit into it. She wasn't fat, not by a long shot, but she'd given birth to four children, and she'd breast-fed them all. Her body had changed and she was no longer the little slip of a thing who had worn that dress.

Standing there and studying her reflection, she thought it wasn't just her body that had changed; she had changed, too. She was much more confident these days and much more assertive than she had been as a young bride. She was more open-minded, too, and less opinionated. Back then, she thought, she'd been a bit of a prig, convinced there was a right way to do things and a wrong way.

Nowadays she was no longer convinced that food colorings were poison, that childbirth had to be natural, and all plastic should be banned.

She realized now that her strongly held beliefs had been a defense against an uncertain world. That had become obvious when she stepped inside the church vestibule on her wedding day and panicked, completely terrified to take that first step down the aisle to the altar where Bill was waiting for her.

"Ready, sweetie?" her father had asked, cocking his elbow and inviting her to take his arm.

Not at all, she'd realized, wanting only to turn tail and run right out the door. She would have fled, she remembered, except for the fact that everything was going black and she was about to faint. It was Beth Gerard, her best friend and maid of honor, who had produced from somewhere a brown paper lunch bag, which she gave to Lucy, instructing her to breathe into it.

Dad had held her up as Lucy breathed in and out, deep breaths, into the paper sack. "I thought this might happen," said Beth.

"I can't do this," said Lucy. "The wedding's off."

"It's rather late for that," said her father.

"Look, if it's no good, you can get a divorce or an annulment. But today, you have to get married," said Beth.

"It's not Bill, it's me. I can't go down that aisle."

"Oh, yes you can," said Beth. "Just imagine they're all naked."

Standing there, in front of her mirror, Lucy smiled, just as she had on her wedding day when she followed Beth and the other bridesmaids down the aisle on her father's arm. Afterward, everybody said they'd never seen such a radiant, happy bride.

It was time, thought Lucy as she replaced the dress in the garment bag, to call Beth. She hadn't spoken with her in a long time, and she knew Beth would love hearing about the Bickersons and reminiscing about the wedding. No time like the present, decided Lucy, knowing that unless she made the call immediately the moment would pass and she would be distracted and forget. She perched on the side of her bed and picked up the phone from the bedside table, punching in the number she knew from memory.

The voice that answered wasn't Beth's; it was male.

"Is Beth there?" asked Lucy, puzzled.

"I'm afraid not. Who's calling?"

"I'm an old friend, Lucy Stone. Could you please tell her I called?"

"I'm afraid not, Lucy," said the voice, which was close to breaking. "This is Dante."

Lucy knew Dante was Beth's son, whom she remembered as a skinny, mischievous kid. Now, from his deep voice, it was clear he was all grown up. And it was also clear to her that something was wrong. "Is everything all right, Dante?"

"No. It's not. Oh, Lucy, everything's wrong." He gasped, letting out a sob. "My mother is dead."